PENALTIES

PENALTIES

STEPHEN LEATHER

IF YOUR TEAM WINS, YOUR FAMILY DIES.
THE BEAUTIFUL GAME HAS JUST TURNED UGLY

CHAPTER 1

Sammy Wu downed his whisky, slammed the empty glass onto the bar and gestured at the barman for a refill. There were four large screens at the far end of the bar, each showing a different football match. Wu was only interested in one of the games. Arsenal at home to Chelsea. Two days earlier Wu's grandfather had come to him in a dream and told him that Chelsea would win 3-1. Wu had placed a bet on the game to the tune of ten thousand pounds, ten thousand pounds that he didn't have. There were five minutes to go and considering that Arsenal were ahead 2-0 it was clear that Wu's grandfather had been full of shit.

The barman refilled Wu's glass. Wu downed it in one. 'Another,' he grunted, in Cantonese.

The barman looked over Wu's shoulder. Wu knew that the barman was checking with the owner of the bar if a refill was in order. 'Just pour the fucking drink,' said Wu. 'My fucking money's as good as anyone else's.' The barman poured the drink. Wu grabbed the glass and swivelled around on his stool.

CK Lee was sitting in the far corner of the bar at his usual table. He was in his sixties but still as hard as iron, as bald as a billiard ball, his eyebrows the faintest of lines and his hands liver-spotted with nails like talons. He was staring impassively at Wu. Wu raised his glass. 'Yámbūi!" he shouted. Cheers. He drank and showed the empty glass to Lee. Lee continued to stare at Wu as he waggled the glass.

There were two other men sitting at Lee's table. Wu didn't know their names but he knew their role. Enforcers. CK Lee was a hard bastard but his enforcers were harder. They were big men wearing matching black leather jackets and blue jeans. One had large silver rings on each of the fingers of his right hand, a makeshift knuckleduster. Wu turned around and banged the glass on the bar. The barman refilled it. He was a big man, almost as big as Lee's enforcers. He was wearing a black leather vest that revealed heavyset tattooed arms. A dragon. A tiger. Skulls. A dagger. 'What's your name?' asked Wu.

'Wang Gang.'

'A good name,' said Wu. It meant strong. 'Let me give you some advice, Wang Gang. If you have a deceased grandfather, and if he comes to you in a dream and tells you the score of a big game, you tell him to go fuck himself.' He raised his glass. 'They know fuck all, the dead.' He drained his glass.

There was a loud roar from the screen showing the Arsenal game. Wu turned to look at it. Arsenal were 3-0 ahead and Wu was in deep, deep shit. He didn't have ten thousand pounds. He'd made the bet because he was already in the hole to Lee to the tune of seven grand. So now he owed seventeen grand. Seventeen fucking grand.

'I need the bathroom,' said Wu.

'Help yourself,' said Wang Gang.

Wu slid off his stool and walked unsteadily towards the men's room, studiously avoiding Lee's gaze. He pushed open the door. The bathroom stank of piss and shit. There was a single stall to the left and by the look of it it'd been used by a Mainlander because the wooden seat was up and there were dirty footprints on the porcelain. Mainlanders never got used to sitting while they shat and always squatted. Most of the staff at Lee's places were brought in from China, usually smuggled in the back of trucks coming in from the continent. They paid for their passage and worked off the debt by toiling in Lee's restaurants, bars and cheap hotels, often for years. Lee had his fingers in a lot of pies.

The urinals were to the right of the door. At the far end of the room was a small window, at head height. Wu went over and put his head on one side as he stared at it. He could probably get through, if he breathed in. He took off one of his shoes and used the heel to smash the glass. It shattered on the first blow and glass tinkled onto the tiled floor. He smashed away at the remaining glass. He was clearing the final shards when the door behind him slammed open. Wu whirled around, the shoe in his hand. It was another one of Lee's enforcers. This one Wu did know. Teddy Kang. Kang was a hard man from Shenzhen, brought up on the docks where he'd broken heads and limbs for money before Lee had noticed him and brought him over to London. He had two tattoos on his left hand, a scorpion and the Chinese character for seven, rumoured to be his lucky number, and also rumoured to be the number of people he'd killed in China.

Kang snarled and moved towards Wu. Wu ducked right and left and then threw his shoe at Kang's face before bolting past him. The shoe smacked into Kang's nose and by the time he'd recovered Wu was already out of the door, running at full pelt.

He crashed into a table, pushed himself off and staggered towards the door, only half aware of Lee staring at him open-mouthed. The two enforcers sat with their hands on the table, and by the time they had reacted he had reached the door and flung it open. There were stairs leading up and down but there were two men in cheap suits heading up so Wu had no choice. He slammed the door behind him and ran up the stairs to the next floor. There was another door there. It was open and a man was coming out. Wu pushed past him. There was a long corridor lit with red bulbs and doors leading off either side. At the far end was a large room, also bathed in a red light. Wu ran towards it, his arms pumping at his side. There were three sofas in the room and half a dozen Asian girls in various states of undress sprawled over them. Wu smelled marijuana and it was clear from the blank looks on their faces that they were off their heads.

Wu came to an abrupt halt as a big man in a dark suit came out of the kitchen at the side of the main room. Another of Lee's enforcers. This one was holding a large knife and had murder in his eyes. Wu turned and ran for the door. A girl with waist-length black hair wearing a long white silk robe that was open at the front had stood up and was reaching for him but he shoved her away and hurtled through the door.

He ran down the corridor but he was less than halfway when the door at the stairs was flung open and Teddy Kang was there, holding a machete. Wu swore and grabbed at the handle of the door to his left. He thrust the door open, dashed inside and slammed it shut. There was a middle-aged Chinese man on a double bed with two naked girls, Asians but with dyed blonde hair. One had two ornate Japanese fish tattooed across her back and they writhed as she rode up and down on the man. The other was bent over the man, kissing his chest as she massaged the other girl's ample breasts.

The man's eyes widened as he stared up at Wu, but the girls carried on, either they were seasoned professionals or like the girls in the main room they were drugged out of their brains. There were red curtains over the window and Wu jumped onto the bed and ripped them open. Light flooded in but there were bars across the glass. He jumped down off the bed and pushed open a door that led to a small shower room. It was windowless.

Wu groaned and turned around. Teddy Kang was standing there, the machete held high, a grin of triumph on his face. Wu threw up his hands to protect himself but he was too slow, Kang upended the machete and brought the handle crashing down against Wu's temple. He fell to the floor without a sound.

Chapter 2

When Wu woke up it was with a throbbing head and the taste of vomit in his mouth. He cleared his throat and spat, then blinked his eyes as he tried to focus. The first thing he realised was that he was tied to a chair. The second thing he realised was that Teddy Kang was standing in front of him, holding a hammer. Wu looked around, He was in a warehouse. There were cardboard boxes all around him, labelled in Chinese. There were boxes of canned food, detergent and toilet rolls. There was a pallet of cans of cooking oil and another pallet of floor cleaner. There were no windows and the fluorescent lights overhead made his eyes water. He blinked away tears.

CK Lee walked from behind a stack of boxes. He was wearing a long brown overcoat that almost reached down to his ankles. 'You think you can run away from your debts, Sammy Wu? Is that what you think.' He ran a hand over his bald head and down to the back of his neck. He stood staring at Wu as he massaged the neck muscles as if trying to ward off a headache.

'I'm sorry,' muttered Wu, blinking as he tried to focus his tear-filled eyes.

'No one runs away from me,' said Lee. 'If one man runs away and isn't punished, then everyone will think they can run. Where would I be then, if everyone ran away from their debts?' He took the hammer from Kang and swung it to and fro.

'I'm sorry,' repeated Wu.

Two more heavies walked into view. They were the ones he had seen sitting with Lee in the gambling joint. The heavy with the ringed fingers cracked his knuckles one by one as he stared menacingly at Wu.

Lee grimaced as if he had a bad taste in his mouth. 'You're not sorry, Sammy. But you will be.' He brought the hammer up and slammed it down onto Wu's left knee. The kneecap cracked with the sound of breaking glass and Wu screamed in pain. 'That'll stop you from running again,' said Lee. He gave the hammer to Teddy Kang and Kang gave him a pair of industrial wire cutters.

Lee waited patiently for Wu's cries to subside.

'Please, I'm sorry,' sobbed Wu eventually. 'I am so, so sorry.'

'I think you are,' said Lee. 'Because you're in pain. You see, Sammy, you should have thought about the pain before you tried to run away from your debt. You should have spoken to me man to man. We could have come to an arrangement.'

'I'm sorry,' said Wu again, and this time Lee brushed the apology away with an impatient wave.

'You need to stop saying that, Sammy. It's too late for sorry. The time for sorry was when you knew you couldn't pay. That was when you should have apologised. But what did you do? You ran. And you threw a shoe at Teddy. You hit him in the face. With a shoe. You know what they're calling him now? Shoe-face. Shoe-face Kang. You think that's funny, ridiculing a man like that?'

'I was just trying to get away,' said Wu. 'I made a mistake.'

'You made a huge mistake, Sammy. And saying sorry isn't going to make it right.' He sighed, then took a step towards Wu. Wu flinched, then turned away, his eyes tightly closed.

'So my question to you, Sammy, is can you pay me what you owe?'

'Yes,' said Wu opening his eyes. He nodded enthusiastically. 'I can. I will. I'll get you your money, I swear on my mother's life.'

Lee sighed and shook his head. 'Now why would you say something like that? You think I hurt mothers, do you? You think what, that if you don't pay me back I'll take it out on your mother? Is that what you think of me?'

'No,' said Wu hurriedly. 'I was just promising, that's all. I will pay you back everything I owe you. I swear.'

Lee smiled. 'That's good to hear, Sammy. That's good to know.' He walked slowly behind Wu and cut the ties that were binding his wrists.

'Thank you, thank you,' said Wu. He rubbed his hands, trying to get the circulation going again as Lee walked back around to stand in front of him again. Wu put his palms together and bowed. 'Thank you.'

'When will you pay me back, Sammy?'

'As soon as I can, I swear on my...' He swallowed back what he was about to say. 'Very soon,' he said.

Lee nodded thoughtfully. 'And how much do you owe me?'

'Seventeen thousand pounds,' said Wu. His voice was shaking now. He didn't have seventeen thousand pounds. He didn't have one thousand to his name. The only way he could get the money would be to borrow it from someone else.

'Plus interest, of course.'

Wu nodded. 'Yes. Interest.'

'Normally I would charge you one thousand seven hundred pounds a week interest,' said Lee.

'A week?' repeated Wu.

'A week. But in your case, I'm going to make an exception.'

Wu's eyes widened. 'Thank you,' he said. 'Thank you so much.'

Lee held up the wire-cutters. 'One week, one finger,' he said.

Wu's stomach lurched. 'I'll get the money, I swear,' he stammered.

'Good,' said Lee. 'That's what I want to hear. But the interest payments start today.' He clicked the cutters. 'For the first payment, I'm going to let you choose the finger.'

'Oh Mr Lee, please, no...' Wu was shaking now and his stomach felt as if it had turned to liquid.

'People have to know what happens to those who do not pay their debts to me.'

Tears were streaming down Wu's face and they were nothing to do with the fluorescent lights. 'Please no...'

'You're right handed so I'd recommend the small finger on the left,' said Lee. 'But it's your call.'

'Please, Mr Lee... don't do this.'

Lee smiled. 'I'm not going to do it,' he said. His smile widened when he saw the look of hope on Wu's face. 'I'm going to let Teddy do it. It'll go some way to making up for the shoe-throwing incident.'

Wu began to tremble.

'Left hand or right hand?' asked Lee. 'If you don't make up your mind, I'll let Teddy choose. And I rather think he'll go for one of your thumbs.' He handed the wire cutters to Kang.

'Mr Lee, I'll pay you back. I swear.'

'I'm sure you will, Sammy,' said Lee. 'Now hold out your hand. Or Teddy will do it for you.'

Wu slowly reached out his left hand, bunched into a first with the little finger extended.

'Good choice,' said Lee. He nodded at Kang. Kang smiled cruelly, grabbed the finger with his left hand and slid the pincers of the wire-cutters just below the knuckle. He squeezed the handles, then applied more pressure as the blades cut into the flesh.

Wu screamed and then bit down on his lower lip.

Kang squeezed harder as the blades met the bone, then he grunted as he forced them through. Blood spurted and the finger hit the floor with a dull plop. Wu sat back in his chair, groaning, his face ashen. Lee stepped forward and handed him a handkerchief. 'Next week it will be another finger,' he said, as Wu wrapped the handkerchief around the bloody stump. 'And next time, Teddy will choose.'

Lee's phone rang and he took it out of his coat pocket. It was another of his enforcers, Rick Zhang. Zhang was one of Lee's smarter men and often functioned as Lee's number two. 'We have a problem, Mr Lee,' said Zhang. 'A big problem.'

CHAPTER 3

Gabe Savage stared at the two X-rays but he didn't know what he was supposed to be looking for. He could see the thigh bones and the knees and the femurs and he knew what he was looking at, he just didn't know what he was looking for. He shrugged. 'They look the same,' he said.

'They look the same because they're both showing the same amount of damage,' said the man in the white coat who was standing to the left of the X-rays. He tapped one of the knees. 'Your cartilage is damaged, and the damage is getting worse.' His name was Craig Parker and he was one of the top joint specialists at London Bridge Hospital. He was in his late fifties and the consultation was costing more than a thousand pounds. Gabe's club reckoned he was worth every penny.

There was another doctor standing to the right of the X-rays, a pretty West Indian in her thirties. She was wearing a low-cut blue dress under her white coat and Gucci heels that made her almost as tall as Gabe. She was holding a clipboard and had a pen tucked behind her right ear and a stethoscope around her neck. Her jet-black hair glistened under the overhead fluorescent lights, and her pink nail varnish was a perfect match for her lipstick.

Standing either side of Gabe were the club's senior coach, Joe McNamara, and the team doctor, Brian Lawrence. McNamara had only been with the team for six months but Lawrence had been around for more than ten years.

'The good news is the ligaments are fine. But you need to address the damage to the cartilage,' continued Parker.

'We've been giving Gabe hyaluronic acid supplements and corticosteroid injections,' said Lawrence. He was in his forties and starting to grey. Usually he wore a team tracksuit but he'd put on a dark blue suit and a tie for the hospital visit. McNamara hadn't bothered to dress up though he had thrown a fleece over his track suit. He was in his fifties, his grey hair windblown and unkempt.

'The problem is that the injections might themselves be contributing to the cartilage breakdown,' said Parker. 'You know as well as I do that corticosteroid injections have to be strictly limited.'

'We haven't been going crazy,' said Lawrence.

'Have you been increasing the dosage?'

'Well, yes. Obviously.'

'And increasing the frequency?'

'We've tried not to,' said Lawrence. 'I mean, let's not get this out of proportion. We can all see the scans, but this has been a gradual thing. This hasn't happened suddenly. We could look at the scans from a year ago and frankly there isn't too much of a difference.'

'But there is a deterioration, that we can all agree on,' said Parker. He kept looking at Lawrence and eventually Lawrence had to nod in agreement. Parker gestured at the West Indian doctor. 'Laura tells me you're often in pain.'

Gabe laughed. 'I'm a professional football player, pain goes with the turf.' He grinned at Laura. 'No pun intended.'

'Specifically knee pain,' said Parker. 'Knees locking up first thing in the morning. Aches that won't go away.'

'Doc, show me a single Premier League player who doesn't need painkillers now and again.'

'Gabe, come on,' said Laura. 'You're among friends here. You can be honest with us.'

Gabe sighed. 'Right. Fine. Yes, sometimes I'm a bit stiff in the mornings. And yes, my legs ache at night. But I had that when I was a teenager after a hard day's training. Your body hurts when you put it under pressure.'

'Sometimes you twist it, right?' asked Laura.

'Everyone puts their joints under pressure at some time or another. They're not designed to be twisted.'

'You also need to consider the long-term consequences of the pressure you're putting on your knees,' said Parker. 'And your hips. There's a very high incidence of osteoarthritis among former top-level players. Long-term that could become an issue.'

'Yeah, well long-term we're all dead anyway,' said Gabe, dismissively.

'Gabe!' protested Laura.

He smiled at her. 'I'm just saying, long-term isn't my concern right now. My concern is Saturday's game and I want to play.'

'My recommendation would be that you didn't,' said Parker, folding his arms.

'But this has happened gradually,' said Gabe. 'I haven't had an accident.'

'Touch wood,' said Laura.

Gabe sighed. 'The point I'm trying to make is that it's wear and tear. So nothing dramatic is going to happen tomorrow.'

'Or you could take the view that the damage is cumulative and one more bad tackle could be the straw that breaks the camel's back,' said Parker. 'You've just turned thirty-one years old. It's generally accepted that in your profession athletes peak at twenty-seven.'

'I'm ready for the scrap heap, is that what you're saying?'

Parker laughed. 'Of course not. Twenty-seven is also the average age of the footballers in the Premier League so there are plenty of top-class players older than that, many in their mid-to-late thirties. What I'm saying is that you've had a good run. But now your joints are showing the effects of, as you say, wear and tear. My advice would be to take a break now and treat these injuries. Do it properly, take some time off to heal, and you could have another couple of years at the top. If you don't…' He shrugged.

'I need to play until the end of the season,' said Gabe. 'Four more games.'

'You need to sort this out, Gabe,' said Parker.

'I will do.'

'Now,' said the doctor. 'You need to fix this now.'

'I don't want you cutting me,' said Gabe.

'There are options that don't involve surgery,' said Parker. 'Not major surgery anyway. There's a new stem cell technique where we harvest cells, grow them and then inject them into the knee.'

'Great. Let's do that.'

'But you have to stop playing, for at least three months.'

Gabe shook his head. 'No way. Not now.'

'Gabe, it's for the best,' said Laura.

Gabe turned to look at McNamara. 'Look, I'm playing. That's all there is to it.'

McNamara held up his hands. 'Gabe, at the moment it's your call. We just want to know what state you're in. That's why we had the scans done. Now analyzing those scans is often a matter of opinion, and we need to respect the opinion of the experts.' He grinned. 'It's costing us enough. But if you're not in imminent danger then whether or not you play is down to you.' It had been twenty years since

McNamara had left Scotland but if anything his Glaswegian accent had strengthened over the years.

Gabe looked at Laura. 'There you go. I'm playing. I'm fine.'

Laura pointed at the X-Rays. 'No, you're not. And you know you're not. And I know you're not. I've seen you first thing in the morning, Gabe, when you can barely get out of bed. I've seen you last thing at night when you need a hot bath to unlock your legs.'

Gabe grinned at her. 'I love it when you're angry.'

'I'm not angry, Gabe. I'm worried. Worried about what's going to happen to your legs if you carry on like this. You could end up in a wheelchair.' She looked at Parker. 'Tell him, Craig. He won't listen to me.'

'Laura's right, Gabe,' said Parker.

'You'll push me around though, if I'm in a wheel-chair?' Gabe asked Laura.

She laughed despite herself. 'It's not funny, Gabe.'

'You're laughing.'

'Because I love you and sometimes you're too cute for your own good.'

Gabe stepped forward and put his arms around her. She made a play of trying to push him away but her heart wasn't in it and she surrendered to his kiss.

'Guys, please, go get a room, this is a hospital,' said Parker.

Gabe broke away from Laura. 'Seriously, you have a room?' he asked Parker

'The interns have to sleep somewhere,' said Parker.

Laura pointed a finger at Gabe's face. 'Don't even think about it,' she said. He grinned and kissed her again and this time she didn't even pretend to try to push him away.

Parker looked over at McNamara. 'Love's young dream.'

McNamara smiled and shrugged. 'We could throw a bucket of water over them.'

'He needs to stop playing. And now.'

'Just a couple more games, Doc. That's all we need. Let's just give him an injection same as we always do and we'll be out of your hair.'

'Joe, this isn't the same as before. There's a very real danger of permanent damage.'

Gabe broke off from kissing his wife. 'Just let me get the penalty record, Craig. Then I'll take a few months off and we'll do the whole stem cell thing.'

'It's not me you have to convince,' said Parker. "I'm just the specialist. Whether you play or not is down to you and the manager. All I can do is give you a medical opinion, and I've done that.'

'Does it mean that much to you, the record?' asked Laura.

Gabe nodded. 'It does. One more penalty and I have the record for most consecutive penalties.'

'You're an idiot.'

'But you love me.'

She nodded solemnly. 'Yes,' she said. 'Yes I do.'

'And you'll push me around in my wheelchair?'

She pulled a face. 'We'll compromise, I'll buy you an electric one.'

'And we can still have sex, right?'

'Guys, we're still here,' said Parker.

'We can have sex, but with no knees you're limited position-wise.'

'Oh good God,' said Parker. He put his hands over his ears and began to make random sounds.

Gabe and Laura started kissing again.

'I'm out of here,' said McNamara.

Gabe waved as he continued to kiss Laura.

CHAPTER 4

E ric LeBrun's two million pound apartment had stunning views over the River Thames, but this was the first time he'd seen it upside-down. The river came into view every ten seconds or so, then he'd continue to turn. He could feel his face flushing red, the result of being suspended by his ankles from the balustrade of the upper hallway. He didn't know who the two men were who had kicked their way into his apartment but the fact they were Chinese left him in no doubt who they worked for. CK Lee. Triad leader and all round bastard.

The doorbell had rung and LeBrun had opened it holding a mug of coffee, assuming it was a neighbour, and one of them had hit him over the head with something hard. LeBrun had staggered to the kitchen but they'd hit him again and he'd collapsed. When he'd woken up he was hanging upside down.

LeBrun had begged and pleaded for the men to cut him down but they had just sat on one of his sofas, drinking from a bottle of brandy they'd taken from the sideboard. It was expensive stuff, a gift from the club's owner, but the two men knocked it back as if it was rotgut. They were waiting for something, or someone, and LeBrun was pretty sure he knew who that someone was. LeBrun knew there was nothing he could say to persuade them to let him go, and nothing he could offer them. It was his financial problems that had led him falling into CK Lee's clutches, so there was no way he could buy his way out of his predicament. LeBrun hoped that this was just Lee applying pressure to make sure that LeBrun did as he'd been told. But he had a horrible feeling that it was more than that. And if LeBrun was right, he was in deep, deep shit.

CHAPTER 5

Gabe drove his black Bentley Continental GT3-R to the club's training ground, some ten miles to the north of the club's stadium. He arrived a few minutes before McNamara and Lawrence, who were both driving their club Mercs. Gabe's car came courtesy of the distributor and was replaced every time a new model came out, though Gabe always insisted on having the same colour – black. Gabe had been enjoying the GT3-R so much he was hoping to keep it, but Laura had been less than enthusiastic, mainly because there was no backseat. It was a fair point and Gabe knew that his wife would probably make the final call, but it was one hell of a joy to drive.

The training facilities were world class, with four full-size pitches, two grass, one artificial and one of sand, a medical and physiotherapy centre, two gyms, a sauna and steam room, and an Olympic-size swimming pool. It was surrounded by high walls topped with razor wire and the main entrance was guarded by two men in fluorescent jackets. Access to the training ground was tightly controlled. On occasions the

Press was allowed in but generally it was off limits to everyone except players and club staff – even wives and girlfriends weren't allowed in.

The guards recognised Gabe and waved him through. The main building was to the left, the car park to the right. There were more than a dozen cars parked and it was easy enough to spot the ones owned by the players. There were two red Ferraris, a white Lamborghini, a black Range Rover with tinted windows and three Porsches.

Gabe got his kitbag from the boot and headed for the changing rooms as McNamara and Lawrence drove up. Ronnie Watts, the team's Liverpudlian keeper, was warming up in one of the goalmouths with two mid-fielders – Jason Wood and Juan Fernandez taking it in turns to lob balls at him. Wood was a thirty-year-old black midfielder who had been with the club his entire career. He was as big as they came, and favoured a shaved head and a goatee beard to cover the fact that his hair had started receding when he was in his twenties. Fernandez was shorter and stockier, an Argentinian who had been in the UK for just one year.

Assistant coach Tommy Brett was taking names in the changing rooms, using his iPad to note the time each player arrived. The club's manager, Italian Piero Guttoso, had instituted a battery of penalties for what he saw as infractions. Late for training was a £100 fine for every hour, five times that on a match day. Failure to turn up on match day without a suit and tie was £200, using a phone on the team coach was £500. The money didn't mean much to players earning thousands of pounds a week, but Guttoso used it as a way of keeping track of who was playing by his rules. He kept a chart by the entrance so that everyone could see who was breaking the rules and it was the embarrassment factor more than anything that kept the players in line. Guttoso was a hard task-master but he got results which meant he had the full backing of the club's Thai owner. Brett was in his late twenties and had been one of the Premier League's top goal-scorers before an ankle injury brought his playing career to an untimely end. Brett tapped his iPad and nodded at Gabe. 'After the warm-up we'll do thirty minutes of ball control then I can sched-ule penalty practise with Ronnie and Jamie if you want.' Jamie McNeil was the number two keeper, a lanky youngster who had recently been signed from Glasgow Rangers during the January transfer win-dow. He was only twenty but was fearless and already had Ronnie Watts looking over his shoulder.

'Sounds like a plan,' said Gabe, dropping his bag in front of his locker. All he had in his bag were his boots and toiletries, the club supplied everything else he'd need.

'How are the knees?'

'All good,' said Gabe, unzipping his kitbag and taking out his boots. Most of the players left their boots at the changing rooms for the apprentices to clean but Gabe always took care of his own. And unlike some of the players who preferred to play in neon yellow or Day-Glo orange boots, Gabe had always stuck with traditional black.

In front of Babacar's lockers were two gleaming boots, one black and one red. A lot of the players had various superstitions they followed and Babacar insisted on the mis-matched boots. He said it was because when he was a kid he stole his first pair of boots and he couldn't manage to get matching ones. Now he was worth millions but the mis-matched boots kept him in touch with his roots, he claimed. Other superstitions were harder to explain. Marco Mancini, for example, always insisted that his socks were rolled up and placed inside his boots, pre-match. And Fernandez wanted his Number 20 shirts on wooden hangers rather than the metal that most of the players had. Stefano Armati always crossed himself before pulling on his Number 18 shirt, and Tim Maplethorpe demanded a fresh pair of laces for every game. Gabe considered himself free of such nonsense, though he couldn't imagine himself playing in any other boots than black.

'The ice bath is yours when we're done,' said Brett.

'Thanks,' said Gabe. He was pulling on his boots when McNamara came into the changing rooms and took Brett over to one side so that he could be brought up to speed. Lawrence sat down next to Gabe. 'Okay?' asked the doctor.

Gabe grinned. 'I've been asked that a hundred times today, give or take.'

'We're worried about you.'

'There's no need, it's wear and tear; I'll be careful and I'll be fine.'

'Make sure you hit the ice bath after training.'

'Yeah, Tommy'll have it ready.'

'And maybe half an hour of physio before you head off.'

Gabe nodded. 'Sure.'

McNamara walked over and stood in front of Gabe, hands on hips. 'Have you heard from Eric?'

Gabe shook his head. 'Not today.' Eric LeBrun wore the club's number 7 shirt and had been captain for almost three years. He was a Frenchman but had played in the English Premier League for more than a decade.

'Any idea where he was last night?' asked the coach.

'We're not joined at the hip, Joe,' said Gabe. 'Last time I saw him was here yesterday.'

'He didn't say he was planning a night out? You know what Eric's like.'

LeBrun had a liking for champagne and casinos, ideally in the company of a pretty blonde or two, a series of vices that had led to him being divorced two years earlier. 'He didn't mention it.'

'I can't believe he's pissing around like this on the day before a big match.' McNamara sighed. 'If he's gone AWOL again there'll be hell to play. The boss won't stand for it.'

'He's not answering his phone?'

The coach slapped his head theatrically. 'Of course, why didn't I think of that?'

'Sorry,' said Gabe. 'I was just trying to help.'

'If he does get in touch, tell him to stop fucking about and call me.'

'I will, for sure,' said Gabe. He stood up. 'He'll be here. He always turns up eventually.'

Chapter 6

The doorbell rang and Teddy Kang went to peer through the security viewer. It was CK Lee, stone faced, his hands in the pockets of his overcoat. Kang opened the door and Lee walked in without a word. He was followed by two more heavies, Jiang and Tan. The two men nodded at Kang, who closed the door then followed his boss into the room.

LeBrun was twisting slowly and it was several seconds before he saw Lee. 'CK, please, get your thugs to let me down,' pleaded LeBrun. 'There's been a mistake. We can sort it out, right. But not like this. All the bloods flowing to my head and I'm close to passing out. Come on CK, get me down and we can talk.'

Kang went over to the marble coffee table and picked up LeBrun's mobile phone, clicked the keyboard with his thumb and then handed it to CK Lee. He said something in Chinese and Lee grunted then studied the screen.

'CK, look, I'll throw the game, just the way you wanted. You've nothing to worry about.'

Lee ignored him and continued to stare at the screen. Tan and Jiang walked over to the window and looked out over the river. Tan cracked his ring-encrusted knuckles and the sound could be heard around the room, like twigs breaking.

'I'll do exactly what you want,' said LeBrun. 'We'll lose and you'll make a fortune. It's a win-win situation. There's no need for this.'

Lee looked up from the phone, scowled at LeBrun, then looked at the phone again.

'I don't know what you think, CK, but I'm on your side. You know I am.'

Lee held the phone out. 'Do you think I'm stupid, Eric? Is that what you think? I'm some dumb chink that you can lie to and I won't find out?'

'CK, please ...'

'I wiped out two hundred grand of your gambling debts!' shouted Lee. 'I own you!'

'I know that. That's why I'm throwing the game.'

'Are you?' snarled Lee. 'Or are you spilling your guts to Ian Johnston on the Mail? That's your plan, is it? Sell your story to the papers?'

'No, CK. You're wrong.'

'I'm wrong?' Lee held up the phone. 'The texts on this tell me all I need to know. You were selling me out, LeBrun.'

'He wanted to talk to me, I said no.'

Lee shook his head. 'That's not what your texts tell me.'

'Mr Lee, please ... I'm sorry ... I just wanted out.. I just wanted ...'

Lee took three quick steps forward and kicked LeBrun in the side of the head. LeBrun screamed.

You fucking idiot!' screamed Lee. 'Have you any idea what you've done?'

LeBrun was spinning around now as blood tricked from between his lips and splattered on the polished wood floor.

'Tell me the truth, LeBrun, or I swear I'll kick you to death.'

'Please ... don't ...' gasped LeBrun.

'You were going to tell him about me, weren't you?'

'He knew already. He said he had proof that I was fixing games for you and that he was going to write the story. I was trying to talk him out of it.'

'Then why didn't you tell me? Why didn't you come straight to me when he approached you?'

'I'm sorry,' gasped LeBrun. 'I'm so sorry.'

'Sorry? You're fucking sorry? I don't think you're fucking sorry.' He turned to Kang and shouted at him in Chinese. Kang took out a gun and gave it to Lee. Lee walked up to LeBrun, pointed the gun at his chest and pulled the trigger, three times in quick succession. LeBrun jerked and then went still. Blood stained his shirt and then began to drip down his face and onto the polished wooden floorboards. Lee sneered at LeBrun as he bled out. 'NOW you're fucking sorry,' he said.

Lee handed the gun back to Teddy Kang. 'Clean up that fucking mess,' he said. 'Then take care of that fucking journalist.'

'Yes, Sir,' said Kang, though Lee was already heading for the door.

CHAPTER 7

With a big match just a day away, the squad's training session was little more than a long warm-up session with exercises and stretching, followed by half an hour of ball control exercises. Gabe had then done half an hour of penalty practise with the team's two goalkeepers, alternating every half a dozen shots, while the rest of the squad were drilled by McNamara and Brett. Eventually McNamara blew his whistle to bring the session to a close. 'Right guys, we'll call it a day on the physical stuff. Jump in the showers and when you're all squeaky clean and you've used all those hair care products you're paid millions to advertise, we'll go through some Chelsea videos.'

There were groans from most of the players. 'It's not the first time we've played them,' moaned Omar Babacar, the lanky forward from Senegal. He had been spotted by a talent scout when he was just ten and emigrated to the UK when he was 19. Ten years later he was one of the league's top scorers, but he was very much a player who relied on his instincts and was bored by strategy briefings.

'Yeah, and last time was a draw, remember?' said McNamara. 'I'm not prepared to have a draw tomorrow so in the viewing room and stop the bitching and whining.'

Babacar raised his hands in surrender and jogged back to the changing rooms.

McNamara went over to Gabe and slapped him on the back. 'Looking good out there, Gabe,' he said.

'All good,' said Gabe.

'Grab fifteen minutes in the ice bath,' said McNamara.

'I'm okay.'

McNamara grinned. 'Doctor's orders.'

Gabe nodded and ran back to the changing rooms. He wasn't a big fan of the ice bath but knew that it was a great way of dealing with aches, pains and swelling. The bath was a large metal container with plastic pillows for comfort. There was no actual ice, the temperature was lowered electronically to between 12 and 15 degrees Celsius. He stepped into the bath and eased himself into the water.

Wood laughed at Gabe's obvious discomfort. 'Makes your nuts disappear, doesn't it?'

'His balls are tiny anyway,' laughed Fernandez. 'Like marbles.'

'Yeah, and why are you looking at my tackle in the first place?' asked Gabe, lying back and gasping as the freezing water covered his chest.

'Tackle?' repeated Fernandez. He had been in the UK for less than a year and his English wasn't great.

'Wedding tackle,' said defender Michael Devereau, punching the Argentinian on the arm. 'Cock and balls. The tackle you use on your wedding night.' Devereau was a relatively recent signing from Everton, a tough no-nonsense Liverpudlian with a reputation for going for his opponents legs as often as he went for the ball.

'Haven't you two got anything better to do?' asked Gabe.

Devereau walked over to the ice bath and pulled down his shorts. 'I could warm that up for you, sir,' he said.

'You piss in my ice bath and I'll make you drink it,' threatened Gabe.

Devereau laughed and pulled his shorts back up. He and Fernadez headed over to their lockers as Gabe concentrated on breathing slowly and evenly. The first time he had used the ice bath, Lawrence had given Gabe rubberized dive booties to protect his toes and rubber briefs to keep his midsection warm, but there had been so much derision from his teammates he'd refused them ever since, prefer-ring instead to get in wearing his full kit. The first couple of minutes were the worst but then his whole body went numb with the cold and he felt nothing. After ten minutes he climbed out, his body as white as a corpse. He stripped off his soaking wet kit and took a cold shower, gradually upping the tempera-ture to warm, then dried himself off and changed into his casual clothes. The squad were all in the briefing room, helping themselves to sandwiches, biscuits, healthy snacks and a range of soft drinks, while Brett was busying himself attaching his laptop to the flatscreen TV. Gabe made himself a coffee and picked up an energy bar. Eventually Brett flashed McNamara a thumbs up and the coach went to the screen and blew his whistle to get everyone's attention. 'Bums on seats, guys!' he shouted. 'School's in session!'

Those players that weren't already seated took their places, and McNamara spent the next hour playing them recent videos of incidents in recent Chelsea games. He'd show a Chelsea move, then play it again in slow motion several times, explaining what was going on and the strategies they were using. Then he'd use a whiteboard to show the best ways of responding to their strategies. Gabe was tired and had to fight to keep his concentration levels up, but he knew it was necessary. Teams spent hours and hours practising set pieces and if you could recognise a set piece you could block it and seize the advantage. That's how Gabe saw it, but several of the players – including Babacar – found the sessions boring and kept sneaking looks at their smartphones.

When the briefing was over, McNamara gave them a brief pep talk about the forthcoming match and then sent them on their way but motioned for Gabe to wait behind. 'Do you fancy going through some videos of Crowley in action?' he asked. Ted Crowley was the new Chelsea keeper, a recent signing from Everton. He was in his early thirties and Gabe had come up against him more than a dozen times over the past few years.

Gabe grinned. 'Hell, yeah.'

'Shouldn't take more than half an hour or so,' said McNamara.

Gabe grabbed himself another coffee and settled down in front of the screen. McNamara had put together several dozen clips of the Chelsea keeper in action, mainly reacting to free kicks and penalties. Crowley was fast and confident, but his main weakness was a tendency to be flamboyant, often launching himself into the air to tip a ball over the goalpost when he could just have easily taken a step and reached up for it.

'He likes to make it look difficult,' said McNamara after they had watched a dozen saves where Crowley threw himself across the goalmouth and tipped the ball over the net. 'But in every case he could have got there in plenty of time to have caught the ball with his body behind it.'

Gabe knew Crowley of old, and knew that he was a showman. Every time a TV commentator came up with his – or her – saves of the month, there would be at least one featuring Crowley. Gabe had taken a penalty against him the previous year and had beaten him, but it had been more by luck than judgement. He was a difficult keeper to shoot against. Most keepers made up their mind which way they were going to move as the penalty-taker ran towards the ball. The ball was probably going to go top or bottom, right or left. Four choices. Depending on how the penalty-taker made his approach to the ball, the keeper would go left or right. The penalty-taker tended to work the same way. The decision was made before the ball was kicked, sometimes even before it was placed on the penalty spot. Gabe favoured the left, and he preferred bottom to top. So his favourite spot would be bottom left, followed by top left, then bottom right and top right. The problem was, if he always kicked to his favoured spot, the keeper would know which way to jump. And if the keeper didn't spot it, the club's penalty coach sure as hell would.

Most penalty-kickers tried to keep their left-right ratios on fifty-fifty, or close to it. Which meant that sometimes they would decide which way to go long before they actually kicked the ball. What gave Gabe his edge was that he was able to change his mind right at the last moment, literally as his foot connected with the ball. He had developed the knack of kicking left or right no matter how he approached the ball and so was able to see how the keeper was reacting and kick accordingly. A good keeper would watch to see where the penalty-taker planted his foot because that would point towards where the ball would go. The hips, too, usually indicated where the ball was going to travel. But Gabe tended to run forward in a straight line, his hips facing the goal, giving the keeper no idea where the ball was going to go.

'He watches the penalty-taker all the time,' said McNamara. 'You need to be careful of that. Some keepers just look at the ball, or they interact with their team mates, but Crowley just watches the eyes. Most penalty-takers will look at where they're going to place the ball at least once and he's quick to pick up on that.'

'Got it,' said Gabe. 'But I'm pretty good about not telegraphing my kick.'

'There's one thing he's started doing over the last few weeks that he might try tomorrow,' said McNamara. 'He's been standing off centre. Not always, maybe half the time. But he moves a couple of feet one way, usually to give the penalty-taker more space in their natural direction. So you being a rightie he'll give you a bit more space on your left. And he does this thing with his left shoulder, raising it just a bit and sticking his left arm out a bit. Let me show you.'

McNamara showed Gabe four clips, and in each case Crowley had moved slightly off centre. The penalty-taker went for the larger space every time and Crowley dived and got the ball without fail.

'It's barely noticeable, but it seems to work for him,' said McNamara. 'He offers the penalty-taker a larger space for his natural kick, the penalty-taker bites and Crowley leaps early.'

'Clever,' said Gabe.

'I think he's been taught to do it,' said McNamara. 'I can't find any examples of him doing it last year.

Now here's the thing. If he does move to his left, offering you more space to your left, from what I've seen he's sure to jump that way.'

'So I do the opposite of what he's expecting?'

'That would be my advice,' said McNamara. 'You make it look like you're going left then do that thing you do and switch to your right and he should already be on the move.'

Gabe nodded. He knew that McNamara was talking sense. Crowley was so used to diving at the last moment that he often didn't start moving until the ball had been kicked. It was called reactionary defending and it was the most problematic keeping for a penalty-taker. Crowley was a master at it. But if his coach had persuaded him to try something different, that could be a weakness Gabe could exploit.

They spent another half an hour studying the footage before McNamara called an end to the session. Gabe was still thinking about what McNamara had said as he pulled up in front of Ollie's school. There was no doubting the use of video and pre-planning, but sometimes it was just better to run at the ball and kick it instinctively. His instincts had stood him in good stead so far, which was why he was so close to breaking the record.

Ollie was in the playground with two of his friends, deep in conversation. Gabe beeped his horn to attract the boy's attention. Ollie waved and ran over, his backpack bouncing on his shoulder. He climbed into the front passenger seat.

'Seatbelt,' said Gabe, and waited until Ollie had buckled himself in before driving off. It was a thirty-minute drive to their home, a six-bedroom house with a double garage on an estate with a dozen similar dwellings. Their neighbours were stockbrokers, doctors and businessmen and a private security firm drove around regularly in a clearly-marked van. Gabe's house, like all the rest, were covered by CCTV and had alarms linked by secure phone lines to the security firm. The developers had wanted to surround the estate with a high wall but the local council had refused planning permission.

The house had been very much Laura's choice – she liked modern and minimalist whereas Gabe would have preferred something older and with more character, but he had been happy enough to let her have her way.

'Is mum home?' asked Ollie, looking around for her car as they drove up to the house.

'Doesn't look like it,' said Gabe and he winced as he saw Ollie's face fall. 'It means we can have a kickaround before tea,' said Gabe, patting him on the leg.

'Cool,' said Ollie.

Gabe took Ollie inside and he dropped his backpack in the hallway before running into the kitchen. 'No soda!' shouted Gabe.

'Oh come on, Dad,' moaned Ollie.

'One on Saturday, one on Sunday, you know your mum's rules,' said Gabe. 'Water or fruit juice.'

'You know there's as much sugar in orange juice as there is in soda,' said Ollie, opening the fridge.

'Who told you that?'

'The internet,' said Ollie. 'How about a Snapple?'

'I suppose so,' said Gabe. Ollie was as good at arguing as his mother and it was often difficult to fault his logic. Gabe figured he'd make a great lawyer.

Ollie grabbed a bottle of Snapple iced tea, unscrewed the top and drank greedily. Gabe opened the kitchen door and went out into the garden. There was a football at the edge of a flower bed and Gabe picked it up and began bouncing it up and down on his forehead.

'To me, dad!' shouted Ollie, putting his bottle of Snapple on the counter and running after Gabe.

Gabe let the ball fall, caught in on his left thigh and let it drop to his right foot. He kicked it over to Ollie who trapped it easily before starting to run across the lawn, dribbling the ball from left to right. Gabe stood with his hands on his hips, grinning at the boy's enthusiasm. Ollie turned, trapped the ball, then kicked it towards Gabe, who caught it on his chest and let it drop to his feet. 'Nice pass,' said Gabe. He kicked it back to his son who ran with it to the far end of the lawn before kicking it back.

'When do you think I could play professionally, dad?' asked Ollie.

'You're eight,' said Gabe.

'I'm just asking.'

'You can be an apprentice at sixteen. And you could play in the Premier League then.'

Ollie wrinkled his nose. 'Eight years? I have to wait eight years?'

'To play professionally, yes. But I think your mum might have something to say about that.'

Ollie picked up the ball. 'Why?'

'Because she wants you to get a good education. And she's right.'

'You didn't go to university.'

'True. But I wish I had.'

'You left school and played for West Ham.

Gabe laughed. 'It wasn't quite as easy as that. I had to clean a lot of boots.'

'But I can join the Academy this year, right. And get extra training?'

'Sure. And we'll arrange that. And you're playing for the school team, which is great.'

'But I want to play in the Premier League.'

'And if you keep going the way you are, I'm sure you will. One day. But football isn't the be all and end all, Ollie. Professional footballers have a relatively short shelf life, you need to have a fallback position.'

'So what's your fallback position?'

Gabe grinned. It was a good question. His worsening knees had made him realise that his playing days were numbered, and frankly he didn't have another career lined up. 'I could coach,' he said. 'Be a manager maybe.'

'You always say you hate managers.'

'That's not true.'

Ollie nodded solemnly. 'Yes it is.'

'Not hate,' said Gabe. 'You should never hate anyone.'

'I've heard you tell mum that you hate Mr Guttoso.'

'I'm sure I never said that.'

Ollie nodded again. 'You did.'

'We sometimes have differences of opinion,' said Gabe. 'And I might say that I hate something he's done. But that doesn't mean I hate him. He's a good manager, he knows what he's doing. But that's not the point here, the point is that even the best players only play for a few years, and some of them have their football careers cut short because of injuries. That's why you need to go to university and get a good degree.'

'Okay,' said Ollie. His head jerked as he heard a car in the driveway. 'Mum's home!' he shouted. He dropped the ball and ran towards the house at full pelt. Gabe grinned as he watched the boy run. Ollie was fast. And he had amazing ball control, too. There was nothing that would make him prouder than seeing Ollie sign professional papers but he had meant everything he had said – football was a precarious career and while Gabe had been lucky, the problems he was having with his knees only emphasised that playing professional football was a young man's game.

CHAPTER 8

CK Lee was sprawled on his sofa watching Sky Sports on the massive flatscreen above his fireplace. He was drinking brandy from a large balloon glass and smoking a cigar. He was only half watching an interview with the Chelsea manager talking about the following day's match. Chelsea were the underdogs and even the Chelsea manager had to admit they had a tough game ahead of them. The Skype logo started to flash in the corner of the screen letting Lee know he had an incoming call. He put down his cigar and brandy, picked up the remote and swung his bare feet off the marble coffee table. He stood up and pressed the button to accept the call.

Sky Sports was replaced by Yung Jaw-Lung, his face almost filling the screen. Jaw-Lung meant Like A Dragon in Chinese, but Yung looked more like a turtle, peering out of its shell. No one knew for sure how old Yung was. He was seventy at least, but he could just as easily be eighty or ninety. He was completely bald and his eyelashes were so pale as to be virtually invisible. His face was smooth and unlined but his neck was mottled and wrinkled and peppered with skin tags. He licked his lips before speaking. 'You killed LeBrun?' said Yung in guttural Mandarin. He had lived in Hong Kong for more than fifty years but he still favoured the mainlander language over Cantonese.

'I had no choice,' said Lee. 'He was going to talk to a journalist.'

Yung nodded. 'And the journalist?'

'Teddy Kang is dealing with him tonight.'

'Killing a journalist is a big thing,' said Yung. 'People will notice.'

'He couldn't be bought off, he couldn't be bribed. He'd already spoken to LeBrun, he has notes and recordings.'

'So the story is already out?'

Lee shook his head. 'The journalist is a freelance. He hasn't approached anyone with the story yet. By acting quickly we can make sure the story stays buried. We are getting his computer tonight.'

'And the bodies?'

'They will never be found.'

Yung nodded slowly. He hadn't blinked once during the conversation. He rarely did.

'What about tomorrow's game? We need them to lose, you know that. We have millions riding on the match.'

'I know, I know.'

'We are depending on it, CK. We are depending on you.'

'I will take care of it.'

'Make sure that you do,' said Yung. The call ended. Sky Sports was back on the screen. It was an interview with Gabe Savage. The interviewer was a blonde woman with an impressive cleavage. She was talking to Gabe in the garden of his house. A small boy was kicking a football around in the background. The woman was asking Gabe about the record he was close to breaking – the most consecutive scored penalties. Gabe was confident, obviously. Then the interviewer asked Gabe about his son – was he destined to play for England. Gabe laughed and called the boy over. 'This is Ollie,' he said, then he asked the boy to show what he could do. Within seconds the boy was doing a very impressive job of bouncing the ball off his feet, his knees, his chest and his head. The boy was good.

Lee bent down and picked up his brandy glass. He swirled it between his hands, then sniffed it as he watched the screen. The boy used his knee to put the ball onto his head, then he span around in a full 360 with the ball on his head and dropped it to his knee again. The blonde was laughing and Gabe was beaming with obvious pride. Lee sipped his brandy and smiled at the screen. He had an idea. An idea that would get Yung Jaw-Lung the Chelsea victory he needed.

CHAPTER 9

Gabe always had pasta and chicken the night before a big game, loading up on carbs and proteins because it was never a good idea to eat a lot on match day. Laura had roasted chicken pieces and cooked spaghetti with an Alfredo sauce, one of Gabe's favourites. There was also a salad and French bread.

Gabe opened a bottle of Chablis. He poured wine into Laura's glass and water for himself and Ollie.

'How did training go this afternoon?' she asked after she'd sipped her wine and smiled her thanks.

'It was okay. Nothing heavy.'

'Your knees?'

'Are fine. Really.'

'What about penalties?'

'What about them?'

She waved a chunk of bread at him. 'You know what I mean? I'm assuming you practised penalties. How did your knees feel?'

'Laura, baby, penalties aren't about banging the ball into the back of the net. It's technique and timing, it's knowing which way the keeper is going to go. It's not about power, it's more of a mental thing.'

She opened her mouth to say something else but her mobile rang. She picked up the phone and grimaced. 'It's the hospital.'

'I thought you were finished for the day.'

She stood up and walked into the hallway to take the call.

'Women don't understand football,' said Ollie.

'She tries,' laughed Gabe.

'But she's a good doctor, dad.'

'Of course she is. The best.'

'So when she says you shouldn't play, she's right.'

Gabe put his head on one side. 'Well, they're my knees,' he said. 'I know how they feel.'

'But she's a doctor,' said Ollie. 'And like you said, she's a good doctor. She always takes good care of me when I'm sick.'

'But I'm not sick, Ollie. It's wear and tear.'

'Because you're old?'

Gabe laughed and ruffled his son's hair. 'Yes, because I'm old.'

'You have to take care of yourself, dad,' said Ollie.

'I will. I just want to break the record. You know about the record, right?'

Ollie sighed as if Gabe was stupid. 'Of course. Rickie Lambert scored 34 consecutive penalties for Southampton. You've scored 34. You need one more to beat his record.'

'And you can see why that's important, right?'

'The most important thing is your health, dad,' said Ollie, solemnly.

'You sound just like your mum.'

'Because she's right. You say she's right when she says I have to go to university. And she's right when she says you need to take care of yourself.'

Gabe played for time by popping a piece of chicken into his mouth and chewing slowly. The problem was that deep down he knew that his son – and his wife – were right.

Laura came back into the kitchen. 'I'm sorry,' she said.

'You've got to go?'

'It's a young boy, not much older than Ollie. He's getting worse and they're going to operate. I need to be there.'

'Of course.'

She walked over and kissed him on the lips. 'I have the best husband in the world.'

'Baby, you're a doctor, you save lives. I just kick a ball around. I'm the one who's proud.'

'I love you.'

Gabe laughed. 'I hope you do.' He gestured at her plate. 'Shall I put it in the oven?'

'I'll be a while,' she said. 'I'll microwave it when I get back.'

She picked up her bag. 'Make sure Ollie does his homework, then bath.'

'It's Friday, mum,' said Ollie. 'I can do my home-work on Sunday.'

'Deal, but bath and make sure you clean your teeth.'

She grabbed her coat and headed out. They heard the front door slam.

'She nags sometimes,' said Ollie.

'Because she loves us,' said Gabe.

'Can we play FIFA 16 later?'

'After your bath.'

'Before?'

Gabe laughed. 'It's not a negotiation.' He pointed at Ollie's plate. 'Eat.'

'I hope you win tomorrow, dad.'

'We will do.'

'How can you be so sure?'

'It's called visualization. If I believe we'll win, we'll win.'

'Does that work on FIFA 16?'

Gabe laughed. 'We'll see.'

CHAPTER 10

Teddy Kang cracked his knuckles and rolled his shoulders. He didn't like sitting and he had been in the car for the best part of two hours.

'Are you okay?' asked the driver. His name was Billy Huang but he was known as Big Billy because he was huge, and not just for a Chinese. Huang was a third generation British Chinese who had benefited from a Western diet his whole life coupled with a love of bodybuilding that had gripped him from his teenage years.

'What the hell is he doing in there?' asked Huang, gesturing at the pub across the road. 'He's taking forever.'

'Drinking, probably,' said Kang

'It was a rhetorical question,' said Huang. They spoke in English. Huang's Cantonese was rough at best and his Mandarin was non-existent. He spoke English with an Essex accent unlike Kang, who had a good grasp of the language but sometimes had trouble making himself understood.

'So why did you ask it?'

'That's the point of a rhetorical question,' said Huang.

Kang didn't want to give Huang the satisfaction of admitting that he didn't know what rhetorical meant so he stared out of the window and cracked his knuckles again. He was wearing tight-fitting black leather gloves and a black bomber jacket.

The van they were sitting in had the name of a Chinese wholesale food company on the side. They had put down sheets of polythene in the back because even though Kang was an expert with a knife there was always some blood.

Ian Johnston lived in a flat in a rundown part of Ealing in a house which had once been home to one large family. In the eighties it had been subdivided into one-bedroom and studio flats with the garden paved over for parking spaces. The house was on a busy road and Kang had realised that it wasn't a suitable place for what he needed to do. Kang had downloaded the man's picture off the newspaper's website. He had the picture on his lap. The pub was a short walk from Shepherd's Bush Tube station so Kang figured the man would take the train home. They had watched the journalist go into the pub at six o'clock and it was now almost eight.

The door opened and Kang stiffened, but then two women in short skirts and tight tops appeared, clearly the worse for wear.

'What if he doesn't come out?' asked Huang.

'He has to leave at some point, it's a pub,' said Kang. 'What time do pubs close? Eleven?'

'Sometimes later,' said Huang. He looked at his watch. 'My wife is cooking won ton soup tonight.'

'It'll keep,' said Kang.

'She won't be happy.'

'She'll get over it,' said Kang. 'If we don't get this done CK Lee isn't going to be happy and when CK Lee isn't happy...' He shrugged and left the sentence unfinished. He looked down at the picture. Johnston was in his thirties, balding with a comb-over, and thick lensed glasses. When Kang looked up he saw the man himself standing on the pavement, wrapping a black and white scarf around his neck. 'That's him,' said Kang.

Huang started the engine.

'Pull up alongside him after he turns into the next road. I'll get out and talk to him.' The journalist had started to walk away from the pub, swinging a battered leather briefcase as he walked. 'Get the side door open.'

Huang did as he was told, indicating before he made the turn to follow the man down the quiet side street. He stopped and Kang jumped out. 'Hey, mate, do you know where Seymour Road is?' asked Kang. He looked left and right. There was no one else on the pavement and the van shielded them from any passing traffic.

Johnston stopped, frowning. 'Seymour Road?'

'Yeah, it's near here somewhere.' He reached into his pocket. 'I've got the address.'

The side door grated open and Johnston turned towards the sound. Kang pulled his flicknife from his pocket, pressed the steel button with his thumb and felt the blade shoot out and click into place. He stepped forward, slapped his left hand over the man's mouth and stabbed him half a dozen times in the kidney. Johnston struggled for a few seconds but went limp as he bled out. Huang grabbed him by the scruff of the neck and pulled him into the van. Kang lifted the man's legs, rolled him over, and then slammed the door shut. It had taken less than five seconds.

Kang retracted the blade of his knife, slipped it back into his pocket and climbed into the passenger seat. Huang joined him.

'You've got blood on your hand,' said Kang.

Huang held up his gloves and groaned when he saw the smear of blood across the knuckles of his left hand. 'Bastard was bleeding all over,' he said, and wiped it on his seat.

'What the fuck are you doing?' said Kang.

'Wiping it off,' said Huang.

'On the fucking seat? Are you retarded? Don't you watch television? CSI? Blood trace?'

'Sorry,' said Huang. 'I'll clean everything later.'

'Make sure you do,' said Kang, folding his arms. 'All they need is one drop and they'll know everything. You've got to be careful. It's not like China where no one gives a fuck if a journalist disappears. This is London and someone will be looking for him.'

Huang drove to a lock-up in Southall, the middle garage in a line of seven with identical green wooden doors. Huang stayed at the wheel while Kang got out and unlocked the up-and-over door and switched on the single lightbulb that illuminated the interior.

Huang reversed in. The lock-up was about four feet longer than the van and up against the far wall were two oil barrels. Kang tapped on the side of the van once the nose was just inside and he pulled down the door.

Huang got out and opened the rear door of the van while Kang took the top off one of the barrels. Together they rolled the body out of the van and tipped it into the barrel. Next to the barrel were twenty one-gallon containers of hydrochloric acid drain cleaner. Hanging on a nail in the wall were two protective masks. Kang put one mask on and gave the other to Huang. Together they emptied the containers of drain cleaner into the barrel. It took them the best part of ten minutes, then Kang replaced the lid and banged it into place. 'We're done,' he said. LeBrun's body was in the other barrel. The barrels would be left in the lock-up for a week while the acid did its work, then someone else would dispose of them.

Huang got back into the van. Kang opened the door, switched off the light, and Huang drove out.

'Why did we kill him?' asked Huang as Kang got back into the van.

'Does it matter?'

Huang shrugged his massive shoulders. 'Not really.'

'So it's a rhetorical question, right?'

Huang chuckled but didn't reply.

CHAPTER 11

Gabe was lying on his back staring up at the ceiling. He was visualising taking penalties. The goalkeeper was Ted Crowley, the man he'd be facing in just fifteen hours time. Gabe placed the ball, took four steps back paused, then ran forward and kicked. The ball powered into the back of the net.

'You're not sleeping?' whispered Laura. She was curled up with her back to him, her hair a jet black curtain across her pillow.

'Sorry,' he said.

'You know you're kicking?'

'Sorry. I'm taking penalties.'

She chuckled. 'Yes, I know. It's your thing.'

'My thing?'

'Your thing. You keep running them through your mind and when you kick, your right leg twitches.'

'It's called visualization.'

'I know what it's called, baby.' She rolled over and draped her arm across his chest. 'Are you worried about tomorrow?'

'No more than usual,' he said. 'I'm just playing all the options, where to place the ball, where to feint.'

'You've done it a thousand times, baby.'

'I know. Like you said, it's my thing.'

She snuggled against him. 'You need your eight hours,' she said. 'You know how grumpy you get if you don't get your eight hours.'

He looked over at the alarm clock on the bedside table. It was just before one. 'It's early,' he said. 'I'll sleep soon.'

Her fingers ran through the hairs on his chest and down his stomach. 'Would a blow job help?'

He smiled. 'That's your prescription?'

'I'm a doctor. You can trust me.'

'I do, baby.'

'So you'll take your medicine?' Her hand found its way between his legs.

'I'd be crazy not to.' She moved down and his hands stroked her soft hair as she went to work on him.

Chapter 12

G abe ate the same thing the morning of every match. Coco Puffs cereal and two bananas. Laura called it the breakfast of champions. She had toast and marmalade, Ollie had two hard boiled eggs. Kick-off was at three and Gabe was supposed to be at the ground by ten for a warm-up and a pre-match briefing. After breakfast, Gabe took Ollie out for a kickabout in the back garden, another pre-match tradition. They kicked the ball back and forth, then Gabe watched as Ollie practised juggling the ball with his feet and knees. He realised Laura was watching him from the kitchen window and he waved. She blew him a kiss back.

Ollie wanted to be in goal and have Gabe kick penalties, but Gabe shook his head. 'You can take the penalties and I'll go in goal,' he said. He knew it was crazy but at the back of his mind was the conviction that if he failed to get a shot past his son, he'd repeat the failure on the pitch.

Ollie beat Gabe with his first two shots but Gabe managed to grab the third. Ollie was about to kick again when Laura appeared at the kitchen door, waving his mobile. 'It's Joe!' she shouted.

Gabe jogged over to her and took the phone. 'Hey, Joe.'

'Have you seen Eric?' asked McNamara.

'Eric? No?'

'Or heard from him?'

'Joe, like I said before, we're not joined at the hip. I haven't seen him since training on Thursday and he seemed fine then. What's wrong?'

'He's still not answering his phone. I called him half a dozen times last night and it keeps going straight through to voicemail. Same this morning. Gabe, just between the two of us, he's not gone off the rails again, has he?'

'I don't think so.'

'You don't think so?'

Gabe sighed. 'Joe, I'm not his best mate, not by a long way. If he's started drinking and gambling and God knows what, I doubt he'd tell me. Look, I'm ready to leave, why don't I swing by his place?'

'You don't mind?'

'No problem, I'll just leave a few minutes earlier. His place is on my way. I'll ring his bell, see if he's overslept.'

'Please, Gabe. And call me as soon as you find out what's going on.'

McNamara ended the call and Gabe called over to Ollie. 'I've got to go, I'll see you at the stadium, yeah?' Ollie and Laura would be watching from the family box with the rest of the team's families and friends.

'See you, dad!' shouted Ollie.

'Is there something wrong?' Laura asked as he went back into the kitchen.

'Eric's gone walkabout, by the sound of it.'

'Is he drinking again?'

'I hope not, but he's not answering his phone.'

'He's got a self-destructive streak,' said Laura. 'He drove away his wife, lost his kids, lost his house. He's got an addictive personality, there's no doubt about that. And his addictions feed off each other – he drinks, then he gambles, then he loses so he drinks even more.'

'Easy come, easy go,' said Gabe. 'The money means nothing to him. He doesn't seem to care whether he wins or loses when he gambles. If anything, he seems to want to lose.'

'That's what I mean. Self-destructive.'

'I told Joe I'd drop by, see if he's at home.'

'Why you, baby?'

'It's on the way.'

'He's not your responsibility.' She laughed. 'Hell, he's the captain. He's supposed to be the responsible one.'

'It's no biggie,' said Gabe. 'I'll just knock on his door, see if he's home.'

'Do you want me to come with you?'

Gabe shook his head. 'I can handle it, baby. He's probably in bed with a hangover. I'll throw a bucket of water over him and drive him in.'

Laura kissed him on the cheek. 'I'd tell you to break a leg, but under the circumstances.'

He laughed, grabbed her, and kissed her on the lips.

Ten minutes later he drove away from the house. He didn't notice the two vans parked at the side of the road. One had the name of a Chinese wholesale food company on the side. The other belonged to a cable TV company. Both drivers were Chinese and both were wearing dark glasses, but Gabe didn't notice that, either.

CHAPTER 13

Laura was pouring orange juice for Ollie when the doorbell rang. She put down the carton and headed down the hallway. She opened the door and frowned when she saw the two men standing there. They were Chinese, both wearing blue overalls and one of them carrying a clipboard. The one with the clipboard blinked at her from behind wire-framed spectacles. 'Mrs Savage?'

'Yes?'

'You have a problem with your cable TV?'

'I don't think so.'

He looked at the clipboard. 'Your husband phoned us, he said there was a problem with the sports subscription channels.'

'He didn't mention it to me.'

'It'll only take us a few minutes to check the signal.'

'What company are you with?'

'Our company is Tele-Service,' he said. 'We carry out technical repairs for most of the cable companies.' He tapped the logo on the breast pocket of his overalls. 'We're everywhere.'

'Well, I don't think we have a problem, so thank you...' said Laura, starting to close the door.

The man without the clipboard put his foot inside the door. 'We should take a look, just to be sure,' he said. Laura looked down at his foot. His shoes were black and white with a buckle on them, not the sort of shoe she would expect a cable repairman to be wearing. She was still staring at the shoe when the man pushed the door, hard. It banged against her head and she staggered back.

The two men rushed towards her. The one who had pushed the door had something in his hand. At first she thought it was a phone but then he pressed a button and blue sparks crackled between two metal prongs. 'No!' she shouted and flailed her arms but the man pushed her in the chest and she staggered backwards. She lost her balance, slipped and fell, banging her head on the wooden floor.

'Mummy!' She heard Ollie shout and she heard him run from the kitchen.

'Ollie, no!' she shouted but then the man was on top of her and had the stun gun against her neck. He pressed the button and her body went into spasm and then everything went black.

Chapter 14

Gabe drove slowly through Wapping looking for the warehouse conversion where Eric LeBrun lived. LeBrun had been living in the riverside apartment in Wapping for just over a year; he'd moved in not long after his divorce had been finalised. His wife had taken the house in Sussex, the cottage outside Nice and the apartment in Paris with its view of the Eiffel Tower. LeBrun hadn't contested any of her demands, much to the chagrin of his lawyer. LeBrun never cared much for money, or for possessions, all he'd really cared about was his children and his wife had been happy enough for him to see them whenever he wanted. He'd rented a three-bedroom apartment so that his son and daughter could have their own rooms when they visited, and he'd stocked it with all the latest electronic gadgets to keep them amused. Gabe had only been once when LeBrun had thrown a moving-in party, and while the booze and models had flowed, LeBrun had been morose throughout.

The apartment was on the top floor of a warehouse conversion and there were double yellow lines along the street outside but Gabe managed to find a parking space down a side road. He walked back to the entrance to the building. LeBrun lived on the top floor and Gabe pushed the button on a stainless steel console to the left of the door. There was no answer so he pushed again. And again. When there was still no answer he walked along to the car park entrance, two massive wrought iron gates with another keypad set into the wall. He peered through the gates but couldn't see LeBrun's car so he went back to the main entrance and tried the bell again.

'Can I help you?' said a voice behind him and Gabe turned to look at a blonde woman in her mid-thirties, wearing a purple track suit and gleaming white trainers. She was jogging on the spot as she smiled at him and Gabe couldn't help but notice how her breasts bobbed up and down. 'I'm looking for Eric, he lives on the top floor.'

She stopped jogging. 'He's not answering?'

'No. I can't get him on the phone, either.'

'You're a friend?'

Gabe nodded. 'Sure.'

'He was there yesterday. I heard him. His flat's above mine.'

'Did you see him?'

She shook her head. 'No. But I heard him banging around at about nine.'

'At night?'

'Nine in the morning.'

'Banging around, you said?'

She nodded. 'Like furniture being moved. And the TV was on loud.'

'What was he watching?'

'I don't know but there was shouting.' She frowned quizzically. 'Oh, maybe it wasn't the TV. Is that what you mean? You think something happened?'

'I don't know. Look, I know this is a lot to ask, but can we go downstairs and see if his car is there? I can't get into the car park.'

'Sure, I can let you in.' She unzipped a waistpack and pulled out a small pink wallet, then went over to a square sensor set in the wall below the keypad. She pressed the wallet against it and there was a loud click and the gates began to open inwards.

She followed him into the car park. There were a couple of dozen cars parked, and as many empty bays. Each parking bay had the number of the flat it had been assigned to, painted in white on the Tarmac but Gabe didn't need the number to recognise LeBrun's car. Gabe pointed over at a gleaming red Porsche. 'That's his,' said Gabe. He pursed his lips and sighed.

'What's wrong?'

'If his car is here, where the hell is he?'

'He could have taken a taxi.'

'Eric liked to drive.' He nodded at the Porsche. 'No point in having a Porsche if you don't show it off, that's what he always said.'

'Do you think something's happened to him?'

'I hope not. But I'm starting to get a bad feeling about this.'

'Have you spoken to Bill?'

'Bill?'

'Bill O'Hara. He lives in the flat opposite. He'll be home. Come on, I'll let you in.'

The gates had closed behind them so she had to touch another sensor in the wall to let them out. 'Oh my God, you're Gabe Savage, aren't you?' she asked as the gates opened.

'That's me.'

She laughed. 'I'm sorry, I should have recognised you straight away. It's just you look different in a suit.'

'The manager makes us wear them on match days,' he said. 'We get fined if we don't.'

'Are you serious?'

'Says it builds team spirit. He's probably right.'

'Well to be fair to him, you do look good in a suit.' She smiled and held out her hand. 'Lisa.'

'Nice to meet you, Lisa,' said Gabe. 'And thanks for your help.'

'My nephews will be made up when they hear I met you,' she said. 'They're huge fans.' She grinned. 'Listen to me babbling away,' she said. 'I'll let you in and you can go up and talk to Bill.'

She tapped a four-digit code into the key pad and pushed the door open. It led into a small reception area where there was an unmanned desk and a bank of mailboxes.

'There's no security guard or receptionist?' asked Gabe.

'There used to be, but there hasn't been for a few months,' said Lisa. She pointed to the left. 'The lifts are that way.' She headed for the mailboxes as Gabe went around the corner and took one of the two lifts up to the top floor. He rang the doorbell to LeBrun's flat and knocked on the door just to satisfy himself that there was no one at home, then rang the bell of the flat opposite. The door opened after a few seconds and a bald man with a bushy beard peered out. He was in his late forties and wearing a brightly-coloured kaftan. The sweet smell of marijuana oozed through the door and by the glazed look on the man's face he was clearly under the influence. 'Bill?'

'You'd better not be trying to sell me something,' said O'Hara. He blinked, rubbed his eyes, then his jaw dropped as he looked again at Gabe. 'Fuck me, you're Gabe Savage.'

Gabe grinned. 'Guilty as charged.'

'You're playing today, right?'

'Hopefully,' said Gabe. He pointed at the door to LeBrun's flat. 'Have you seen Eric recently?'

'Sure. Yesterday.'

'He was okay?'

O'Hara frowned. 'Sure. Is there a problem?'

'I'm not sure,' said Gabe. 'He missed training yesterday and he's not answering his phone. But his car is in the car park.'

'He was fine yesterday. He was checking his mail box.'

'What time would that have been?'

'Nine. Nine thirty.' O'Hara grinned. 'He was wearing his dressing gown. Never was an early riser, Eric.'

'Do you think he was hung-over?'

O'Hara grinned. 'Come on, you know Eric. He likes his drink.' He frowned. 'You think something's wrong?'

'I don't know,' said Gabe. 'But I'm wondering if I should call the police and get them to check the flat.'

'No need,' said O'Hara. 'I've got a key. Eric and I swapped spare keys a few months back after he locked himself out one night.'

'Do you mind?'

'Of course not.' O'Hara disappeared back into his apartment and reappeared thirty seconds later with a key on a chain with a plastic football. They crossed the corridor to LeBrun's flat and Gabe knocked on the door. When there was no response he stepped to the side and let O'Hara unlock the door. O'Hara pushed the door open. 'Eric. Are you there? It's Bill. Are you OK?"

When there was no reply he pushed the door fully open and motioned for Gabe to go in first. 'Eric, are you there?' shouted Gabe as he walked slowly along the hall.

The two men walked into the main room with its spectacular views over the Thames. Gabe saw a half-empty bottle of brandy on the floor by the sofa and he cursed under his breath. Then he saw the broken chair by the open plan kitchen, and a shattered coffee mug on the floor behind the front door.

'He's not here,' said O'Hara, stating the obvious.

Gabe picked up the brandy bottle. LeBrun was a champagne drinker, or vintage red wine, the spirits were usually for visitors. He put the bottle on a sideboard. The coffee had pooled on the varnished wood floor, some had dried which suggested it had been spilled hours earlier. 'That doesn't look good,' said O'Hara, nodding at the broken coffee mug.

'You didn't hear anything?' asked Gabe.

O'Hara shook his head. 'No, but I was out most of the day. I didn't get back until about eight. Want do you think? He had an accident? Fell over?'

'I don't know,' said Gabe. 'It's possible. Maybe. He might have fallen and gone to hospital. Maybe an ambulance came. Shit.'

'He might be fine. You can wait forever in A&E these days.'

'So why isn't he answering his phone?'

O'Hara looked around and then pointed at a sideboard. 'Because it's there,' he said. There was an iPhone next to a bowl of fruit. Gabe went over and picked it up. There were several dozen missed calls, mainly from Joe McNamara, and as many text messages. 'That doesn't make sense,' said Gabe. 'Why didn't he take his phone with him?'

CHAPTER 15

When Laura came to she was lying on her side and everything was dark. She blinked her eyes several times and then realised there was something over her face. She tried to take off whatever it was but she couldn't move her hands. They were bound behind her back. 'Ollie!' she shouted. 'Ollie where are you?'

Something clipped the side of her head. 'Be quiet!' snarled a man.

'Where is my son?' she asked. 'Where's Ollie?'

'He's here. He's fine. Now shut up.'

'I want to see my son!' There was no answer. She realised she was in a vehicle, she could hear the sound of traffic and there was the vibration of an engine. 'I demand that I see my son!' she said. There was a crackling sound and something pressed against her neck and her whole body went into spasm and she passed out.

When she awoke a second time the vehicle had stopped moving and she heard a door opening. Her head was throbbing and she felt awful. Hands grabbed at her, at least four, and they pulled her out and she was thrown over someone's shoulder. She tried to speak but this time her mouth was so dry she couldn't do anything other than cough.

She heard male voices, guttural and talking a language she didn't recognise, then the crunch of feet on gravel, then the thud of feet on something harder. Her head banged against something and then she could tell she was inside. She heard more voices, then she felt herself being carried up a flight of stairs, then her head banged against a wall and she was taken to the left. They stopped, she heard a door being opened, and she was carried again and then suddenly she gasped as she was thrown through the air. She hit something soft. A bed, she realised.

'Hello?' she croaked.

There was no answer. She heard a thud on the other side of the room. 'Is there someone there?' she said.

She strained to listen. Whatever had been pulled over head was muffling most of the sounds around her, but then she heard a door being closed.

'Hello?' she said again. She tried to sit up but with her hands tied behind her and her legs also bound, that was impossible. She lay back, gasping for breath, her face bathed in sweat. 'Ollie, are you there?' she said. There was no answer, and she began to cry.

Chapter 16

Gabe went back downstairs. Lisa was still in reception by the mailboxes, holding half a dozen letters and clearly waiting for him. 'Any joy?' she asked.

Gabe shook his head. 'He's not there. But it looks as if something happened.'

'Like what?'

'There's a broken chair. That might have been the noise you heard. Were you in all day yesterday?'

'Most of the time, yes.'

'And no ambulance came?'

'I would have said.'

'I know, I know. Sorry. It's just I can't work out why he would have left the flat without his phone.'

Lisa grimaced. 'I wish I could help. I hope he's all right.'

Gabe looked at his watch. 'I've got to go,' he said.

'Can I ask you a favour?'

'Sure.'

'Can I take a selfie with you? My nephews won't believe I actually met you if I don't show them a picture.'

Gabe laughed. 'Of course.'

'Brilliant,' she said. She stood close to him, held the phone out, and pouted. Gabe couldn't help grinning. She took a picture, then another for luck, and then thanked him effusively.

Gabe hurried outside to his car and climbed in. He drove off and slotted his iPhone onto its holder on the dashboard before calling Joe McNamara on hands-free. 'Eric's not in his flat,' said Gabe. 'But his car is parked there. There's some damage in the flat as if he'd fallen over. A neighbour heard some noise yesterday morning.'

'What do you mean, damage?'

'A broken table. A smashed mug.'

'You got into his flat?'

'A neighbour had a key. Oh, his phone was there.'

'This is not good, Gabe.'

'The only thing I can think of is that he had some sort of an accident and is in hospital.'

'I'll get someone to phone around,' he said. 'Look, Gabe, I hate to ask but were there any signs that he'd been drinking?'

'No,' said Gabe. 'There was a cup of coffee spilled on the floor. No booze.' Gabe thought it best not to mention the half-empty brandy bottle because he was fairly sure that LeBrun hadn't been drinking it.

'That's something, I suppose. Where are you now?'

'Driving to the training ground. I should be there in about half an hour.'

'See you there,' said McNamara. 'Look, if Eric is off the grid, how do you feel about taking over as captain for the match?'

'Hell, Joe, I've got enough on my plate with the penalties.'

'Just for this game, Gabe. Please. You'd be doing me a big favour.'

'Okay, okay,' said Gabe.

'You're a star,' said the coach, and he ended the call.

Gabe drove for five minutes and then his phone rang again. He looked over at the screen. It was Laura, calling on FaceTime. He swiped the green phone with his finger and then concentrated on the road. 'Baby, I'm driving,' he said.

'Gabe!' she said and he could tell from her voice that something was wrong. His eyes flicked across to look at the screen. Her face was fearful and there were tears in her eyes. 'Baby, what's wrong?'

'You have to do what they say, Gabe,' said Laura. 'Just do what they say.'

'Baby, what are you talking about?' Red lights flashed ahead of him and he realised the car ahead of him was breaking. It was a black cab, slamming on the breaks to avoid a cyclist. The cab squealed to a halt and Gabe only just managed to avoid smashing into the back of it. He looked back at the screen. Tears were running down his wife's face.

'Gabe, they say they'll kill me and Ollie if you don't do exactly as they say.'

'Laura, what the hell's going on?'

'Please, Gabe, don't let them hurt Ollie.'

'What do you mean? What the hell are you talking about?'

The picture lurched and Gabe realised Laura wasn't holding the phone. The phone pulled back and he saw that Laura was sitting on a chair, her arms at her side. Then he saw the grey duct tape around her arms. 'Laura!' he shouted.

'Gabe!'

The camera panned to the left and Gabe caught a glimpse of a man wearing a ski mask His stomach lurched. The taxi in front of him moved off. 'Laura, what's happening?' he shouted, pulling the phone off its mount and holding it in front of him.

The phone continued to pan to a sofa. Ollie was lying on it, bound with duct tape. There was a strip of tape across his son's mouth. 'Ollie, no!'

Horns began to sound impatiently behind him but all his attention was on the screen. The phone moved closer in on Ollie, so close that Gabe could see the fear in the boy's tear-filled eyes. 'Ollie, don't worry, I'll get you out of there,' he said.

The phone moved back and Gabe saw there was another man in a ski mask standing behind the sofa, holding a gun. His hands were trembling but he managed to press the sleep button on the top of his phone and immediately hit the home button, capturing a screen shot of the image. He did it twice more. The horns behind him were more insistent now with half a dozen cars joining in the cacophony. The phone tipped back down again, giving him a view of the duct tape around Ollie's arms and legs.

More horns sounded and Gabe pulled the car over to the side of the road and switched on his hazard lights. A white van drove by and the driver glared at him, flashed him a 'V' sign and mouthed obscenities. Gabe was already staring at the screen of his phone.

The camera had panned back to Laura. 'We have your son and your wife,' said a voice. 'Now listen carefully to what I have to say.'

There was a view of the man standing near Laura and Gabe took two more quick screenshots, then another ski-mask filled the screen.

'You are to make sure that your team loses today. Do you understand me?'

'What?' asked Gabe. 'What the fuck are you talking about?'

'You will lose the match today. If your team wins, or if it is a draw, your family dies.'

'I can't throw a whole game, I'm just one player,' said Gabe.

'You can and you will,' said the man. 'But if you don't, your wife and son will die. And that will be on your head. And if you talk to the police, they will die. Tell no one. Just throw the match and you'll get your family back, safe and sound.'

'Why are you doing this?' asked Gabe.

'Do you understand?'

'Let me talk to my wife!'

The phone lurched and Laura was on the screen. 'Gabe, please, do what they say.'

'Have they hurt you?'

'No, but they said they'll hurt Ollie if you don't do what they say.'

Gabe heard something in a language he didn't recognise, then the man standing next to Laura grabbed her by the hair and pulled her head back before pushing the barrel of his gun under her chin. Gabe saw a tattoo on the man's hand and he fumbled to get a screenshot. 'Please, don't hurt her!' he said.

'Do as we say and we'll release her and your boy unharmed. All you have to do is to make sure your team loses this afternoon. Do you understand?'

'Yes,' said Gabe.

The man released his grip on Laura and she slumped forward, sobbing.

The man's ski-mask filled the screen. 'You lose the game. You don't contact the police. You don't tell anybody. Follow those three rules and you'll have your family back safe and sound.' The call ended and Gabe stared at the blank screen in disbelief.

There was a loud knock on the passenger side window and Gabe flinched. It was a policeman. 'You can't park here,' said the officer. 'Red lines. Move on.' He was in his twenties and his helmet seemed a size too big for him.

Gabe held up his phone. 'I was just making a call.'

'You need to do that somewhere else or I'm going to give you a ticket.'

'Sorry,' said Gabe.

The policeman made a 'wind the window down' gesture with his hand and Gabe did as he was told. The officer leaned forward, then his face broke into a smile. 'You're Gabe Savage.'

'Yes,' said Gabe. 'Look, I'm sorry, I had to pull over to use the phone. I'll be on my way. Sorry about the inconvenience.'

'No problem, Gabe. Bloody hell, Gabe Savage. You've got a big match today.'

Gabe forced a smile. 'I know.'

'Think you'll win?' asked the cop.

'I hope so.'

'You're the bookies favourite.'

'That's what they say.'

'I was going to put a bet on, but the odds...' He shrugged. 'And you've got that record thing, for the penalties.'

Gabe nodded. He was finding it hard to concentrate on what the cop was saying. Images of a tearful Laura and Ollie gagged and bound kept filling his mind.

The policeman was looking at him intently and Gabe realised he had said something and was waiting for a reply. 'Sorry, what?' said Gabe.

'I said, do you practise penalties a lot, to get that good?'

'Pretty much every day,' said Gabe.

'The way you make that ball curve, it's something,' said the cop. He pointed at the road ahead. 'Anyway, you get on your way, Mr Savage. And good luck today.' He patted the car door and straightened up.

'Thank you, officer,' said Gabe.

The cop bobbed down again and gestured at the phone. 'And don't hold that as you're driving. That'll get you a ticket even if you're not actually using it.'

'Right, officer, thank you,' said Gabe. He put the phone on the passenger seat and pulled away from the kerb.

His mind raced and he could barely concentrate on the traffic around him. He indicated left and pulled into a side street. He found a parking space and reversed into it, then grabbed the phone and stared at the screen. He called up the screenshots he'd taken and flicked through them, his heart pounding. He felt suddenly trapped by the car and he got out and paced up and down the pavement. It was as if he was trapped in a nightmare and if he could just force himself to wake up everything would be all right and he'd be lying in bed next to Laura. He took deep breaths, trying to calm himself down, but the screenshots of the men in ski masks just made it worse.

A woman in a long coat walked by with a poodle on a lead. She looked at him inquisitively and he turned away from her. He had to do something but he had no idea what. Call the police? What could they do? And the warning had been clear – talk to the police and Laura and Ollie would be killed. Could he throw a game? Maybe. Especially if there were any penalties. But what if he couldn't, what if he tried and the team still won? Laura and Ollie would be dead and how would he be able to deal with it. He felt light-headed and he realised he was hyper-ventilating. He tried to slow his breathing but it was an effort. He wanted to run and scream and punch something. He folded his arms gripping the phone tightly, his mind racing. 'Fuck, fuck, fuck, fuck,' he repeated like a mantra. 'Fuck, fuck, fuck, fuck.'

He stopped swearing and leaned against a brick wall, and began banging the back of his head against it. He needed help. But who? Who the hell could do anything to help him?

CHAPTER 17

Ray Savage had his game face on. Jaw set tight, lips thin, eyes shielded behind impenetrable sunglasses. He was wearing a black Versace suit and a blue checked Ted Baker shirt and in a holster under his right arm he had a fully loaded Glock pistol. He was standing with his back to the wall with his hands at his side.

To his left was Mike Tyler; he was a few inches shorter than Ray and several kilos heavier. His suit wasn't quite as expensive and he wasn't wearing sunglasses but he had a matching Glock in a shoulder holster. Like Ray he had his game face on, his lips tight and his eyes ever watchful. The two men were there to watch over their boss, Den Donovan, one of the country's major cannabis importers. Donovan spent most of his time in a palatial villa in the Caribbean, but whenever he was in the UK he never went far without Mike or Ray. Today was special, a face-to-face meeting with the leader of a Yardie gang who controlled a large chunk of the crack cocaine market in Brixton. No one knew what Wesley's other name was, or even if Wesley was his family name or his given name. Everyone called him Wesley, or Mad Wesley if he was out of earshot. He was a big man, close to seven feet, with short dreadlocks and a rash of tribal scars across both cheeks. He was wearing a denim shirt with cut-off sleeves that revealed bulging forearms and puckered skin close to his left shoulder where a bullet had ripped through his flesh. There were another three similar wounds under the shirt, the result of an assassination attempt three years earlier. Two men had between them put four bullets into Wesley but he had still managed to pull out his own gun and fight them off. He had spent two weeks in intensive care but within three months both his attackers were dead and buried out in the New Forest. Wesley put his lucky escape down to the talisman that he always wore around his neck, but the emergency room doctors were of the opinion that it was his bulk that had saved him.

Donovan had been the one who had requested the meeting so Wesley had insisted it be on his turf. They were in the back of a car-wash he owned, a mainly cash business that he used to launder his illicit gains. They were in a storage room at the rear of the main cleaning area and outside they could hear the splash of water and the slap of wet sponges against metal. It was a labour-intensive business with most of the cleaning, inside and out, done by hand.

There were no windows in the room, and it stank of detergent and stale water, but there was no chance of them being seen or overheard, so as far as Donovan was concerned it was fit for purpose. Donovan and Wesley were sitting either side of a wooden table covered with empty bottles and ashtrays overflowing with the butts of cannabis cigarettes. Whereas Wesley ran his drugs operation with a steel hand, he was clearly much more relaxed about what his car cleaners did in their down time.

Everyone in the room was armed. There were two ways to arrange a meeting. One was to insist on no weapons, but that was always difficult to enforce as it meant searching everyone and there was always at least one person who took offence. Having everyone unarmed also left them vulnerable to a surprise attack so no one was happy about giving up their weapons. Ray preferred the second option – weapons were just fine so long as they stayed concealed. Everyone then just assumed that everyone else was armed and behaved accordingly.

There were eight men in the room. The principals and three heavies each. That had been agreed in advance. The third member of Donovan's security detail was Barry Chisnall, he was only in his twenties but he was a former squaddie and as hard as nails. He was standing on one side of the door, his arms at his side. On the other side of the door was one of Wesley's heavies – a lanky Rastafarian with waist length dreadlocks tied back with a knotted yellow, green and red handkerchief. Wesley's two other heavies were standing by the wall facing Ray and Mike. The three Yardies who were looking after Wesley hadn't bothered with holsters, their guns were tucked into their belts, which in Ray's opinion showed a distinct lack of professionalism. Belts could easily snag a weapon – pulling a gun from a holster was always smoother and faster.

Donovan wasn't a big fan of face-to-face meetings but Wesley had insisted and made it a deal-breaker. Donovan had decided that since there were no drugs and no money involved, the sit-down was probably worth the risk.

'Thanks for seeing me, Wesley,' said Donovan. 'I know you by reputation, obviously.'

Wesley nodded, accepting the compliment.

'We've got a problem with the Turks, and I gather you're having problems too.'

'What makes you say that?' asked Wesley.

'It's no secret that three of your people have been shot in the past couple of months. The boys at Operation Trident put it down as black-on-black but we both know it's the Turks. They're encroaching on your turf and you can't have that, right?'

Wesley nodded slowly. 'Go on.'

'We're in the same boat,' said Donovan. 'Last month a consignment of mine was hijacked on the way from the docks to London. Two of my men were put in hospital and I lost half a ton of very high grade cannabis. It came out of the blue and I had no inkling of who might have done it, then suddenly Stoke Newington and half of north London is awash with the stuff. So much of it that the price dropped by a third.'

'The Turks only deal heroin,' said Wesley. 'Protection rackets and prostitution among their own communities, but outside of that their only interest is heroin.'

'In the past, that's true,' said Donovan. 'Which is why they've never been a problem in the past. I bring in my bit of puff, you handle the crack and the coke, the Turks import their heroin, everyone makes money. But that's all gone to fuck now that the EU has gone and allowed 70 million Turks visa-free access to Europe. Their criminals are flooding into Europe and a lot of them are getting across the Channel now. The heroin trade alone isn't enough to keep them all occupied, so they're starting to spread their wings.'

Wesley's brow creased into a deep frown. 'And you know this, how?'

'Because I've got my ear to the ground, mate,' he said. 'It's happening right across the country. Same as when Yugoslavia fell apart in the Nineties and all the Bosnian and Serbian mafia flooded in.'

Wesley grinned, showing a single gold tooth at the front of his mouth. 'Before my time,' he said.

'Mine too,' said Donovan. 'I was just pointing out the historical precedent. It happened when Communism folded in Russia and we had all the Russian gangsters piling in. Now it's the Turks. There are just too many of them to stay confined to the heroin trade, and that means they're going to start treading on our toes.

Ray's phone rang and both men looked over at him. The James Bond theme. Ray was a big fan of the Bond movies, especially the Daniel Craig ones because the general view was that Ray was the spitting image of the actor, albeit a few kilos heavier.

Donovan shook his head angrily. 'Are you fucking serious, Ray?'

'Sorry, thought I'd put it on silent.'

'Yeah, well you clearly didn't,' said Donovan. He looked over at Wesley. 'Sorry that my associate is such an arsehole.'

Wesley shrugged. 'S'okay. So long as it's not the cops calling.'

'See now, that's not funny,' said Donovan. The theme tune continued to ring out. 'Fucking hell, Ray, will you deal with that?'

Ray reached for his phone but as he did the two Yardies opposite pulled out their guns and aimed them at him, gangster-style, the butts parallel to the floor. Ray raised his hands. 'Guys,' he said, 'it's a phone.' He pointed at his left armpit with his right hand. 'This is where my gun is.' He pointed at his right jacket pocket. 'This is where my phone is. Now I'm going to take it out slowly and you'll see it's a bloody iPhone and not a Heckler and Koch. Okay?'

One of the Yardies waved his gun at Ray's chest, his finger on the trigger. 'Let's see it, man.'

'For fuck's sake, how many guns do you know that play the James Bond theme?' asked Ray.

Mike pulled out his gun and aimed it at the Yardie who was threatening Ray. 'Put the fucking gun away,' he said.

The second Yardie took a step towards Mike and aimed his gun at Mike's face. 'You drop your gun first!' he shouted.

The third Yardie pulled his gun from his belt and waved it around as if unsure who he should be pointing it at, then Barry produced his Glock and aimed it at him, his face impassive.

Wesley stood up slowly and pulled out his gun, a large chromed automatic with a mother-of-pearl handle. He pointed the gun at Donovan. 'What the fuck's going on, man?' he shouted.

Donovan smiled and raised his hands. 'For fuck's sake, Wesley, will you fucking chill out.' He looked over at Ray. 'See what you've fucking started here?'

Ray sighed and raised both his hands high up above his head. 'Guys, look, I'm sorry, OK?' he shouted. 'My fucking bad. I'm an arsehole for not switching my phone off but what's done is done. It's a fucking phone. It's an iPhone 5 for fuck's sake. It's not even a 6 or a 7. So let me take it out and switch it off and we can carry on with business. OK?' He kept his left hand above his head as he reached down slowly with his right hand to fish out the still-ringing phone.

Wesley relaxed slightly but still kept his gun pointed at Donovan. 'Are you fucking happy now, Wesley?' asked Donovan. 'It's a phone for fuck's sake. Put your pea-shooter away.'

'Who the fuck is it?' asked Wesley.

'What the fuck does that matter?' Donovan pointed his finger at Ray. 'Turn that fucking thing off, Ray, or I swear I'll shove it so far up your arse that you'll be burping text messages.'

Ray stared at the screen, frowning.

'Ray, turn that fucking thing off now,' growled Donovan. 'Or I swear to God I'll shoot you myself.'

Ray turned his back on Donovan and took the call. 'What?' he said.

'Ray?'

'You dialled my number by mistake, did you?'

'Are you in London?' asked Gabe.

'You don't talk to me for what, ten years, and now you want to know where I am.'

Donovan stood up, pulled out a Glock and gestured at Ray with it. 'For fuck's sake, Ray, we're in the middle of something here, if you hadn't noticed. Put the fucking phone away.'

Ray waved him away without turning around. 'You've got a fucking cheek, Gabe.'

'I need your help, Ray.'

'What?' It was the last thing Ray expected to hear.

'I need your help. It's Laura. She's been kidnapped. And Ollie. I'm in deep shit, Ray. I didn't know who else to call.'

'What the fuck?'

Donovan walked over and put his left hand on Ray's shoulder but Ray shook him off. 'Ray, what the fuck are you playing at?' snapped Donovan.

Ray turned to glare at him. 'It's Gabe. He's in trouble.'

Donovan frowned. 'I thought him and you never spoke.'

'We don't. He wants fuck all to do with me. But he needs my help. It's serious. I've got to go, sorry.'

Donovan stared at him for several seconds and then he nodded. 'Okay. Fuck off.'

'Will somebody tell me what the fuck's going on?' shouted Wesley. 'Are we doing this fucking deal or not?'

'Ray's got to go,' said Donovan.

Ray started walking towards the door. Wesley pointed his gun at Ray's back. 'You ain't going anywhere!' he shouted.

'Leave him be,' said Donovan. 'He's got family troubles.'

'Family troubles? What the fuck?'

'Just let him go.'

'How do I know he's not going to get the cops?'

Donovan laughed harshly. 'Ray Savage talking to the cops? Give me a fucking break, Wesley.'

Ray reached the door, pulled it open and left the building.

Donovan put his gun into his holster and raised his hands. 'Look Wesley, all's good. Ray's just got some personal business to take care of. We're all good.'

Wesley jutted up his chin, then nodded slowly. 'Yeah, okay.' He put his own gun away and nodded at his team to do the same. Mike was the last to lower his gun and slide it into his holster. Wesley gestured at the door. 'Families always fuck you over, one way or another.'

'That's true,' said Donovan.

'Always asking for money or help or whatever. Mine drive me fucking crazy. Three wives, eight kids. I should learn to keep my dick in my pants, right?' Wesley sat down and sighed. 'Okay, let's get down to business. How the fuck are we going to handle the Turks?'

Chapter 18

Ray walked away from the carwash, his phone clamped to his ear. 'What the fuck's going on, Gabe?'

'Laura's been kidnapped. If I don't throw this afternoon's game, they'll kill her. And Ollie.'

'Who'll kill her?'

'I don't know.'

'You don't know? How can you not know?'

'All I got was a call. From Laura. She was with some guys in ski-masks. They said we had to lose. If we don't lose, they'll kill her. And Ollie.'

'For fuck's sake. Where are you?'

'I'm heading to the training ground to get on the team bus. The match starts at three.'

'Have you called the cops?'

'No. Do you think I should?'

'No, mate. The cops'll only fuck it up.' He stopped walking. 'Look, Gabe. You're sure it's not a con? Have you tried calling her?'

'It goes straight through to voicemail. And there's no answer on the home phone. Ray, what do I do? I'm at my wit's end here.'

'Just stay calm, Gabe. I'll find her. Where was she last time you saw her?'

'At home. This morning. They were coming to the match later.'

Ray started walking again. His BMW was parked next to the black Range Rover that Donovan, Mike and Barry had arrived in. 'And you've no idea who they might be?'

'Of course not.'

'You haven't been dealing with any shady characters?'

'What the fuck are you talking about?'

Ray took his key fob from his pocket and clicked it. 'Don't snap my head off, Gabe. I'm just asking. Maybe it's someone you know, someone you've crossed paths with.'

'You think someone I know has done this?'

'That's what I'm asking you.'

'I'm not in bed with match-fixers, if that's what you mean.'

Ray pulled open the car door and climbed in. 'What about the guys in the ski-masks?'

'What do you mean?'

'What can you tell me about them?'

'Hell I don't know.'

'What did they look like?'

'Are you not fucking listening? They were wearing ski-masks.'

'I heard you. But were they white? Black? Asian?'

'Not black. White maybe. I don't know, Ray.'

'Big, small, short, tall?'

'Difficult to say.'

'Taller than Laura? Shorter?'

'She was in a chair. They were standing over her.' There was a silence of a couple of seconds. 'Yeah, they weren't tall. And they didn't look big. Not that big, anyway. Average.'

'Anything else? Anything you can remember?'

'They had guns.'

'Okay. But what about the men?'

'I keep telling you, Ray. They were wearing fucking ski-masks.'

'Clothes, Gabe. Jewellery. Watches. Anything that might help identify them.' He started the engine.

'I took screenshots,' said Gabe.

'You what?'

'Screenshots. While they were talking.'

'Why the fuck didn't you say so. Send them to my phone.'

'I will do. Ray, what are you going to do?'

'I'm going to check your house. Just to make sure they're not there and that someone's not pulling your chain.'

'This isn't a fucking prank, Ray. Do you want the address?'

'I know where you live, Gabe. Don't worry, I'll get this sorted, one way or another.' Ray ended the call, tossed the phone onto the passenger seat and drove out of the car park. Two minutes later his phone beeped to say that he'd received a text message. Then another. And another. Ray ignored them and concentrated on cutting through the Saturday morning traffic.

CHAPTER 19

Gabe drove into the training ground. From the number of luxury cars in the car park it looked as if he was the last to arrive. He hurried into the changing rooms. Tommy Brett pointed at the wall clock. It was 10.15. 'I'm going to have fine you, Gabe,' said the assistant coach. 'You know the rules.'

'I was checking on Eric for Joe,' said Gabe, tossing his kitbag down in front of his locker.

'He didn't tell me, sorry,' said Brett.

Gabe's training kit was hanging up inside his locker, freshly laundered. He kicked off his shoes, then took off his suit and hung it up.

'So, what's the story with Eric?' asked Brett.

'He wasn't home, but his car was there,' said Gabe, taking off his tie and shirt.

'Do you think he's drinking again?'

'I don't know, Tommy. He's been off the booze for months.'

'Either that or he got good at hiding it,' said Brett. 'He's gone off the rails before.'

'That was two, three, years ago,' said Gabe.

'Leopards don't change their spots,' said Brett.

'Once a drunk, always a drunk? Is that what you're saying?'

'If the cap fits,' said Brett. "I'm just saying, it's not the first time he's fucked up. Okay, see you on the pitch.' He jogged off before Gabe could say anything.

Gabe finished changing, grabbed himself a bottle of water and headed out. The training sessions on match day were always a relaxed affair, an hour and a half of warming up and rehearsing a few set pieces. Joe McNamara was running things, wearing a dark blue tracksuit and with his whistle on a club lanyard. He waved at Gabe when he saw him and jogged over. 'You okay?' asked the coach.

'Sure.'

'Still no sign of Eric?' Gabe shook his head. 'Did you check the hospitals?'

'I got Tommy to call around but getting information from the NHS is like getting blood from a stone. So if he is in a hospital somewhere, we're none the wiser. I'm thinking of calling the cops, see if they can get anywhere.'

Gabe's stomach lurched at the mention of the police. If he was seen speaking to the police, the kidnappers might think he had called them in. 'Wouldn't be great publicity for the club,' said Gabe. 'You know the cops always talk to the Press. Guttoso will hit the roof if he read about it in the papers.'

McNamara swore. 'Yeah, you're probably right.' He looked at his watch. 'I suppose there's still a chance he'll turn up.' He patted Gabe on the back. 'Okay, let's get you warmed up.' He blew a sharp blast on his whistle to attract the attention of the squad. 'Right guys, just want to let you know that we're having problems locating Eric LeBrun, so in his absence Gabe here will be acting captain!' shouted the coach. 'Gabe here didn't ask for the job, he's had it thrust upon him as it were, so give him your best and don't give him any grief.'

'What's happened to Eric?' asked Devereau.

'He's not available,' said McNamara. 'That's all we know.' He pointed over at Johnnie Reid, a young mid-fielder who had joined the squad from Newcastle six months earlier but who had yet to play for the first team. 'Johnnie'll take Eric's place mid-field.'

'So Eric's been dropped?' asked Stefano Armati, an Italian player with movie star looks and a seven-figure contract to be one of the faces of Hugo Boss.

'He's not been dropped, Stefano. We're just not sure where he is.' He clapped his hands together. 'Right come on, let's get moving. Those highly-paid muscles won't warm themselves up.'

CHAPTER 20

There was a red Honda CRV parked in front of Gabe's house and Ray parked behind it. He ran up to the front door and pressed the bell, long and hard, then shouted through the letter box. There was no reply and he hurried around to the rear garden. The kitchen door was locked and so was the sliding door into the conservatory.

Ray picked up a rock and weighed it in his hand. Gabe's house was fitted with an alarm system but if Laura and Ollie had been kidnapped the kidnappers were unlikely to have set the alarm when they left. He threw the rock with all his strength at one of the conservatory windows and it shattered. Ray pulled out the remaining shards and then stepped through into the conservatory. He moved quickly through the ground floor. There were breakfast things on the table in the kitchen but no signs of violence or a struggle. There was a fashion magazine open on a coffee table and an open Chanel handbag on one of the sofas. Ray picked it up. Inside was a purse, make up and keys.

He doubted that Laura had left the house voluntarily without taking her keys with her.

There was a selection of framed family photographs on a low sideboard, mainly of Gabe, Laura and Ollie, including several when Ollie was a babe in arms. There was a large photograph of Laura and Gabe's wedding with the bride and groom surrounded by friends and family. Ray wasn't in the photograph. He hadn't been invited and had only found out about it three months after the event. Gabe had been playing for Oldham Athletic and his agent had just started negotiations with Liverpool. Laura had been five months pregnant at the wedding, but there was barely a bulge to be seen. Gabe and Ray's parents were there, as proud as punch, and Ray had never forgiven them for not telling him about the wedding. Ray shook his head sadly as he stared at the photograph. He didn't blame Gabe for cutting him out of his life. He'd probably have done the same if the roles had been reversed.

He went upstairs and checked the bedrooms and bathrooms, though he knew he wasn't going to find anything. Ollie's bedroom was a mess, the quilt half off the bed and clothes thrown around the floor, but Ray was sure that was just the result of general untidiness rather than signs of an abduction. The master bedroom was the opposite, the bed had been neatly made and there were half a dozen cushions arranged perfectly against the headboard.

The bathroom was spotless with gleaming marble his-and-her sinks. On the side that was obviously

Laura's was a row of perfume bottles. One of them was Chanel Coco. Ray recognised the black bottle. He picked it up and squirted it onto the back of his hand, then sniffed it and smiled.

He replaced the bottle, went back into the bedroom, sat down on the bed and took out his phone. There were six messages from Gabe, each a screenshot. He flicked through them. There were three men in the pictures, all wearing ski-masks. One of the pictures showed the hand of one of the men. Ray zoomed in on the hand. There was a tattoo between the thumb and the first finger. A scorpion and what looked like a Chinese character.

He went through the screen shots again, slowly this time. He zoomed into the faces. The eyes could be Chinese, it was hard to tell. One of the men sported a green ring, jade maybe. Another indication that the kidnappers might be Chinese. It made sense. The kidnappers wanted Gabe to throw the game and the Chinese bet millions on UK football matches.

He called Gabe's number and it went through to voicemail. 'Gabe, mate, I'm at the house. I got the pictures. I'm thinking they're Chinese. I know someone in Chinatown who might help us ID these bastards. Chin up, mate. I'm on it. You play your game, I'll play mine.'

He ended the call and stood up, taking a quick look at his watch as he headed downstairs. It was just coming up to eleven. Just four hours to go before kick-off.

CHAPTER 21

McNamara had the squad jog slowly around one of the pitches, just to loosen up, then started them on a few passing exercises. It was all gentle stuff, the coach didn't want any pulled muscles or stupid injuries. The pre-match training was more about building team spirit than anything. Some managers allowed their teams to arrive at the ground on match day, get changed and play, but Piero Guttoso insisted that they meet first at the training ground and travel together to the stadium. He also insisted that players didn't use phones or headphones on the coach, he wanted them socializing and talking so that when they ran out onto the pitch they were a true team and not a group of highly-paid individuals. Despite there being more than a dozen nationalities on the squad, Guttoso insisted that everyone spoke English. He followed his own rules; there were three Italians on the Walford United team – Luca Moretti, Stefano Armati and Marco Mancini – and whenever he spoke to them he did so in English. Being caught speaking any other language than English was an automatic £200 fine.

Guttoso rarely attended the training ground himself, he believed in letting his coaching staff do their jobs and judged them by their results rather than micromanaging them. So far his faith in the coaches had paid off and the team were third in the Premier League with the bookies giving even odds of them being on top by the end of the season, now just two months away.

After half an hour of warming up, McNamara split the squad up into groups of five and they put on coloured vests. Gabe was teamed up with Watts, Mancini, Wood and Babacar, the green team. 'Let's have a few quick games,' said McNamara. 'Green against Blue, Red against Yellow.'

Blue team consisted of Reid, Tim Maplethorpe, Devereau, and two of the reserves. 'Tenner says we trounce you,' said Devereau.

'I'll take that bet,' said Wood.

McNamara blew his whistle. 'Don't even joke about gambling on games!' he shouted. 'You know the boss will have you off the squad for that! Right, Blues and Greens on Pitch A, Yellow and Red on Pitch B with Tommy. And take it easy. No pushing, no shoving, no silly tackles. And I want to see you all creating space. Chelsea are going to keep you all on tight leashes.'

Wood started to howl like a wolf and the squad laughed. 'Very funny, Jason,' said McNamara. 'Let's see if you're still laughing at three o'clock.' He blew his whistle again. 'Come on, let's get started.'

Gabe looked over at the changing rooms. More than anything he wanted to call Ray to find out what was happening.

McNamara blew his whistle again. 'Come on, Gabe!' shouted the coach. 'Look lively.'

Gabe waved in acknowledgement and jogged over to join the rest of the Green team on Pitch A, though football was the last thing on his mind. All he could think about was how terrified Laura and Ollie must be, and how powerless he was to do anything to help.

CHAPTER 22

Ray left his car on double yellow lines and jogged into Chinatown. Ray was a big fan of Chinese food and over the years had visited most of the restaurants in the area. Den had done business there to, and it was through one of the business deals that Ray had met Jimmy Chen. Jimmy was British-born but his parents had flown him back to Hong Kong during his school holidays to stay with his grandparents to make sure he remained fluent in Cantonese and Mandarin. What they didn't expect was for Jimmy Chen to fall in with the 14K Tai Huen Chai triad when he was in his early teens and by the time he graduated from South Bank University with a degree in economics he was a fully-fledged White Paper Fan, a triad administrator. During the week Jimmy worked for a bank in the City from where he laundered much of the triad's London profits, but at the weekends he still helped out at his parents' Chinese supermarket.

Den used 14K's connections to ship cannabis from Thailand to the UK, and much of the money he had paid had gone through Jimmy. Money was taken in cash to the supermarket and Jimmy always insisted on giving them a receipt, in Chinese, saying that his bosses at 14K insisted on it. Ray knew that Den wouldn't be happy about him calling on Jimmy unannounced, but Ray didn't see that he had any choice.

The supermarket was busy, packed with Asians stocking up with the products that they couldn't get at a regular British supermarket, things like duck's feet and pig entrails and all sorts of exotic vegetables. Jimmy was sitting behind one of the cash registers and his eyes widened in surprise when he saw Ray. 'What's up?' he asked.

'I need a word in private,' said Ray.

'I'm busy, mate. Up to my eyes.' He gestured at the queue of Asian housewives lined up in front of him.

'It won't take long,' said Ray.

'Mate, seriously, you'll have to come back.'

Ray opened his jacket just enough for Jimmy to see the butt of his gun. 'I could fire a shot into the ceiling and see what that does for trade,' he said.

'What the fuck is wrong with you?' hissed Jimmy. One of the Chinese housewives barked at him in Cantonese but he ignored her.

'Jimmy, back room, now. Or I'll start making a fuss.'

Jimmy cursed in Chinese, stood up, and apologised to the customers. An elderly man sitting at the other cash register shouted over at Jimmy and Jimmy waved his hands and shouted back. Jimmy pushed open the door that led to the store room and Ray followed him inside. It was where Jimmy wrote out his receipts. There were shelves piled high with sacks of rice and cans of produce, with a small metal desk and chair in the far corner next to a metal filing cabinet. 'What the fuck is going on?' asked Jimmy, trying to act aggressively but failing miserably. He was a good six inches shorter than Ray and probably half the muscle mass and from the look of him wasn't privy to any of the exotic Chinese martial arts. Ray back-heeled the door shut. 'I need your help, Jimmy,' he said.

'What the fuck are you doing here, Ray?'

'If you'd shut the fuck up I'll tell you.' Ray took out his phone.

'You shouldn't be here. This is my business, what if the cops are watching me, this isn't….'

Ray held up a hand to silence him. 'Chill, Jimmy.'

'Chill? What the fuck do you mean, chill? You come in here waving your gun around…'

Ray slapped him across the face and Jimmy fell back. 'I did not wave my gun Jimmy, will you shut the fuck up and listen to me. I don't have much time.'

Jimmy's lip had split and blood trickled down his chin. Jimmy touched the blood and then stared at is fingertips. 'What the fuck, Ray?'

'Just fucking chill, Jimmy. Take deep breaths and calm the fuck down.' Ray held the phone in front of Jimmy's face. 'You ever seen a tattoo like this? Probably some Chinese enforcer. Triads maybe.'

Jimmy squinted his eyes. They were watering and he was having trouble focusing. Ray thrust the phone into his trembling hands. 'Zoom for yourself.'

Jimmy fiddled with the phone, stared at the screen, then nodded. 'Yeah, that's Teddy Kang. What's he done?'

'You're sure?'

Jimmy nodded. 'Yeah, I'd recognise that scorpion anywhere. And the Chinese character for the number seven. That's how many men he's supposed to have killed in China.'

Ray took the phone back and put it in his pocket, ignoring the question. 'Who is he?'

'Enforcer for CK Lee. You heard of him?'

'No.'

'Lee's a nasty piece of work and Kang's his red pole.'

'What the fuck's a red pole?'

'That's what the triads call their enforcers.'

'This CK Lee is 14K?'

Jimmy shook his head. 'Wop Hop To. His boss is a guy called Yung Jaw-Lung. He's even nastier than Lee. Wop Hop To are mega in Hong Kong and San Francisco, not so big here.'

'Where can I find this Lee?'

Jimmy shrugged. Ray drew back his hand to slap Jimmy again and Jimmy flinched. 'For fuck's sake, Ray, what's wrong with you? If I knew, I'd tell you. I know him, but I don't know where he lives.'

'What about Kang?'

Jimmy wiped his bleeding chin again. 'Ray, mate, they don't hand out business cards. It's like, I don't know where you live, right? But I know you.' He dabbed his chin with his sleeve. 'Though I'm starting to wish I didn't.'

'What do you know about Lee? What's his story?'

'Like I said, he's a nasty piece of work. Extortion, protection rackets, gambling.'

'Drugs?'

'Not that I know of. Gambling is his big thing.'

'Football?'

Jimmy nodded. 'Football, sure. Horses, too. And he runs illegal casinos. Chinese places, you wouldn't get a look-in. What's your problem with him?'

'That's for me to know, Jimmy.'

'No problem. But be careful. I heard that Lee just hacked the finger off a guy who owed him money. That's his thing. He charges interest in fingers.'

'This guy who lost a finger? You know him?'

Jimmy nodded. 'Sammy Wu. Been around for ever.'

'Got an address?'

'What do you think I am, the Yellow fucking Pages?' He flinched as Ray drew back his hand. 'No, I don't have an address for him.'

'Where does he hang out?'

'If he fell foul of CK Lee there's a good chance he'd have gone to his illegal gambling den, above a restaurant in Lisle Street. The one with the ducks in the window. Top floor.'

'Like a casino?'

'Some mahjong but mainly sports betting. You're wasting your time, though. There's no way they'll let a gweilo in.'

'Gweilo?'

'Foreigner.'

'Fuck me, Jimmy. This is my country. I'm not a fucking foreigner.'

'You are in Chinatown. And here you always will be.' He wiped his still bleeding mouth. 'Are we done?'

'Yeah. Thanks.' Ray headed for the door.

'Why are you so fucking grouchy?' asked Jimmy, dabbing at his chin again.

Ray stopped and turned to look at him. 'My family's in trouble, this Lee's behind it, I think.'

'You should have said,' muttered Jimmy. 'Nothing matters more than family. I get that.'

'I'm sorry.'

'It's a bit late for sorry, Ray.'

Ray hurried out, ignoring the accusatory stares of the Chinese housewives queuing at the tills.

CHAPTER 23

Laura rolled over as she heard the door open. It was one of her captors, as always wearing a ski mask. She fixed him with her eyes and grunted through the duct tape that had been wound around her mouth after she had made the FaceTime call to Gabe.

'No one can hear you,' said the man. He was dressed in black and had a brown leather shoulder holster on top of his pullover in which nestled a grey gun.

She increased the urgency of her grunts until eventually he walked over to the bed and looked down at her.

'I told you, shut up.'

She shook her head, held his gaze, and grunted again.

The man reached into his back pocket and pulled out a flicknife. He pressed a chrome button on the side and the blade flicked out. It was at least six inches long and it glinted as he waved it back and forth over her face. Laura kept trying to talk. She doubted that he would kill her, at least not while they needed Gabe to carry out their orders. And if he was going to hurt her, a slap would be more effective. The knife was to intimidate, that was all. 'Shut up,' said the man. She could see two tattoos on his right hand. A scorpion and a Chinese character. He was Chinese, she realised. She hadn't noticed the eyes before but he was definitely Chinese.

She began breathing hard and fast, the duct tape pulsing in and out. The man snarled at her, stuck the blade between her flesh and the tape, and cut off the gag. 'Just let me talk, just for a minute,' she gasped.

'If you don't shut up I'll put the bag back over your head,' said the man.

'Listen to me, please. There's no need to gag us.'

'You don't tell me what to do,' said the man.

'My son can't breathe.'

'He's okay.'

'He's not okay. I'm a doctor and I can tell you he's not okay. If you gag a child like that and he throws up he can choke on his own vomit.'

'He won't throw up.'

'And he's asthmatic. He has breathing problems.' That was a lie but she would say anything to get them to take the gag off Ollie.

'Asthmatic?'

'He has trouble breathing. If he gets upset, and what you're doing is upsetting him.'

The man turned to look at Ollie, and he shrugged. 'He looks okay.'

'Are you a father?'

'Why do you ask that?'

'Because if you were, and something like this happened to your child, you'd want them to be as comfortable as possible. You wouldn't want him to be tied up like an animal would you.' The man looked at Ollie, then back at her. 'Look, we won't shout or scream, and even if we did I don't think anyone would hear us, would they? We're tied up so we can't run away. Can't you just take off our gags? At least then if he's scared I can reassure him.' She forced a smile. 'Please? Can you do that?'

The man held her gaze for several seconds, then he nodded slowly. 'Okay,' he said. 'But if either of you make a sound, I'll have to put the tape back on.'

'Sure,' said Laura. 'We'll be quiet.'

The man went over to the sofa. Ollie looked up at him, his eyes wide with fear. 'It's okay, Ollie, don't worry,' Laura called over to him. 'He's going to take the gag off your mouth. Just take deep breaths and relax, everything is going to be fine.'

The man used the knife to carefully cut the duct tape away from Ollie's mouth. 'Mum!' he said. 'Mum what's happening!'

'Shush, Ollie,' said Laura. 'We have to be quiet.'

'But what's happening?'

'Ollie, listen to me. Everything is going to be all right but we have to be quiet. Can you do that for me? Just for a while.'

'Okay, mum,' said Ollie, but she could hear the uncertainty in his voice.

'Just pretend it's a game,' said Laura.

The man straightened up, still holding the knife. He tossed the pieces of duct tape onto the floor. 'Thank you,' said Laura. 'You're a good man.'

'Just keep quiet,' said the man.

She tried to smile as brightly as possible. 'Can I bother you for something else?'

His look hardened. 'What?'

'Just water,' she said. 'I'm really, really thirsty and I'm sure my son is too. If you could get us some water that would be wonderful.'

The man waved the knife at her and then nodded. 'Okay,' he said. 'I will get you water.'

Her smile widened. 'That's so nice of you, thank you.'

The man grunted and left the room. Laura listened intently and heard the man head down stairs. 'Ollie, can you hear me?' she whispered.

'Yes, mum.'

'It's going to be all right,' she said. 'I promise.'

'Who are they, mum?'

'They're just bad men, but they won't hurt us.'

'They want daddy to lose the game, right?'

'That's right.'

'Will he do that?'

'He'll do whatever he has to so that we get home safely,' she said. 'Just trust in him, and trust in me. Everything is going to be okay. I know this is a bit scary, but think of it like a movie. It'll be all right by the end.'

'Okay, mum.'

Laura bit down on her lip as she heard the uncertainty in her son's voice. Was it going to be all right? Life wasn't like a movie, everything wasn't always all right by the time the credits rolled. Bad things often happened to good people, especially when the bad people were wearing ski masks. But the ski masks were a good sign, Laura realised. If they didn't want them to see their faces, that meant there was a good chance they would be released when it was all over. That was the hope she clung to as she lay on her side and stared at the wall.

Chapter 24

'Earth to Gabe!' shouted McNamara. The coach was standing some ten feet away from Gabe but the footballer didn't react. 'Gabe!' shouted McNamara.

Gabe shook his head. 'Sorry, what?'

McNamara jogged over. 'Are you ok?' asked the coach. 'It's like you're a million miles away.'

'Sorry, Joe. I didn't sleep well last night.' Gabe couldn't think of a better lie.

'I need you on top form for this game, Gabe,' said McNamara. 'You're the captain and you need to be leading from the front.'

Gabe nodded enthusiastically. 'I'm fine,' he said. He jumped up and down on the spot. 'Raring to go.'

McNamara patted him on the back. 'I'm depending on you, Gabe.' He put his whistle between his lips and blew hard. 'Right guys, pair up and let's do some stretching.'

Gabe paired off with Michael Devereau. Following McNamara's instructions, they stood back to back and linked arms, taking it in turns to bend forward and take the other man's weight. Gabe did the moves on auto-pilot. All he could think about was Laura and Ollie and the danger they were in.

CHAPTER 25

Ray hurried down Lisle Street. Chinatown was busy and there were people waiting outside most of the restaurants. He found the one with a line of roast ducks hanging from a stainless steel bar in the window. To the left of the entrance was a red door. There was an intercom next to it with a single button. He stabbed at it with his finger and after a few seconds someone spoke in guttural Chinese. 'Yeah, it's me,' he said. There was no response. He stabbed at the button again but there was only silence. He looked up and saw a CCTV camera pointing down at him. He grinned and flashed the camera a thumbs up but nothing happened. 'Bastards,' he muttered, and walked across the road to stand in front of a dim-sum restaurant. He looked up at the top floor of the building opposite. The windows had been covered with what looked like aluminium foil. The roof seemed to be flat and he could see the rims of two large satellite dishes. He paced up and down as he considered his options, which basically came down to abseiling down from the roof or finding someone to let him in.

He looked at his watch and cursed. It would soon be mid-day, just three hours from kick off. As the minutes ticked by he considered going back to see Jimmy Chen and press him for more information, though he guessed that would be flogging a dead horse.

Two middle-aged Chinese women in long wool coats and with almost matching floppy hats walked by the duck restaurant, deep in conversation. But when they reached the red door they stopped talking and the shorter of the two reached up and pressed the button. Ray put his phone to his ear and faked a call as he jogged across the road. The women were just disappearing into the hallway when Ray reached the door, and he caught it just before it closed. He eased it open and slipped inside. The women were chatting away again and hadn't noticed him. He let them go up the stairs and around the corner before he headed up after them.

There was a door on the first floor but the two women kept on going. Ray followed, treading softly so as to make no sound. There was another door on the second floor. Ray heard them knock and he hurried up so that he arrived just as the women were going inside. Ray heard loud clicking noises and the occasional dull thud. He followed them, keeping his face away from whoever had opened the door. There was one long room with a bar to the left and a dozen small tables where mahjong was being played, mainly by elderly Chinese women. They were banging their tiles on the table with every move, and no one seemed to care about the near-deafening noise. At the far end of the room were four large screen televisions, all showing sport. One was tuned to horse racing and three were showing football programs, including Sky TV. Ray looked over at the screen and realised the view was the pitch where Gabe would be playing. More than a dozen Chinese men were standing around watching the screens. Moving among them were two Chinese teenagers in grey suits who were constantly tapping on iPads, presumably collecting bets. There was a gents toilet and a ladies at the end of the bar.

Off to the right was a roulette table with more than a dozen Chinese crowded around it, and there were two fully-occupied blackjack tables beyond it.

The men were busy watching the screens and the women were caught up in their mahjong games so Ray got halfway along the bar before anyone realised there was a non-Chinese in the room. One of the barmen shouted at a heavy in a black suit who was standing by the roulette table croupier. The heavy came over. He was a few inches shorter than Ray but looked like he could handle himself. 'This is for members only,' grunted the heavy.

Ray smiled easily. 'I'm only passing through,' he said. 'I'm looking for Teddy Kang.'

The man frowned. 'You know Teddy?'

'Yeah, I know Teddy.'

The man scowled. 'I don't think so.'

'Don't fuck me around, where is he?'

The man grabbed Ray's arm and tried to pull him towards the door but Ray stood rooted to the spot. The man tried harder but Ray was a good deal heavier and stronger and he didn't budge. Ray grinned then he moved, so quickly that before the man had any idea what had happened his right arm was wedged up behind his back and he was being frogmarched to the toilets. Ray kept the hold on with his right hand and opened the toilet door with his left. He pushed the man inside and bolted the door. There was a line of urinals, a small sink with a paper towel dispenser above it, and one foul-smelling unoccupied stall. The man struggled but Ray yanked his arm up higher until he went still, then he put his foot behind the man's right knee and pushed him down to the floor. The man yelped in pain but his cries were silenced when Ray pushed his head into the toilet and pressed the flush button. Water gushed around the man's head and he struggled frantically but Ray's grip was too strong. 'Where's Teddy Kang?' shouted Ray. He pulled the man's head up. 'Where the fuck is Teddy Kang?'

The man gasped for breath and Ray pushed his head down into the water again and held him there for twenty seconds or so, ignoring the banging on the door.

Ray pulled the man's head out of the toilet bowl again. The toilet had stopped flushing and the cistern was refilling. 'I can do this all fucking day,' said Ray. 'Now where is Teddy Kang?'

'I don't know,' spluttered the man. 'Not seen him all day.'

'Is he with CK Lee?'

'Probably.'

'What about Sammy Wu? Where does Sammy Wu live?'

The man hesitated and Ray shoved his head back into the toilet and hit the flush button. The man struggled but Ray kept his face pressed into the water for a full thirty seconds before pulling him out. The man coughed and spluttered and then gasped for breath.

'Where's Sammy Wu?'

'At home. Teddy worked him over pretty bad.'

'Where's home?'

'Camden.'

'Where in Camden?'

'I don't know,' said the man. Ray started to push his head back into the toilet but the man struggled. 'Okay, okay,' he said, and gave Ray the address.

Ray grabbed the man by his collar and yanked him to his feet. 'Thanks for your help,' said Ray, then slammed the man's dripping wet head against the tiled wall and let him slump to the floor.

He unlocked the door and pulled it open, then cursed when he saw the four Chinese heavies waiting for him. They were all wearing ill-fitting suits and cheap shoes but unlike Jimmy Chen their stances suggested they could handle themselves. 'I'm done here,' said Ray. 'Just let me on my way.'

The four heavies didn't move. From the look of the way they were standing, three were right-handed and one was a leftie. The leftie looked as if he favoured kicking to punching, and the man closest to him had his forward hand open telegraphing his intention to grab. The customers who weren't sitting at the tables had moved to the far end of the room, like sheep huddling away from dogs.

Ray reached into his jacket and pulled out his Glock. 'I'm going,' he said. 'I've got things to do.'

He stepped to the side, moving towards the exit. The four heavies moved with him, their eyes watchful.

'Easy does it,' said Ray. The leftie started bobbing from side to side as if he was about to attack so Ray pointed the gun at his chest. 'Take it easy, mate,' said Ray. 'I've never seen a kung fu move yet could block a bullet.'

A heavy had taken the opportunity to move closer and he warned him off with his gun. 'I'm going,' he said. 'No harm done.'

One of the heavies said something in Chinese and spat on the floor.

'I know, I know,' said Ray. 'But I'm the one with the gun so you're just going to have to get over it.'

The heavy to his left also said something and they all started to move towards him. Ray moved his gun from side to side, trying to cover them all. 'Come on then,' he said. 'Which one of you wants a bullet in the balls?' he said, still moving towards the door. He had his game face on but it was clear that they weren't buying it. And he knew why, if he did pull the trigger then the shots would be heard outside in the street and he was the intruder, he was the one with a weapon. If the cops arrived, he'd be the one hauled off to jail. But even before the cops could get there the ones that he hadn't managed to shoot would beat him to a pulp.

He continued to back towards the door, his finger on the trigger. 'Let's just call this a day, shall we? No hard feelings? Live and let live?'

Another heavy had appeared from a side room. He was big, his shoulders straining the material of his cheap black suit. He had a black metal tube in his right hand and he flicked it out and it extended to two feet of metal. He walked confidently towards Ray, swinging the baton back and forth. Ray pointed the Glock at the man's chest but that didn't seem to faze him in the least. He barked something in Chinese and the leftie answered, then grinned savagely.

Ray's mind raced while his face stayed a blank mask. There were fifteen rounds in the clip, enough to put three bullets in each of the heavies, but being responsible for a massacre in a Chinese gambling den meant his future would be bleak to say the least. He kept the gun moving from side to side, figuring that none of them would want to be the first to take a bullet. But once he pulled the trigger it would all move into overdrive, he was sure of that.

He couldn't risk a look over his shoulder but he knew that he had about ten feet to go before he reached the door. At least in the hallway outside he'd have more of a chance of fighting them off because they'd have to come at him in single file.

The big guy was holding the baton above his head and Ray was considering the merits of firing a warning shot when a bottle of Sing Tao beer arced through the air and slammed into his shoulder. Froth sprayed across his face, temporarily blinding him, and when his eyes cleared the guy with baton was lashing out. Ray jumped back but the baton caught the barrel of the Glock and sent it clattering to the floor.

The heavy to Ray's right kicked at his groin but Ray grabbed his ankle with his left hand and smacked him in the mouth with his right fist, sending him crashing into the wall. A second heavy threw a punch at Ray's face but it was slow and Ray had all the time in the world to pivot on his back leg, grab the wrist and then twist it up and around so that man had no choice but to go with it. That left him with his face looking down and his right arm up in the air. Ray brought his knee up and felt the man's nose crack and splinter. He let go of the arm and jumped back, hands close to his head.

The big heavy with the baton swung it around and despite his bulk he was fast so all Ray could do was use his hands to block the arm. The blow knocked him back but as he moved he managed to back-fist the man in the face, smashing his nose. Blood spurted down his chin but other than that the blow didn't seem to affect him. He raised his baton again and Ray dropped and punched him several times in the solar plexus, putting all his weight behind the punches. The man grunted but stood his ground. Ray threw a final punch, this time at the man's groin, and finally he had the satisfaction of hearing the man scream in pain.

Ray straightened up but as he did a foot caught him the small of the back and he fell against the big man. The big man grabbed him in a bear-hug and began to squeeze. The man snarled in Ray's face and Ray smelled stale garlic and onions. Ray drew back his head then smashed his forehead down on the man's already broken nose. The man released his grip on Ray and Ray chopped him hard across the throat before turning around just in time to catch the leftie mid-way through a vicious kick that would have felled him if it had landed. Ray had just enough time to twist away from the kick then he swept the other man's leg away from him. The man seemed to freeze for a second, parallel to the floor, then gravity kicked in and he hit the ground hard. Ray kicked him in the side then headed for the door. As he grabbed for the door handle he remembered the Glock but he took a quick look over his shoulder and realised there was no way he could get to it.

He pulled open the door and ran into the hall-way and down the stairs. He heard the thud of feet behind him so he stopped, turned, and punched his pursuer twice in the stomach. The man's breath exploded from his lungs and Ray pushed him back.

As the man hit the stairs Ray turned and continued to run down, taking the stairs two at a time. He threw open the door to the street and almost fell on to the pavement. Shoppers turned to look at him and he straightened up and forced a smile. There were more footsteps behind him. Ray turned again just in time to confront the last of the heavies who had produced a knife and was charging towards him, his face contorted with rage. Ray waited until the last second then pulled the door hard, smashing it into the man's shoulder and sending him crashing against the wall. Ray pushed the door open then kicked the man between the legs with so much force that the man flew through the air and crashed into the stairs. Ray pulled the door closed and walked away, breathing slowly and evenly.

A West Indian parking warden was standing by the BMW, tapping on his hand-held terminal. 'You can't park here,' said the warden.

'Yeah, but I did, didn't I?' said Ray. He had scraped the knuckles of his right hand and he licked them as the warden printed out a ticket and held it out. 'You know where you can shove that,' said Ray, pulling open the door and climbing in.

The warden pulled up a windscreen wiper and shoved the ticket under it. 'Doesn't matter whether you take it or not, you have to pay,' said the traffic warden.

Ray scowled at him and drove off. The parking ticket wasn't a problem. He never paid them, or speeding tickets. The car wasn't registered in his name. It was taxed and insured through a shell company. He never held onto a car for more than three months and he bought and sold them for cash through a dealer he knew in Battersea. This one he'd be dumping by the end of the day, no matter how things played out.

CHAPTER 26

At twelve noon on the dot, McNamara brought the practice to an end with a long blow on his whistle. 'Hit the showers, guys,' he shouted. 'We're leaving at twelve-thirty sharp.'

Gabe ran to the changing rooms and pulled open his locker door. He grabbed at his phone. One missed call, from Ray. He stabbed at the screen and listened to the brief message that Ray had left, then called him back. McNamara came into the changing rooms as the phone was ringing out and he pointed an accusatory finger at him. 'That's five hundred quid, Gabe. You know the rules.'

'Joe, this is important.'

'Doesn't matter,' said the coach. 'No phones in the changing rooms. Manager's rules.'

'It's a stupid rule,' said Gabe.

'Take it up with the boss,' said McNamara. 'Me, I think he's right. Now's the time to be focussed on the game.'

Gabe put his phone back in the locker. 'Fine.'

'Are you okay?'

Gabe opened his mouth and was about to give McNamara a piece of his mind, but then he got a grip on himself and forced a smile. There was no point in antagonising the coach and he was right, they were the manager's rules. 'Just feeling the pressure, Joe. I've never been captain before.' He took off his boots and put them in his kitbag, then sat down and ran his hands through his hair.

'You'll be fine,' said McNamara. 'The guys look up to you. The role could have been yours irrespective of Eric going walkabout.'

Gabe nodded. 'Thanks.'

'I mean it, Gabe. You've always been an asset to this team, not just as a bloody good player but as a calming influence for the younger lads as well. They listen to you. They respect you.'

Gabe looked up and smiled, and this time he meant it. 'Thanks, Joe.'

McNamara patted him on the shoulder. 'I'm not blowing smoke up your arse, Gabe. I mean it.' He jerked a thumb at the showers. 'Now get showered and we'll be on our way.'

McNamara went over to talk to Second Assistant Coach Martin Jessop, a grey-haired former England winger who was the longest serving member of the coaching staff. The two men stood by the door and there was no way that Gabe could take out his phone without them seeing him, so he stripped off his kit, grabbed a towel and headed to the showers.

CHAPTER 27

Teddy Kang and Billy Huang were sitting on a low grey leather sofa, their feet up on a marble coffee table as they watched the large screen TV mounted above an ornate fireplace. They had helped themselves to a bottle of brandy and two balloon glasses, taking care to choose a bottle from inside the drinks cabinet rather than one of the expensive brands on display. They weren't expecting CK Lee to return any time soon and they figured they had earned a drink.

On the screen, two former footballers were discussing the upcoming Chelsea match against a backdrop of the stadium. Huang waved his glass at the screen. 'Did you put a bet on?'

Kang grinned. 'Be stupid not to. You?'

'I wasn't sure.'

'You weren't sure? How could you not be sure? You know who's going to win.' He shrugged. 'Up to you.' There was a bowl of shelled peanuts on the table and Kang leaned over and grabbed a handful.

'What happens afterwards,' asked Huang.

'Kang frowned. 'What do you mean?'

Huang gestured up at the ceiling. 'When the game's over. What happens to them?'

'I don't know. It's up to CK.'

'Do you think he'll want us to kill them?'

'Maybe. Maybe not.'

'I think he'll want us to kill them.'

'It's possible,' said Kang. He looked across at Huang. 'Is that a problem?'

'I've never killed a woman or a kid.'

Kang looked at the television and sipped his brandy. 'It's no different to killing a man. Killing's killing. Same as eating. Do you care how old the cow was when you eat a steak? Meat's meat.'

They sat in silence for more than a minute, watching the television and sipping their brandy, before Huang spoke again. 'Have you?'

Kang kept his eyes on the screen. 'Have I what?'

'Killed a woman? Or a kid?'

Kang held his hand out, showing Huang the two tattoos. 'The seven I killed in China. One was a woman. One was a boy.' He shrugged and took back his hand. 'It was no big thing.'

'What happened?'

Kang sighed. 'Why do you want to know?'

'Because I want to know what it's like.'

Kang sipped his brandy again. He kept his eyes on the screen as he spoke. 'It was about a year before I left Shenzhen. Someone had stolen money from Yung Jaw-Lung. A couple of million Hong

Kong dollars. He knew it was one of three men who worked for him. But he didn't know which one it was. So we worked them over, for days. No one talked. The one who'd done it knew that if he confessed, he was dead. So no one confessed. No matter what we did to them. And we did a lot.' He took another drink before continuing, in a low, dull monotone. 'So Yung Jaw-Lung tells us to get their wives and children. They had one each. One child policy. Two had sons, one had a daughter. We lined the wives up and Yung Jaw-Lung tells the men that if one of them doesn't confess, all three of the women will die. But if the culprit confessed, all three women would be spared.' He shrugged. 'No one confessed.'

'So you killed them?'

'I killed one of them. There were three red poles. I was the youngest, still making a name for myself.'

'And how did you kill her?'

Kang made a throat-cutting gesture with his hand.

'And the kids?' asked Huang, fiddling with his jade ring. Kang recognised it as a sign of nervousness. Huang always played with the ring when he had something on his mind.

Kang shrugged. 'Yung Jaw-Lung had us line the kids up in front of the men. He told them the same thing. If the culprit confessed, the kids would live. If he didn't.' He shrugged.

'And what happened?'

'No confessions. So the kids died.'

'You used the knife again?'

Kang nodded. 'One clean cut.'

'And that didn't worry you?'

Kang shrugged, his eyes still on the screen. 'Meat's meat.'

The two men drank in silence for a while, but Huang had more questions. 'So who stole the money?'

'We never found out,' said Kang.

'They all died?'

'We killed the wives. We killed the kids. Then we killed the men.'

'Why would the man do that? Why would he stay silent while you killed them all?'

Kang sighed, bored with the conversation. 'He probably thought that he was dead anyway. Which is true. If he had confessed he would have had to give the money back to Yung Jaw-Lung. Then he would have been killed, and his family too. You know what Yung Jaw-Lung is like. At least this way someone in his family would still have the money.' He shrugged. 'As to the other families. He wouldn't care. Why would he? Does anyone really give a fuck about anyone else?'

They both sipped their brandy.

'There is another possibility,' said Huang eventually.

'What's that?'

'Maybe none of them stole the money. Maybe it was someone else. Maybe all those people died for nothing.'

Kang turned to look at him, his eyes cold. 'Why don't you shut the fuck up?' said Kang. 'And that's not a rhetorical question.'

CHAPTER 28

The squad filed out of the main building at 12.30 on the dot. The team bus was waiting for them, engine running. Mancini, Armati and Moretti were the first on, as usual, so that they could grab the three seats at the back. All the players were dressed in suits and ties at the insistence of the manager. They were all dark haired but other than that had little in common physically. Mancini was dark-skinned and sported designer stubble; he was heavy-set and well muscled. Armati was taller and had his hair gelled into place and cultivated a perfectly-trimmed goatee, and Moretti was balding with a large cleft in his chin and a nose that had been broken several times. The three Italians competed to buy the most stylish suit and it looked as if Armati was winning, no doubt helped by his Hugo Boss connection.

The manager's insistence on suits and ties was one of his more esoteric rules because the players stayed on the coach until they arrived at the stadium and there were no photograph opportunities as they got off the coach. But Guttoso insisted, claiming that it was necessary to build team spirit. Not wearing a suit incurred a fine of a thousand pounds and missing a tie was another two hundred and fifty.

Gabe hung back, looking for an opportunity to use his phone. He saw Tommy Brett looking at him and Gabe faked a grimace and rubbed his stomach. 'Tommy, I need to use the toilet.'

'Use the one on the bus,' said Brett.

'I'll stink the place out,' said Gabe. 'I had vegetarian last night. You wouldn't want to put the guys through it.'

'More information than I needed,' laughed Brett. He gestured at the building. 'Get a move on.'

Gabe waved his thanks and jogged back to the main door. Tim Maplethorpe was the last to leave, knotting his tie. He was tall and wide-shouldered and his suits always seemed to be a size too small for him. 'Where are you going?'

'Toilet,' said Gabe, hurrying inside.

Maplethorpe grinned. 'Nerves, huh?'

Gabe let the door slam behind him before pulling out his phone and calling Ray's number. Ray answered on the third ring. 'Ray, what's happening?' asked Gabe, his voice trembling.

'I'm on my way to see a guy called Sammy Wu. I'm hoping he knows where CK Lee is.'

Gabe frowned. 'Who the fuck is CK Lee?' he asked.

'One of the guys in the pictures you sent me is a triad enforcer who works for a Chinese gangster

139

called CK Lee. Lee is big-time into gambling so he could well be trying to rig this match.'

'You think this Lee has my family?'

'I think he's behind it, yeah.'

'So let's call in the cops? Get them looking for Laura and Ollie.'

'Look where, Gabe? All I have is the name. I don't know where he lives. And if he finds out the cops are involved, he might just have them killed. I'm on my way to see a gambler that Lee has gotten heavy with. His name's Sammy Wu. I'm hoping this Wu will tell me where I can find Lee.'

'Ray, kick off is in two and a half hours.'

'I know. So we've got time.'

'And what if the match starts, what am I supposed to do?'

'That's your call, Gabe. But I won't let you down. Where are you?'

'Training ground. We'll be on the coach at half past and at the stadium about one.'

'I'll call you when I have something,' said Ray.

'I might not be able to answer, they have a thing about us using phones.'

'I'll text you,' said Ray. 'Don't worry, I'll keep you in the loop.'

Gabe ran a hand through his hair. 'Thanks for this, Ray.'

'Fuck that,' said Ray. 'You're my little brother and no one fucks with my little brother.'

CHAPTER 29

Ray ended the call and concentrated on the road. Then his phone rang again. Ray picked it up and looked at the screen. It was Donovan. Ray cursed and took the call. 'What the fuck's going on, Ray?' snapped Donovan.

'What do you mean?'

'You know what I fucking mean. You want to tell me why you're charging around Chinatown waving your gun around?'

'That's not what happened?'

'Then explain to me why you beat the fuck out of Jimmy Chen. You don't want to piss off the 14K, Ray. They take no fucking prisoners.'

'I didn't beat him up.'

'You slapped him around, that's what I heard.'

'Look, I'll send him flowers, okay. I just didn't have time for please and thank you and he was playing silly buggers.'

'Which brings me back to my first question. What the fuck is going on?'

Ray took a deep breath. He and Donovan went back a long way, but at the end of the day Ray was the hired hand and Donovan was the boss. 'Den, I can't tell you.'

'You see how that doesn't cut any ice with me, don't you? The 14K do a lot for me, and if I lose their trust it'll cost me an arm and a leg. And I mean that figuratively and probably fucking literally as well.'

'This isn't about the 14K.'

'Then tell that to Jimmy Chen.'

'He had some information I needed and I didn't have time to fuck around. I didn't hurt him, Den. Not as much as I could have.'

'What's going on, Ray? It's not like you to go maverick.'

Ray took another deep breath. 'It's Gabe. He's in trouble.'

'With the 14K?'

'No. But maybe another triad.'

'How the fuck does a professional footballer get mixed up with triads?'

'I don't know.'

'Don't fucking lie to me, Ray. I deserve better than to have you bullshitting me.'

'Telling you won't help,' said Ray.

'No, but it might stop me having you put down like a mad dog.'

'Are you threatening me, Den?'

'You're the one who's threatening me, mate. Threatening my business. Threatening relationships I've spent years building up.'

'This is personal, it's nothing to do with your business.'

'Where are you Ray?'

'I'm in North London.'

'I need you back here.'

'No can do, Den. Sorry.'

'Don't fucking "sorry" me, Ray. You're my attack dog and I need you to come to heel, now.'

Ray opened his mouth to reply but then realised there was nothing he could say to placate Donovan. 'I'll call you back,' he said, and switched off the phone. Donovan rang back a few seconds later. Ray let the call go through to voicemail.

He reached Camden. He'd put the address the triad heavy had given him into the BMW's SatNav but from the look of the map on the screen it was planning to take him the long way around. He swore. He didn't know the area well enough to try a rat run and the SatNav was telling him he was nine minutes away. He saw a car park to his left and he drove in. He took a ticket from an automatic dispenser and drummed his fingers on the steering wheel while he waited for the barrier to rise. He found a space and took a last look at the SatNav before locking up the BMW and starting to jog through the crowded streets.

CHAPTER 30

Sammy Wu was lying on his sofa, a bottle of Johnnie Waller Red Label whisky and a carton of day-old fried rice on the coffee table next to him. He was watching Sky Sports. The Walford United-Chelsea teams were on the screen and being discussed by two pundits who appeared to love the sound of their own voices. Wu had five thousand pounds wagered on the game. Not with CK Lee, obviously because CK Lee had stopped taking his bets. Wu had found a Vietnamese guy who would let him bet on credit, but only on condition that Wu used his car as security, along with two Rolex watches that Wu had owned for years. The Vietnamese had taken the watches and made Wu sign over his car before giving him a five thousand pound line of credit. The man was cheating him because the watches alone were worth twice that, but Wu knew that beggars couldn't be choosers, especially beggars who had already lost one finger for late payment.

The bookies all rated United as sure-fire winners but Wu had been able to get half-decent odds on goal difference. He was sure he'd double his money, at the very least. His door intercom rang and he ignored it. He wasn't expecting anyone. He sipped his whisky. The doorbell rang again, more insistent this time. He put down his glass and reached for his walking stick. The bell continued to ring as he pushed himself up off the sofa and hobbled over to the door. His left hand was still to painful to use so he tucked the stick under his arm and picked up the phone with his right. 'Who is it?' he asked in Cantonese.

'Sammy Wu?'

It was a gweilo. 'Yeah.'

'I need to talk to you.'

'I'm busy. And I don't know you.'

'Sammy, stop fucking about. If you don't buzz me in right now I'll kick the fucking door down and then do the same to you.'

Wu shook his head contemptuously and hung up the intercom. He was just settling back on the sofa when he heard rapid footsteps on the stairs outside He frowned, then flinched as someone banged on the door. 'Open up, Sammy, or I swear I will blow your fucking house down!'

Wu struggled to his feet and limped over to the small kitchen at the back of the flat. He pulled open a drawer and took out a carving knife just as the front door slammed open with a splintering sound. The man who had kicked it open stepped into the room. He was tall, well over six feet, broad-shouldered and with murder in his eyes.

Wu held the knife out. 'I've got a knife,' he stuttered.

'Yeah, I can see that,' said the man. He slammed the door shut behind him and it banged against the splintered jamb. 'Look, my name's Ray Savage, I'm a friend of Jimmy Chen's. I just want to talk to you.'

'About what?'

'CK Lee.'

Wu shook his head. 'Never heard of him.'

'See now Sammy we both know that's a lie. Now stop being a dickhead and put down that knife.'

'Get the fuck out of my flat!' shouted Sammy. He limped towards Ray, slashing with the knife. Ray waited until the blade had swung past him before stepping forward to grab the wrist and twist it savagely. Wu yelped and the knife fell to the floor. Ray pulled Wu out of the kitchen, pushed him into the middle of the sitting room and back onto the sofa. 'I'll call the cops!' shouted Wu.

'Yeah, of course you will,' said Ray, picking up the knife. 'Same as you did when CK Lee chopped off your finger. He walked over to the sofa, and pointed the knife at the cast on Wu's leg. 'He did that to you, too, did he?'

'I don't know anyone called CK Lee,' said Wu, but there was no conviction in his voice as he stared at the knife in Ray's hand.

Ray lifted his leg and stamped down on Wu's cast. Wu screamed in pain.

'I need to know where CK Lee is, Sammy, and you're going to tell me one way or another.'

Wu gritted his teeth and stared fearfully up at Ray.

'So talk,' said Ray. 'Or I'll start cutting off the rest of your fingers.'

'You can't do that.'

Ray grabbed Wu's left wrist and placed the edge of the blade against Wu's thumb. 'I can do what the fuck I want!' he shouted. 'And when I've finished on your fingers I'll start on your toes. Now tell me, where the fuck is CK Lee?'

'Wu shook his head fearfully. 'He'll kill me.'

'He won't know it's you that told me. Now where the fuck does CK Lee live?'

'I don't know!' shouted Wu, then he screamed as Ray drew the blade across the base of his thumb. Blood spurted across his palm. 'Okay, Okay!' shouted Wu. 'For fuck's sake, stop!'

'Just tell me where he lives and I'm out of here,' said Ray.

'I don't know,' said Wu.

Ray reached out for Wu's wrist and Wu folded his arms hurriedly. 'For fuck's sake, I don't know where he lives.'

'Tell me something about him, Sammy. Something that will help me find him.'

'He runs a gambling place on Lisle Street. In Chinatown.'

'Tell me something I don't know, Sammy.' He brandished the knife and reached for Wu's wrist.

'For fuck's sake!' shouted Wu. 'Why are you doing this?'

'I need to find him. I need to know where he lives?'

'Why the fuck would I know where he lives? We're not friends. I owe him money and he cut off my finger and shattered my knee. If I don't pay him what I owe him he'll take all my fingers, one at a time.'

Ray put his face near Wu's. 'Listen to me Sammy, and listen to me good. When I get my hands on Lee, he's not going to be collecting any debts. Trust me on that.'

Wu licked his lips nervously. 'You're going to kill him?'

'That's for me to know, Sammy. But take my word, he won't be bothering you again. Now give me something. Something I can use.'

Wu nodded quickly. 'He's got a mistress. Had her for a year or so. Name of Lilly. She should know where he is.'

Ray grinned. 'And where do I find this Lilly?'

Wu screwed up his face. 'I don't know. I'm sorry.'

'Then that's no bloody help, is it? What about a phone number?'

Wu shook his head. 'I just know that he has a mistress, that's all. She used to work in a brothel in Gloucester Place.'

'Where in Gloucester Place?'

'I don't know the number. It's a basement.'

'You've been there?'

Wu nodded. 'It's run by Mrs Wei. She's been around for ever.'

'Tell me how to find it,' said Ray, and he listened as Wu ran through the directions. When he'd finished, Ray tossed the knife onto the sofa. 'If I ever find out you've called Lee to warn him, I'll come back and cut off your dick, I swear to God.'

Wu held up his bandaged hand. 'I don't owe him any favours,' he said. 'And if you kill him, make sure it's painful.'

Chapter 31

A large steel gate rattled to the side and a steward in a fluorescent jacket waved the coach through. The driver opened the door and Joe McNamara and Tommy Brett got off first, followed by Martin Jessop. It was a short walk to the door that led to the changing rooms, which was being held open by another steward. Gabe stayed on the coach. He took out his mobile phone and called Ray but it went through to voicemail.

'Gabe, that's a five hundred pound fine!' shouted McNamara, pointing at him through the window. 'You know the rules!'

Gabe scowled and put the phone away. He jumped as a hand fell on his shoulder. It was Ronnie Watts. 'You okay, mate?' asked Watts from the seat behind him.

'Yeah,' said Gabe.

'You worried about the penalty thing?' Gabe grimaced but didn't reply. 'Mate, you'll be fine. You're in great form.' He squeezed Gabe's shoulder. 'I'd hate to be facing you, I can tell you that much.' He stood up.

'Thanks, Ronnie,' said Gabe. He'd completely forgotten about his penalty record but he could hardly tell the keeper what was worrying him. He forced a smile. 'Butterflies. I'll get over it.' He followed Watts off the coach, his kitbag over his shoulder.

'Gabe?'

Gabe turned around to see a steward standing next to a young boy who wasn't much older than Ollie. It was Gerry McGee, one of the longest-serving stewards at the ground. He was in his sixties and had been a fan of the team for more than half a century. 'Gerry, how are you?'

'Just wanted to wish you luck, Gabe,' said the steward. 'And introduce you to my grandson, Alfie.'

The boy was clearly nervous and biting his lower lip as he looked up at Gabe. Gabe smiled and offered the boy his hand. 'Pleased to meet you, Alfie.'

The boy looked up at McGee and he nodded encouragement. 'Go on, lad.'

The boy tentatively shook Gabe's hand. He was decked out in a team shirt with Gabe's number 10 on the back and a team scarf around his neck and was holding a program. 'Let me sign that for you,' he said, and took out a pen. He signed the front cover and handed the program back.

'I got Alfie and his dad seats in the main stand,' said McGee.

'You should be with them,' said Gabe.

McGee shook his head. 'The club needs me, Gabe.'

Gabe grinned. 'That's true. The place wouldn't be the same without you around.' He smiled at Alfie. 'Your grandad's been here every time I've played. Never missed a game.'

'And I've seen you score some amazing goals,' said McGee. 'Remember that shot two years ago, against Villa?'

'The cross from Eric, you mean? Perfect, wasn't it?'

'His cross was a bit high, to be honest,' said McGee. 'But you got it, brought it down and that volley?' He shook his head in admiration. 'It was a blur, the ball. The keeper didn't even see it.' He patted his grandson on the shoulder. 'Anyway, we don't want to keep you. You have a great game, Gabe. And congratulations on being captain.'

'Acting captain,' said Gabe. 'How did you know?'

McGee tapped the side of his nose with his finger. 'We stewards know everything,' he said.

Gabe laughed and hurried over to the door to the changing rooms where McNamara was waiting impatiently. 'Fan club?' said the coach.

'Gerry's been with the club longer than almost anyone,' said Gabe. 'And he'll probably be here long after we've gone.'

Through the door was the yellow-tiled corridor off which led the changing rooms. To the left were the facilities for the visitors. A cramped room that hadn't been painted in years, with small lockers on the floor and hooks for larger items. There was a whiteboard that had been screwed unevenly by the fire doors, and two of the fluorescent bulbs in the ceiling didn't work. They had never worked, just one of a dozen minor irritants that had been put in place to hopefully put visiting teams on the back foot. The showers were set to blast out cold water when switched on, with the thermostat only kicking in after ten seconds or so. There was a treatment area with just two ancient massage beds, and three sinks, one of which had a note on saying that it was blocked and wasn't to be used.

To the right was the changing room used by Gabe and his teammates. It was four times the size of the away team's facilities. The physio area had an ice-bath and half a dozen state-of-the-art massage beds, a medical station, a gym area with a range of exercise machines, and a huge locker area with floor to ceiling doors. On the front of each locker was a life-size picture of the player in action. Gabe went over to his locker and pulled it open. His kit was already hanging there, including a choice of long or short-sleeved shirt. The players were given brand new shirts for every game and afterwards they were free to swap them or offer them to charities or fans.

Gabe dropped his kitbag onto the bench in front of his locker. Inside the locker was a charging point for phones even though the manager had forbidden their use in the changing rooms. There was an individual air-conditioning unit and Gabe turned his onto full cold and let the breeze play across his face.

He flinched as McNamara blew his whistle to get everyone's attention. Gabe turned to see that Piero Guttoso was standing next to the coach, his hands thrust deep into the pockets of his cashmere overcoat. Guttoso was close to being obese and his large feet were splayed out for balance giving him the look of a King Penguin looking for a fight. He had a mane of grey hair combed back and permanent flushed cheeks, and there was a small chunk of his left ear missing, rumoured to be the result of a brutal brawl when he was a teenager. 'I just dropped in to wish you luck,' he said, in his heavy Italian accent. 'Not that you need luck.' He nodded at McNamara. 'Not with a coach like Joe. I just need you to go out there and do your best, because I know your best is more than enough to kick their arses.'

There were several whoops and cheers from the team, but Gabe stayed silent. Guttoso was right. They were more than capable of beating Chelsea, but if they did, if United should win... He shuddered at the thought of what the consequences would be. If anything were to happen to Laura and Ollie and it was his fault... He shuddered again.

'The owner's in his box with his family and a dozen monks, so we need to put on a good show today,' continued Guttoso. 'He wants me to watch it in the box with him so please, don't fucking let me down.' He turned on his heel and walked out.

'If he really has got a dozen monks with him then we're in deep shit,' said Armati.

'Why's that?' asked McNamara.

'They only have even numbers of monks at funerals,' said Armati. 'When it's a wedding or a blessing, it's always an odd number.' He shrugged. 'I used to have a Thai girlfriend.'

The team laughed. Armati changed his girlfriends about as often as he changed his wristwatch, which was pretty much on a daily basis.

'Well I know we all appreciate the boss's pep talks, but I've got a few words to say myself,' said McNamara. 'The pundits have us down as easy winners, but we all know there are no easy victories, only easy defeats. I want you to go out there and play as if you're the underdogs. With heart. No slacking off, no thinking we've won the game before we set foot on the pitch. Got it?'

The players nodded.

'Excellent. Okay, grab yourselves a snack and a drink and then Tommy will go through their line up with you and give you the weather briefing.' He looked at his watch. 'I know Marco and Michael want the physio to work on them, anyone else need it?'

Armati raised his hand and Devereau laughed. 'You know you won't be getting a happy ending,' he shouted.

Armati frowned. 'What is a happy ending?'

The players laughed and headed for the side room where a range of healthy snacks, sandwiches, tea, coffee and soft drinks had been arranged on a large table. On the far wall was a large flatscreen TV on which the coaching staff would replay highlights from the first half at half time.

McNamara walked over to Gabe. 'You okay?' he asked.

'Sure. Fine.'

'How are the knees?'

'Knees?'

'Those funny-shaped things that connect your thighs to your shins,' said the coach. 'Gabe, seriously, are you okay?'

'Yes, sure. All good, Joe.'

'Are you hurting? Do you need to see the doc?'

'Joe, I'm fine,' said Gabe. In fact he hadn't given a thought to his knees from the moment he'd received the FaceTime call from Laura. 'Pre-match jitters.'

'You never get worried before a game,' said McNamara. He patted him on the back. 'This is your big day, Gabe. One more penalty and you're in the record books.'

Gabe nodded.

McNamara's eyes narrowed. 'Seriously, Gabe. You're okay?'

'Of course. Sure.' He smiled as confidently as he could. 'I'll give it a hundred and ten per cent, Joe, you know I will.'

McNamara grinned. 'I know you will. You always do.' He handed him a black armband with the word CAPTAIN on it. 'You'll be needing this.'

CHAPTER 32

The address Sammy Wu had given Ray was a basement flat in a long line of white stucco houses. There was a gate set into the black railings at the front of the building with a flight of metal steps leading down to a black door. A handwritten sign stuck to the wall stated the obvious – BASEMENT FLAT. Underneath were five Chinese characters which Ray assumed meant the same in Chinese. He went down the stairs and pressed the doorbell. A few seconds later the door was opened by a middle-aged Chinese woman in a dark blue denim dress. 'I'm a friend of Sammy Wu's,' said Ray.

'Come in, come in,' she said brusquely. 'Not stand on doorstep.'

She ushered him inside and closed the door. They were in a hallway with a laminated wood floor and a narrow black table on which an incense stick was smouldering, filling the air with the scent of jasmine. Two open doors led off to the left and at the end of the corridor was another door, closed.

'In, there,' she said, pointing at the door closest to him.

'Are you Mrs Wei?' he asked.

'Talk in room,' she said impatiently. 'In, in.'

Ray did as he was told. It was a small bedroom with a double bed covered in a red sheet with matching pillows. Thick curtains were drawn across the window and the only light came from a bedside lamp over which had been draped a red silk scarf. On a bedside table was a glass bowl containing a variety of condoms, a box of tissues and a tube of KY Jelly that from the look of it had been well-used. Ray suppressed a shudder as he turned around to look at Mrs Wei. Close up, even under the red light, it was clear that Mrs Wei was well over sixty. Her face was smooth and unlined, but unnaturally so, as if her skin was made of wax, but it was her hands that gave her age away. They were rough and wrinkled and dotted with liver spots, and the nails were yellowing. The skin around her neck was mottled and loose and Ray realised she was closer to seventy. 'I have four girls today,' she said. 'All young and all pretty. I will show you them and you can choose.'

Ray put up a hand to silence her. 'Sammy told me that Lilly used to work here.'

'She left,' said Mrs Wei. 'Rose is same Lilly. Young and sweet. I will get Rose for you.'

'Mrs Wei, I just want to talk to Lilly.'

Mrs Wei sighed. 'She not here. I tell you already.'

Ray reached into his trouser pocket and pulled out a money clip with a thick wad of fifty pound notes. 'Sammy Wu said you might know where I can find Lilly.'

Mrs Wei screwed up her face as she peered at the notes. 'Why you want Lilly?' she barked.

'I just need to talk to her. It's nothing bad, I promise. I'll pay her, too.'

'How much?' she said, her eyes still on the wad of fifty pound notes.

'Five hundred pounds, if you can give me her address.'

She looked up from the notes and tilted her head on one side. 'How I know you not police?'

'Because I'm offering to pay you for information.'

'The police pay. Entrapment.'

'Do I look like a cop?' He held up the money. 'Do cops carry money around like this?'

She shrugged. 'Who knows what cop look like? Take off clothes.'

'What?'

'Take off clothes,' she repeated.

'I don't want a massage. I want information.'

'You want information, you take off clothes.'

'Are you serious?'

Mrs Wei didn't say anything, she just folded her arms and stared at him impassively. Ray sighed and took off his jacket. He tossed it onto the bed, then kicked off his shoes and took off his trousers. He stood in his boxer shorts, his arms out to the side. 'Happy now?' he said.

'Take off everything,' said Mrs Wei.

'For fuck's sake,' said Ray.

'No need for bad language,' she said. 'Policeman can not take off clothes. That is rule.'

'I'm not sure that's true,' said Ray. When he saw that Mrs Wei was serious, he sighed and took off his shorts. 'Okay?'

Mrs Wei turned her head and shouted in Chinese. A few seconds later he heard soft footsteps in the hallway and a Chinese girl appeared in the doorway. She was in her late twenties with a pageboy haircut and bright red lipstick. She was wearing a white knee-length nightdress cut low to show a cleavage that was so impressive that her breasts must have been enhanced.

Ray shook his head. 'I don't want a massage.'

Mrs Wei ignored him. She spoke to the girl in Chinese and the girl got down on her knees in front of Ray. 'No fucking way,' said Ray, taking a step back.

'I told you, no bad language,' said Mrs Wei sternly. 'She give you oral, I know you not police. She not give you oral...' Mrs Wei shrugged. 'This way I know for sure. Policeman can not have oral. That is a rule.'

'Mrs Wei, this is crazy.'

She looked at him and shrugged again.

Ray sighed. 'Okay. Fine.' He looked down at the girl and she smiled up at him. 'Go ahead.'

Mrs Wei spoke to the girl in Chinese and her smile widened. Her teeth were perfectly even and gleamingly white. She moved towards him and from the way her breasts moved Ray figured they were probably real after all. Ray closed his eyes as she took him in her soft, warm mouth. Her hands stroked the inside of his thighs and Ray felt himself grow hard, then Mrs Wei clapped her hands. 'Okay, enough,' she said. The girl moved back, licking her lips.

Ray opened his eyes. Mrs Wei spoke to the girl in Chinese and the girl stood up. 'Give her fifty pounds,' said Mrs Wei.

Ray bent down and retrieved his money clip from his trousers. He gave the girl a fifty-pound note and she took it and left the room. Mrs Wei held out her hand. 'My money,' she said.

Ray gave her five hundred pounds. 'Okay if I get dressed now?'

'If you want to stay naked, up to you.'

Ray dressed quickly as Mrs Wei checked the banknotes. 'So what you want to know?' she asked.

'I just want to know where I can find Lilly,' pulling on his trousers.

'She stay in Knightsbridge. Near Harrods.'

'CK Lee takes care of her now?'

Mrs Wei's face hardened. 'You know Mr Lee?'

'I know of him.'

'Bad man,' she said. 'You be careful.'

'Yeah, I'm not hearing good things about him,' said Ray. He buttoned up his shirt and slipped on his shoes. 'He took Lilly?'

Mrs Wei nodded. 'I paid a lot to get her into the country. Many thousands of pounds. But Mr Lee said he wanted her. He likes young girls. Lilly was the third girl he took from me.'

'So why do you let him come here?'

Her eyebrows arched. 'You think I can stop him? You think I can stop him doing what he wants?' She shook her head. 'Mr Lee always gets what he wants.' She held up her dainty left hand and for the first time he realised that the tip of her little finger was missing. 'This is what happened when I tried to stop him,' she said. 'I had a girl here, before Lilly. Mr Lee wanted her and I said no.' She waved the hand in front of Ray's face. 'He did this to me and I never said no again.'

'Bloody hell,' said Ray, putting on his jacket. 'Why didn't you go to the police?'

'Police can not help,' she said. 'And if I tell the police, I lose more than finger.' She shrugged. 'Mr Lee does not care about the police. Not here and not in China.'

Ray nodded. 'I'm sorry,' he said, and he genuinely meant it. 'But thank you for your help.'

Mrs Wei held up the fifty-pound notes. 'No need for thank you,' she said. 'Money is thank you enough.'

CHAPTER 33

The team sat for half an hour listening to Martin Jessop go through the opposition line up and fine-tuning their set pieces to take account of the fact that Chelsea's main defender had been dropped because of a tendon injury and replaced with a left-footer. Gabe sat with a coffee trying to listen but all he could think of was his wife and son being held at gunpoint. Could he really do that? He was just one man in a team of 11. Could one man actually throw a game? What if he tried and failed? Would the kidnappers carry out their threat? And if they did, how could he live with himself? And what if he did throw the match – how could he be sure the kidnappers would release his family. He realised he was gritting his teeth and he took a deep breath. Now wasn't the time to be tensing up.

He slipped his phone out of his pocket and stole a quick look at the screen. Ray hadn't called. He put the phone away and sipped his coffee. His heart was pounding so hard it felt as if it was about to burst out of his chest. He took another sip of coffee and realised that the players in front of him had twisted around to look at him and that Jessop was looking at him expectantly.

'Sorry,' said Gabe. 'I missed that.'

'Focus, Gabe,' said Jessop. 'I know that you find the pre-match briefings as dull as ditchwater but you might at least pretend to be listening.'

'Sorry, Martin. My bad.' He raised his coffee mug. 'Won't happen again.'

'All I said was that any penalties will of course be down to you, unless you say otherwise. For any of you who have been living under a rock the past week, Gabe is just one penalty away from breaking the record for the most consecutive penalties scored. I'm not suggesting that any of you start diving in the opposition's penalty box, but every little helps.'

Gabe raised his coffee mug in salute.

'That's all for now guys,' said Jessop. He looked over at a wall-mounted clock. 'It's now one-forty-five, we'll be out for a warm up at two, until then do whatever you have to do.'

Gabe stood up and hurried over to the toilets. He waited until he was in a cubicle with the door closed before pulling out his phone. He called Ray's number but it went straight through to voicemail. 'Ray, what the hell's happening?' he hissed. 'Just over an hour to go. Where are you? Did you find that guy Lee?' He ended the call, then slammed his hand against the side of the cubicle, hard. He called again and left a second message. 'Let me know what's happening,

Ray. They make it difficult for us to use our phones on match day so send me a text or leave me a message.' He felt tears stinging his eyes and he blinked them away. 'I'm scared, Ray. I'm so scared. I don't know what to do.' He took a deep breath and let it out slowly, annoyed at himself for getting so emotional. 'If I don't hear from you, I'll do what I can to throw the game. Like I said, just over an hour to go.' He closed his eyes, trying to think what else he should say, but nothing came to mind. 'Thanks, Ray,' he said eventually. 'Thanks for this.' He ended the call and wiped his eyes with the back of his hand.

CHAPTER 34

It was residents parking only in the street but it was Saturday so there were no restrictions and Ray found a parking space close to where the SatNav said Lilly lived. Lilly's flat was in a mansion block in a side street, a redbrick building with a flight of stone steps leading up to a front door with symmetrically-patterned stained glass windows. He pressed her buzzer and after a few seconds heard a hesitant 'hello?'

'Lilly, hi, I'm a friend of Mrs Wei's,' said Ray.

'Mrs Wei?'

'She gave me your address.'

'Mrs Wei gave you my address? Why?'

'I just need to talk to you, Lilly.'

'I am not allowed visitors.'

'I just need to talk to you, that's all.'

'And Mrs Wei sent you?'

'Yes.'

There was a silence lasting several seconds and then the door lock buzzed. Ray pushed open the door. He headed up a green-carpeted stairway. Lilly's flat was on the third floor and she already had the door open when he reached it. She had put the security chain on and was peering nervously through the gap. At first he thought it was a child, she was barely five feet tall, but as he got closer he realised she was older. But not much. She had long black hair and all he could see was one almond-shaped eye. He smiled. 'Hello,' he said.

The eye stared back at him suspiciously. 'Who are you?'

'My name's Ray. Mrs Wei gave me your address.'

'You are a client? I don't see clients any more.'

'No, I'm not a client. I just want to talk to you.' He held up his hands and flashed her his most disarming smile. 'I'm a nice guy, really.'

'I'm not supposed to let anyone in.'

'I understand. But I won't be long. And it's not a good idea to talk out here, the neighbours might hear.'

She bit down on her lower lip, then unhooked the chain and opened the door. She was wearing a white shirt and light blue jeans ripped at the knee. Her bare feet were tiny, the toenails spots of scarlet. Her bright red lipstick matched her nail polish. 'You can't stay long,' she said.

As she closed the door, Ray could see that although she was tiny, she was definitely not a child. But she was still a teenager, no doubt about that. She walked down the hallway, her waist-length hair brushing the top of her jeans. From the way she swung her hips, Ray was pretty sure she knew he was watching her. She took him past a small red shrine in which a joss-stick was burning into a small sitting room with a low black leather sofa and a coffee table across which were scattered a dozen fashion magazines. There was a big screen television on a stand that was filled with DVDs of Chinese movies and soap operas. She turned and put her hands together, like a waitress about to tell him the day's specials.

'Is Mrs Wei okay?' she asked.

'She's fine.'

'Please tell her that I miss her. A lot.'

'I will,' said Ray, though he doubted that he would be seeing Mrs Wei again.

She sat down on the sofa and smiled at him. At least her lips smiled, her eyes seemed to be full of sadness, as if she was close to tears. 'And you can tell her that I am well. I don't want her to worry about me.'

'Why don't you call her, tell her yourself?'

She gave a barely audible sigh, then shook her head. 'It is forbidden,' she said quietly.

'Forbidden?'

She frowned. 'Is that the wrong word? I mean I do not have permission. It is not allowed.'

'By who? CK Lee?'

She nodded but didn't reply, as if she was afraid of uttering his name.

'Your English is good.'

She smiled at the compliment. 'Thank you.'

'Do you go to school here?'

'No, Mr Lee won't allow that. But I watch a lot of television. It was hard at first but I'm getting better.'

'Well it's working. How old are you, darling?'

She jutted up her chin like a defiant child. 'Twenty,' she said.

'You don't have to lie to me, I'm not a cop.'

'Seventeen,' she said, quietly.

'And how long has Lee been taking care of you?'

'A year or two.'

'Since you were sixteen?'

'Fifteen,' she said. 'My parents sent me here to work.'

'From where?'

She wrinkled her nose as if she didn't understand the question.

'Where were you before?' asked Ray.

'China, of course,' she said.

'They sent you to London to work?'

She nodded. 'They are poor. This way I can send money back to them.'

'Lee pays for you?'

She nodded again. 'He takes care of me.'

'And you're okay with that?'

She shrugged. 'What can I do? My family need money.'

'And your parents knew what you would be doing here?'

'The man who arranged it said I was to be a waitress.'

Ray rubbed the back of his neck. 'I'm sorry, darling.'

'It's okay.'

'You like this CK Lee?'

Her eyes hardened. 'I hate him.'

'Why?'

She turned her back on him and undid her shirt. She let it fall down to her waist and he saw a large dragon tattooed on her back, mainly black with green eyes and red flames shooting from its jaws. 'He made me have this.'

'He made you?'

'After he took me away from Mrs Wei he took me to a tattoo shop.' She pulled her shirt back on and turned around to face him as she buttoned it up. 'He said he liked to look at the dragon while he fucked me.'

'I'm sorry,' he said.

She shrugged, her face blank. 'It's not your fault.' She sat down and put her hands in her lap.

'Is this better than working for Mrs Wei?'

She shrugged again. 'Before I had to see a lot of men every day. Now I see only Mr Lee. But he doesn't come to see me often. I'm like his prisoner.' She shrugged again. 'It's boring.'

'Did he ever take you to his house?'

'Sometimes,' she said.

'Where is it? His house?'

'I don't know.'

'North London? South? West?'

'I always went in his car. It was a big house, Modern. Very expensive. But I don't know where it was. I don't know London very well. Mr Lee doesn't like me going out on my own. He says if I go out the police will catch me and send me back to China.'

'Did you cross the river?'

She frowned. 'I don't think so.'

'So north of the river,' said Ray. He smiled. 'That's something, anyway.'

'You should ask Mr Zhou. He's a good friend of Mr Lee. Mr Zhou will probably know where Mr Lee lives.'

'Who is he?'

'He owns a restaurant in Kensington. Mr Lee took me to eat there sometimes.' She smiled. 'Very good food but so expensive.'

'What's the name of the restaurant?'

She said something in Chinese and then put her hand over her mouth. 'I'm sorry. In English it's called the Peach Garden. It's near Harrods.'

'Thank you, Lilly.'

She smiled coyly. 'Do you want to fuck me? You can.'

Ray's jaw dropped. 'God, no.'

'You don't like young girls? All men like young girls.'

'Lilly, darling. You're as cute as fuck but you're way too young for me. No offense.'

She frowned. 'What do you mean, no offense?'

'I mean I don't want to upset you. You're lovely, but I'm not here for sex. I just want to find CK Lee.'

'Have you got children?'

Ray nodded. 'A son.'

She smiled. 'I bet you're a good father.'

Ray shook his head. 'No. I'm not a father.' He shrugged. 'It's a long story.' He looked at his watch. 'I'm going to have to go, Lilly. You know, you can go to the police.'

'They'll send me back to China.'

'But at least you'll be away from Lee.'

'And my family will have no money.' She shrugged. 'Better I stay.'

Ray turned to go, then stopped. 'Have you got a phone?'

She nodded.

'Can I borrow it?'

'Of course.' She picked up an iPhone off a table and handed it to him. He tapped in his number and gave it back to her. 'If you have any problems, you call me. My name's Ray.'

'Ray,' she repeated.

'If anything happens, if you need help, just call me.'

'I don't think anyone can help me,' she said, and lowered her eyes. Ray had a sudden urge to wrap his arms around her but he knew how that would end and he had a job to do.

CHAPTER 35

The hour before going out to warm up on the pitch was the time Gabe hated the most. Once he was out and kicking a ball around and the crowd were cheering, the adrenaline kicked in and the body did its thing. But after the briefing and before the warm-up, there was nothing to do, nothing to occupy the mind. Before Guttoso's arrival at the club most of the players would lose themselves in their phones or iPads, fooling around on social media or watching videos or listening to music. The ban on electrical equipment might have helped build team spirit, but it slowed time to a crawl.

He wandered into the briefing area and grabbed an energy bar. He chewed on it as he went back into the changing room. Mancini, Devereau and Armati were lying on massage beds as physios worked on them. Brian Lawrence was examining Reid's shoulder, getting him to raise and lower his left arm as he watched the muscle groups move. Babacar was on a rowing machine, maintaining a slow and steady pace. Wood and Fernandez had already changed into their training kit and were on exercise bikes, apparently racing. Gabe usually spent ten or fifteen minutes on one of the bikes to loosen up and get the blood flowing, but he couldn't be bothered exercising and instead he sat down on the bench in front of his locker and put his head in his hands.

'You okay, Gabe?' asked Fernandez. Gabe looked up. The Argentinian was sitting in front of his locker, reading a glossy car magazine. Like Gabe, he hadn't gotten around to changing into his training kit.

Gabe forced a smile. 'Yeah.'

'You look like shit.'

'Thanks.'

'Do you want to play cards or something?'

Fernandez was a keen poker player, well known around the city's casinos. Gabe had played with him a few times and the Argentinian tended to win more often than he lost.

'Think I'll get some air,' Gabe said. He headed out of the changing room and back to the exit. He went outside and found Moretti and Maplethorpe smoking. They reacted like guilty schoolboys, palming their cigarettes and holding their breath. McNamara was vehemently against smoking, his hatred of the vice honed by his ten years of abstinence. But Guttoso was a heavy smoker so cigarettes hadn't found their way onto the list of finable activities, providing it was done outside. Maplethorpe blew smoke up at the cloudless sky. 'You had me going there, Gabe,' he said. 'Thought it was Joe.'

'Joe's not in there, he's probably checking the pitch,' said Gabe. He took out his phone. Ray hadn't called back.

'You got a bit on the side, Gabe?' asked Maplethorpe.

Gabe frowned. 'What?' he said, as he slid the phone back into his pocket.

'The way you keep checking your phone. Got something on the go?'

'Behave, Tim,' said Gabe. 'My missus is a doctor. Can you imagine the damage she could do with a scalpel?'

'I'm just pulling your chain,' said Maplethorpe. 'Laura's the real deal. She and Ollie coming today?'

Gabe tried to smile but he felt his lips scrape across his teeth. 'Should be,' he said. His eyes filled with tears of anger and frustration so he turned around and went back inside. He let the door close behind him as he blinked away his tears. He had never felt so helpless. His wife and son were in mortal danger and he had to pretend as if life was going ahead as usual. It was a regular Saturday match day, something he had been through hundreds of times before. Except he had to make sure that his team lost. And if they didn't, Laura and Ollie would die.

'You know what would relax you?' asked Maplethorpe.

Gabe hadn't been listening. 'What?'

Maplethorpe repeated the question and held out his pack of cigarettes.

Gabe laughed and waved them away. 'I'm not going to start smoking at my age, you soft bastard,' he said.

'You need something, Gabe,' said Maplethorpe. 'You're very tightly wound at the moment.'

'No I'm not.'

'You were gritting your teeth just then,' He gestured with his cigarette at Gabe's temple. 'And you've got a vein just there that's throbbing like it's set to burst.'

Gabe put his hand up to his head but then realised Maplethorpe was joking. He pointed his finger at Maplethorpe's face. 'Fuck off,' he said.

'I'm just saying, you need to chill. You're captain now.'

'Acting captain.'

'You know what I mean,' said Maplethorpe. 'If you're tense, the team gets tense. Eric was a prick sometimes, but he was quietly confident when it came to match day. And that rubs off on everyone else. Okay?'

Gabe knew that Maplethorpe was talking sense. His role as captain – acting captain – was to lead from the front. On any normal Saturday he'd have absolutely no problem with that and would even relish the responsibility. But this was no ordinary Saturday and this was no ordinary match. If his team won, his family would die. But there was no way he could ever explain that to Maplethorpe so he forced a smile and nodded. "Yeah, you're right,' he said.

'We've got this game in the bag,' said Maplethorpe. 'Chelsea are in a right state at the moment. We'll run rings around them. Your first time as captain and you win. That's a result, right?' He punched Gabe lightly on the shoulder. 'Fuck me, I wish I was in your shoes.'

CHAPTER 36

The Peach Garden was a high-end restaurant with crisp white tablecloths and tall glasses containing orchids on every table. The place was pretty much full even though it was after 2pm. At least half the customers were Asian which suggested the cuisine was authentic, but Ray wasn't there for the food. A pretty Chinese girl in a gold and red Cheongsam standing at a lectern asked him if he had a booking.

'I need to see Mr Zhou.' said Ray.

'He's busy,' said the girl, but the quick glance she gave a door at the rear of the restaurant was enough to tell Ray which way to go.

A waiter blocked his way but two quick jabs to his solar plexus had him doubled over, coughing and wheezing. There was a PRIVATE sign on the door but Ray pushed through and headed up a flight of bare stairs. There were two doors at the top and one had a sign saying OFFICE. Ray threw it open. A middle-aged man in a dark suit was sitting at a computer terminal, peering at the screen over a pair of half-moon spectacles. He jumped as if he'd been hit when the door slammed open. His mouth worked sound-lessly as Ray kicked the door shut and walked quickly across the room. There was a television screen on the wall opposite the desk showing a sports programme.

'Are you Zhou?' asked Ray.

The man nodded. 'Who are you?'

'I'm the guy who's going to break every bone in your body if you don't tell me what I want to know.'

The man frowned. 'What?'

Ray swept the computer off the desk with his arm and it crashed to the floor. Zhou's high-backed chair was on rollers and he pushed himself back until it hit the wall. Ray moved quickly, sidestepping the desk and grabbing Zhou by the throat.

'You can't do this to me,' stammered Zhou.

Ray grinned savagely. 'I'm pretty sure I can.'

Zhou pointed up at a black plastic dome by the entrance. 'I've got CCTV.'

'And I've got a couple of mates who'll put a bullet in your head and bury you in concrete if that CCTV footage goes anywhere near the cops,' said Ray. 'Now this can go one of two ways. You tell me what I want to know, or I beat the crap out of you and then you tell me what I want to know. There is a third option, and that's that I beat you so bad that you can't tell anything to anyone, but that's unlikely because I'm pretty good at hurting people.'

'Please ...'

Ray tightened his grip on the man's throat. 'I don't want to hear please, I don't want to hear you offer me money, or promise me the world if I just let you go. All I want to hear are the answers to my questions. Understand? Just nod if you understand.'

Zhou nodded fearfully.

The door opened and a waiter stood there. He wasn't the one Ray had punched downstairs. He was bigger and holding a large kitchen knife. He froze in the doorway when he saw Ray with his hand on Zhou's throat.

'Tell him everything's all right and to go back downstairs,' said Ray. 'If you don't I'll beat you to a pulp and then I'll rip your restaurant apart.'

Zhou nodded fearfully and then said something to the waiter in Chinese.

The waiter replied, and Zhou spoke again, louder this time.

'Tell him not to call the cops,' said Ray.

'I'm not fucking stupid,' said the man, lowering his knife. 'I can speak English.'

'This is between me and Zhou,' said Ray. 'But if you don't get the fuck out of here it'll be between you and me and that knife won't worry me a bit. Now fuck off downstairs and don't even think about calling the cops.'

'Do as he says,' croaked Zhou.

The man nodded and left the office, giving Ray a final glare before he closed the door.

'Good,' said Ray, tightening his grip on Zhou's throat. 'Now I need an address for CK Lee. I need to know where he lives.'

Ray relaxed his hand slightly and Zhou gasped for air. 'I don't know where he ...'

Ray cut him off by tightening his grip. 'I don't want to hear don't know,' he said. 'That's not what I want. You're his friend, you have to know where he lives.' Zhou tried to shake his head but Ray's grip was relentless. 'Are you going to make me hurt you, Mr Zhou? Because I've hurt a lot of people already today and the gloss has kind of gone off it.' He put his face right up against Zhou's so their noses were almost touching. 'The next words out of your mouth had better be Lee's address or I'm going to start bouncing you off the walls.'

Ray let go of Zhou's throat and the man began to babble. 'I don't know, I promise you I don't know,' he said, the words coming out so fast that they practically ran together. 'He's never taken me to his house I've no idea where he lives I swear please don't hurt me.'

Ray snarled and drew back his fist. Zhou's arms began to flail and his eyes almost popped out of their sockets. 'But I know where he is right now!' he stammered. 'I know where you can find him.'

Ray's eyes narrowed suspiciously. 'Where?'

Zhou pointed at the television screen with his left hand. 'He'll be at the United match. He's got a box. He'll be watching the game.' Ray looked over at the screen and realised that it was the stadium where Gabe would soon be playing.

'Are you sure?'

'Yes. I've been there. It's one of the best boxes, close to the halfway line.'

'So why aren't you there with him?'

'He didn't offer. Sometimes he does, sometimes he doesn't.'

Ray released his grip on Zhou's throat and pointed a warning finger at the man's face. 'If you're lying to me, I'll be back to rip you limb from limb, CCTV or no CCTV.'

Zhou wiped his mouth with his sleeve. 'It's the truth.'

Ray jabbed his finger at Zhou's face again. 'And if you warn Lee, I swear to God I'll kill you. I'll do it personally and I'll do it with pleasure.'

Zhou put up his hands. 'I won't tell him. It's none of my business. This is between you and him and I want nothing to do with it.'

Ray stared at Zhou for several seconds, then nodded slowly. 'Okay,' he said. 'We're good.' Zhou flinched as Ray reached out to adjust his shirt and tie, then straightened the shoulders of his jacket. 'No harm done, right? We're good?'

Zhou swallowed nervously. 'Yes. We're good.'

Ray patted Zhou on the shoulder and he flinched again. 'I'll be on my way, then,' he said. 'You have a nice day.'

Ray turned to go, then gestured at the television. Two commentators were discussing the match against the backdrop of the crowded stadium. 'Have you got a bet on the match?'

Zhou nodded.

'Yeah? Who do you think's going to win?'

'Chelsea,' croaked Zhou. 'By two goals.'

'Good luck with that,' said Ray, as he headed for the door.

Service was carrying on as normal when Ray stepped into the restaurant. The three waiters turned to glare at Ray as he walked by but he ignored them. He looked at his watch. Two twenty. Kick off in forty minutes.

Chapter 37

McNamara let the Chelsea team go out to warm up first. He always let the visitors go ahead so that they would bear the full brunt of the home team supporters as they jeered and cat-called. The Chelsea fans were segregated in a corner section of the stadium, four and a half thousand in all and no matter how hard they cheered they would always be drowned out by the home fans. McNamara let Chelsea have the pitch to themselves for two minutes, then had the team line up in the tunnel. Gabe was at the head of the line, bobbing from side to side, the adrenaline coursing through his system. The coach patted him on the back. 'Give them another minute,' he said.

Gabe grinned. He knew all to well how unpleasant it was to be on the receiving end of the naked hostility of tens of thousands of chanting fans. Eventually McNamara nodded and pointed down the tunnel. Gabe started jogging down the tunnel. As he reached the entrance, the crowd saw him coming and the stadium filled with roars and cheers. As always the hairs on the back of Gabe's neck stood on end and he felt a chill run down his spine. There was no other feeling like it in the world, the open adoration of thousands of fans, many of whom loved the club almost as much as they loved their families.

Gabe left the tunnel and jogged between the seats where the coaching staff and substitutes would sit, and on to the pitch. The sound was deafening, a vibration as much as a noise that had his stomach churning. He looked around at the sea of Walford United colours and forced a smile, He waved his right hand in salute and headed for the goalmouth to his left. The Chelsea team were passing a couple of balls around at the other end of the pitch and their goalkeeper was doing some warm up exercises.

Gabe jogged on the spot, then did a few star jumps. The pre-match warm-up was more for marketing reasons than anything else. The players could do all the warming up they wanted in the changing rooms, but an on-pitch warm-up meant the club could sell advertising space on the training kit so all the players had to turn out and go through the motions.

He heard his name being called and he turned to see Maplethorpe kicking the ball towards him. Gabe reacted instinctively, trapping the ball on his chest, dropping it down to the ground and kicking it back. He jogged on the spot then ran over to intercept a ball that Mancini had sent skidding across the grass.

Gabe could feel the anticipation building. Kick off was just thirty minutes away. He looked up at the windows of the family box. That was where Laura and Ollie would usually be. Ollie would always wave and give him a thumbs up. But not today.

CHAPTER 38

R ay had the route to the stadium on the BMW's
SatNav but the traffic was bad on the route it
selected so he ignored it and took a series of rat runs
through east London. He took a left down a narrow
road, then a hard right. A man on a bike shouted
at him but Ray barely heard him over the roar of
the engine. He took another left, then a right, then
braked at a line of traffic stopped at a red light. Ray
cursed and beat a rapid tattoo on his steering wheel.

There was a knock on the driver's window and
Ray turned to look at an angry cyclist. 'Oi, you cut
me up back there.'

Ray scowled at the man. He was in his thirties
with a black and white swept-back helmet that had a
small camera mounted on it. He was wearing a tight
yellow shirt and even tighter black pants and bright
blue gloves. Ray doubted that the man could see
through the tinted windows of the BMW.

'You owe me an apology for what you did back
there!' shouted the man. He knocked on the window
again.

Ray looked ahead. The lights were still on red.

The cyclist knocked again, harder this time. 'You're on video, you know. Caught on camera. I'll be downloading this on You-Tube when I get home.' Ray stared straight ahead. 'Come on, wind this window down and apologise or I'll report you to the police.'

The man had one of those whiney upper-class voices that suggested a lifetime of entitlement and he clearly wasn't going to stop harassing Ray, so Ray opened the door and slammed it against the man's leg. The man yelped and Ray pulled the door back and slammed it even harder the second time. He heard the satisfying crack of something breaking and the man and his bike toppled into the road. The man began sobbing like a little girl. Ray closed the door. The light turned green and the cars ahead of him began to move. Ray pounded on his horn, encouraging them to move faster. He looked at the clock on the dashboard. Kick-off was just fifteen minutes away.

CHAPTER 39

Laura pushed herself up the bed, using her heels against the duvet and rolling her shoulders. 'Mum, what are you doing?' She could hear her son but not see him.

'I'm trying to sit up, honey. That's all.' The man who'd brought them water had refused to untie them. He had helped her sit up while he held the bottle to her mouth, and then did the same for Ollie. When he'd finished giving them water he had been about to replace the duct tape around their mouths but Laura had begged him not to. He'd agreed not to gag them, but promised that if he heard any noise, any noise at all, he'd be back upstairs.

'I'm scared,' said Ollie.

'I know, but it's going to be all right.'

'Why are they doing this?'

'They want daddy to lose his game today.'

'That's stupid,' said Ollie. 'Why would they want him to lose? Anyway, he's not going to lose, is he?'

'I don't know,' said Laura. She pushed herself again and managed to get her head against the headboard. She grunted and pushed harder and got her shoulders up and with a final shove forced herself into a sitting position. She could see Ollie lying on his back on the couch. 'Ollie, over here,' she said.

Ollie turned to look at her. 'Mum!'

'Keep your voice down, honey,' she said. 'We don't want the men to hear us.' She looked around. To her left was a large window, the blinds drawn. Next to the window was a dressing table and facing her was the door. The couch was to the right of the sofa and above it, on the wall, was a flatscreen TV. To her right was an open door leading into a bathroom.

'What are you going to do, mum?' asked Ollie.

'Let me think, honey,' said Laura. She stared at the duct tape binding her feet. It was presumably the same tape they had used to bind her hands behind her. She needed something to cut through the tape. But what? She looked around. There was a comb on the dressing table but it was plastic and she doubted that would work. There was a framed photograph of a couple, a man and a woman. The frame looked as if it was made of metal, silver perhaps, but the edges didn't look sharp enough to cut the tape. She looked over at the bathroom door. There might be something there she could use.

'Mum?' said Ollie.

'Hush, honey,' said Laura. 'Let me think.'

She rolled her legs over the side of the bed. They had taken her shoes off and her bare feet brushed the thick pile carpet. She stood up slowly. There was

190

no movement in the tape around her ankles, she was going to have to jump and she had no idea how much noise she would make. She hopped forward a few inches and the floorboards creaked under the carpet. She stayed still, listening intently until she was sure no one was coming upstairs, and she jumped again. The boards creaked louder this time. She sat back on the bed. 'Ollie, do you think you can sit up?' she asked.

'Why?'

'I need something to cut the tape,' she said. 'There might be something in the bathroom.'

'Like scissors?'

'Like scissors, yes. But we need to be quiet. Now can you stand up?'

'I'll try,' he said.

'Good boy.'

CHAPTER 40

Ray knew that parking anywhere close to the stadium was going to be impossible on a match day so he started looking for somewhere to leave the BMW once he got within half a mile. He saw a garage in a railway arch and pulled in. A mechanic in stained blue overalls was looking under the bonnet of a Mini Cooper and he straightened up as Ray climbed out. 'Sorry, mate, I'm fully booked, you'll need to come back on Monday,' said the mechanic in a heavy Geordie accent.

Ray took out his money clip. 'Mate, I just need to leave my car here for an hour or so.' He gave the mechanic a fifty pound note. 'There's another one in your hand when I pick it up.'

'I'm shutting up at five,' said the man.

'If I'm not back by five, leave it on the street,' said Ray. He tossed the keys to the man. 'Just put them on the back nearside wheel.'

The mechanic slipped the note into the pocket of his overalls. 'Five sharp, mind,' he said, but Ray was already running down the street towards the stadium.

CHAPTER 41

Chelsea finished their warm-up first and jogged back to the tunnel to a tirade of abuse from around the stadium. When the visitors had left the pitch, McNamara waved his team back to the changing rooms. They jogged off the pitch and down into the tunnel. Gabe was first into the changing room and he pulled open his locker and grabbed his phone. He stared at the screen but his heart fell when he saw that Ray hadn't called, He flinched as McNamara blew on his whistle. 'Five minutes, guys,' shouted McNamara.

The squad began stripping off their training kit and changing into their match shirts. They all had two shirts to choose from – one short sleeved and one long – but both covered with the same advertising, the brewing company that belonged to the Thai owner. Gabe went for the long sleeve version. He pulled on his shirt, then sat down and adjusted his laces and shin pads. Armati was checking his hair in his locker mirror, then used some gel to get his quiff just right. He looked across and saw that Gabe was watching him. 'It's important to look good,' said the Italian.

'Is it, though?' said Gabe. 'Or is it going to mean you fuck up the first time you head the ball?'

'Head the ball?' said Armati. 'Why would I head the ball? This game, it's called football, you know? Not headball.' He finished adjusting his hair and nodded at his reflection, then blew himself a kiss. 'Now I am ready,' he said.

Wood walked by and ruffled Armati's hair. The Italian cursed and launched a kick at Wood's back-side but Wood was too quick for him and skipped away. 'You bastard!' shouted Armati. 'You're only jealous because you're as bald as a…' He struggled for the word and looked over at Gabe.

'Coot,' said Gabe.

'Bald as a coot!' shouted Armati, but Wood had already disappeared into the toilets. The Italian looked down at Gabe. 'What is a coot?'

'Some sort of bird.'

'A bald bird?'

'I guess so.' Gabe shrugged. 'I don't know.' His phone rang inside his locker and he sprang to his feet. He pulled open the door and grabbed his phone. 'Yes, Ray, what's happening?'

'I'm outside.'

'Outside? Outside where?'

'The stadium.'

'What the fuck are you doing here? Laura and Ollie aren't here.'

'No, but CK Lee is. He's got a box'

'So we call the cops?'

'No, that won't work. If they arrest him there's a good chance you'll never see Laura or Ollie again. I'll take care of it. But I can't get inside.'

'Which entrance?'

'The main one.'

'See if there's a steward there called Gerry. Gerry McGee.'

Gabe flinched as a whistle blew close to his left ear. He turned to see McNamara glaring at him. 'What the hell do you think you're doing?' shouted the coach.

'This is important, Joe,' said Gabe.

'Important? Are you having a laugh?' McNamara jerked a thumb at the door. 'Out there is important. For the next ninety minutes that's all that matters.'

Gabe turned his back on the coach and walked away. 'Which entrance are you at?' he asked Ray.

'The main one. At the front.'

'Go left to the players' entrance,' said Gabe. 'Find a steward called Gerry McGee and let me talk to him.'

'Okay,' said Ray. 'Stay on the line, whatever you do.'

McNamara walked around to stand in front of Gabe. He pointed his finger at Gabe's face. 'A grand. I'm fining you a grand.'

Gabe put his hand over the phone. 'Terrific. I'll give you the cash the moment the game's over.'

'Put that bloody phone down!'

Gabe glared at the coach, then pushed past him, kicked open the door and hurried into the corridor. He heard McNamara shouting after him but all that mattered was getting Ray into the stadium.

CHAPTER 42

Ray ran at full pelt, his arms pumping at his sides as his shoes slapped against the pavement, his phone clutched in his left hand. There were only a few latecomers still filing into the stadium but they all turned to watch him run. He flew by two stewards, missing one by inches, and the man swore at Ray's back. He saw a sign saying 'PLAYERS ENTRANCE' and a steward in a fluorescent jacket standing in front of the turnstile. Ray ran up to the man. 'Are you Gerry?'

'Gerry?'

'Gerry McGee.'

The man shook his head. 'Gerry's inside.' He was in his forties with receding ginger hair and a transceiver clipped to his belt.

'Can you tell him I want a word?'

'He's busy, pal. There's a game about to start, in case you didn't know.'

Ray resisted the urge to smack the man in the mouth and instead smiled and held up the phone.

'I'm Gabe Savage's brother,' he said. 'He's on the phone. Says I have to talk to Gerry.'

The steward looked at his watch. 'Like fuck he is, the team is getting ready to go onto the pitch. The game's about to start.'

Ray thrust the phone at the man. 'Speak to him yourself.'

The steward took the phone, frowning, and put it to his ear. 'Who is this?' he said.

He listened for a few seconds, then muttered 'Yes, sure, no problem,' and gave the phone back to Ray. 'Fuck me,' he said. 'Wait here.'

The man used a keycard to operate the turnstile and disappeared into the stadium. He returned a couple of minutes later with another steward. 'I'm Gerry,' said the man. 'You're Gabe's brother?'

'Yeah.' Ray held out the phone. 'He wants to talk to you.'

CHAPTER 43

Gabe paced up and down the corridor as he waited for McGee. The door to the visitor's changing room opened and players began to file out. The Chelsea captain appeared and grinned at Gabe. 'I thought your boss fined you for using the phone,' he said.

Gabe turned his back on him and walked down the corridor. McNamara came out and pointed a finger at Gabe. He was about to shout at him when he realised the Chelsea team were watching so instead he stormed over to Gabe. 'Put that fucking phone away,' he whispered.

'I can't,' said Gabe.

'What do you mean?'

'I have to take this call, Joe. I just have to. I understand the rules, and you are going to have to do what you have to do, but I have to take this call. I'm sorry.'

He heard Ray on the phone. 'He's here. Talk to him.'

'One minute,' Gabe said to the coach. 'That's all I need.' McNamara looked as if he was going to argue, but then the fight went out of him. 'One minute,' he said. 'Or you can get dressed and fuck off.' He turned and walked away, slamming open the door to the changing rooms and disappearing inside.

'This is Gerry,' said the steward in his ear.

'Gerry, mate, I need a big favour,' Gabe said.

'Sure, Gabe. No problem.'

'My brother Ray's there. Can you let him in? I didn't have time to get him a ticket or put him on the list.'

'Sure, I'll do that, no problem. Do you want me to take him to the family box?'

'He'll be okay, Gerry, I know you've got a lot to do. Thanks for this. I owe you.'

'Anything for you, Gabe. And good luck out there.'

Gerry ended the call and hurried back into the changing room as the rest of the United team were filing out. McNamara threw Gabe a withering look as he rushed over to his locker and tossed the phone inside. He went back into the tunnel and took his place at the head of the line, taking deep breaths to steady himself. McNamara looked at his watch then gestured for Brett to open the door. 'Here we go, lads. Let's give it our best.'

Gabe led the team out into the corridor. The opposition was already there, lined up, and the two teams walked quickly down the tunnel towards the pitch. The crowd began to cheer and chant and Gabe felt the familiar vibration in his stomach that had the hairs on the back of his neck standing up. Gabe nodded at the Chelsea captain and he nodded back. 'All right?' he said.

'Yeah,' said Gabe.

'According to the bookies you're going to wipe the floor with us.'

'That's what I heard.'

'Fucking bookies, hey? What do they know?'

McNamara patted Gabe on the shoulder and pointed towards the stadium. Gabe took a deep breath and then started walking. The stadium erupted with cheers and chants and he felt the familiar chill run down his spine as he stepped out into the daylight and the sound washed over him.

Chapter 44

McGee pointed at a concrete stairwell in the corner of the stand, next to a burger outlet where several home supporters were stocking up before taking their seats. 'The family box is on the next level,' said the steward. 'Are you sure you don't want me to walk you up?'

'I'll be fine,' said Ray. 'You're a star.' He hurried to the stairs and ran up, taking them two at a time. There were boxes on all four sides of the stadium, on the first and second levels and Ray had no way of knowing which one CK Lee was in. All Zhou had said was that Zhou's box was close to the halfway line. It wasn't quite a needle in a haystack, but it wasn't far off.

He reached the first level. There was a wide corridor leading the full length of the stand. The doors to the boxes were to his left. Most of them were open. The boxes were pretty much identical, with an inside area with sofas and a dining area, then full length glass sliding doors that led to the seating area. To the side of each door was a small metal cardholder containing the name of whoever had use of the box. The first one was a well-known double-glazing company and half a dozen men in dark suits were drinking glasses of champagne. The second was in the name of G. HARRINGTON and the occupants were a mix of men and women – the men looked like drug dealers in leather jackets and Versace jeans and the women almost certainly hookers. Again champagne appeared to be the drink of choice, though this time it was Cristal and not the Bollinger that the double-glazing team were knocking back. Ray heard the crowd start to roar. He stopped at the doorway to the third box. The door was open and he could see through the box and onto the pitch where the two teams were jogging out. Ray could see Gabe, leading out the United team. Ray smiled to himself. It had been ten years, give or take, since he had seen his brother in the flesh.

A sour-faced woman with scraped-back hair and a Botox-smooth forehead closed the door in his face. Ray grunted and continued down the corridor.

CHAPTER 45

There were 42,000 people in the stadium, but all Gabe's attention was focussed on one man, the referee. He was in his forties, balding and slightly bow-legged. His name was Davie Scott but he was Welsh. He had a cheap Casio watch on his right wrist and a chunky red Goal Decision System watch on his left wrist. The watch functioned as a secondary timepiece but was connected to the stadium's half a million pound Hawk-Eye system which used cameras to monitor the two goal lines between the posts and under the crossbars. When a ball crossed the goal line the watch would vibrate and display the word GOAL. On his left arm, under his sleeve, was the bulge of his Touchline Powerflags paging system through which the Assistant Referees could communicate with him using a system of beeps and vibrations. In a nylon holster secured to his shorts was an aerosol can of vanishing spray that he could use to mark where he wanted free kicks to be taken and to draw a line ten yards from the ball to make sure that the defence kept their distance. The marks would disappear after a minute or so.

The referee tossed the coin he was holding high in the air. 'Heads,' said the Chelsea captain.

The coin landed on the turf and Scott peered down at it. 'Heads it is,' he said, straightening up so that both men could see it. Chelsea made the obvious decision to play towards the home stand so that in the second half they would be playing towards their own supporters. Chelsea took their places and Gabe trapped the ball on the centre spot. He took a deep breath, knowing that the next ninety minutes would change his life for ever.

The referee blew his whistle and Gabe tapped the ball to Babacar on his left. Babacar sent it zipping along the grass to Jason Wood and Wood tapped it across to Reid. It was a set piece they had rehearsed hundreds of times. As the Chelsea forwards rushed towards the ball, Gabe and Babacar sprinted towards the Chelsea goal. The Chelsea defenders moved to mark them. The crowd was buzzing in anticipation and a loud aggressive chant started in the North Stand.

Reid made his move, running hard and fast with the ball at his feet. Gabe scanned the pitch as he ran. There was an opening to the left where Reid could easily reach him with the ball but Gabe broke right. He saw Reid frown in annoyance and then kick the ball over to Babacar. Babacar caught the ball on his chest but as it dropped to the ground he was tackled from behind and went down. One of the Chelsea defenders booted the ball towards the United goal and the crowd groaned in frustration.

CHAPTER 46

Ray reached the final box on the first level. It was the family box, from where Laura and Ollie were supposed to be watching the game. Two stewards were standing outside the door and Ray moved over to the far side of the corridor as he walked by. The stewards looked at him but realised he wasn't a gate-crasher or a threat so they just smiled and nodded. Ray nodded back and headed for the stairs. There was another row of boxes on the second level, pretty much identical to the ones on the floor below. The problem was there were also boxes in the other stand, several dozen in all, and Ray was running out of time. He heard a roar from the crowd, and cheers, then a chant started. 'U-NI-TED. U-NI-TED. U-NI-TED.'

He ran up the stairs and started walking quickly down the corridor. The door to the first box was closed but the card in the holder on the wall said it was being used by a supermarket group. There was another loud cheer from the stadium that seemed to make the floor vibrate, followed by tens of thousands of people groaning in unison. Ray hurried down the corridor.

CHAPTER 47

The Chelsea striker wrong-footed two United defenders and kicked the ball towards the goal but the United keeper was already in position and he caught it easily before taking three quick steps and booting it halfway down the field.

'What the fuck was that?' asked Billy Huang, gesturing at the television. 'He wasn't even trying. How much do these fuckers earn a week? A hundred grand? My aunt can kick better than that.'

The United team were passing the ball back and forth, looking for an opportunity to press forward.

'Come on!' shouted Ricky Zhang. 'Move yourselves. What are you doing?'

Teddy Kang looked up at the ceiling. 'Did you hear that?' he asked. Zhang and Huang were engrossed in the game and neither paid him any attention. Kang picked up the remote and muted the sound.

'What the fuck?' said Zhang.

'Shut up,' said Kang, getting to his feet. 'I heard something.' He listened for a few seconds but there was no repeat of the noise he was sure he'd heard.

'Yes!' hissed Zhang. Kang looked over at him. Zhang was staring at the screen, his fists clenched. A Chelsea defender brought down a United attacker and the ball rolled over the sideline. 'No!' said Zhang, throwing himself back on the sofa. 'Did you see that? Did you fucking see that? He was heading for the goal and that bastard brought him down with a late tackle. And what does the referee do? Nothing.'

Kang tossed the remote onto the coffee table and headed for the door. He pulled on his ski mask and took his gun from its holster as he padded up the stairs. Behind him he heard the television sound go on again. He reached the door to where the woman and kid were being kept and he placed his ear against it. He listened for several seconds and then pushed the door open. The woman was lying on her side, facing away from him. The boy was lying on his back, his eyes closed. Kang stepped into the room and the woman rolled over and looked at him. Her eyes widened when she saw the gun in his hand and he lowered the barrel so that it pointed at the floor.

'Can you check that my son is all right?' she asked.

Kang ignored her as he walked around the room, looking for anything out of place. Then he checked the bathroom.

'Can he breathe all right?' asked the woman.

Kang came out of the bathroom and stared at her for several seconds. 'I heard a noise.'

'He was coughing.'

Kang looked over at the boy. 'He's not coughing now.'

'I think he's having trouble breathing.'

Kang walked over to the couch. The boy's eyes were closed but his chest was rising and falling as he breathed. 'He's asleep.'

'Okay. Thank you.'

Kang reached down and checked the duct tape around the boy's ankles. It was secure.

'Has the match started?' asked the woman as Kang straightened up.

Kang nodded. 'Yes.'

'Who's winning?'

'No one yet.'

'That's good, right? Good for you?'

Kang walked over and stood looking down at her. 'Your husband's team has to lose.'

'What if they don't lose?' asked Laura.

Kang shrugged. 'That depends on my boss.' He checked the tape around her ankles.

'You can't hurt a child, not because of a football match.'

Kang shrugged again. 'Your husband was told what he has to do and what will happen if he disobeys.' He grabbed her arm and rolled her over so that he could check her wrists. They were tightly bound.

'But it's not our fault,' said the woman over her shoulder. 'And it's not my son's fault.'

Kang looked around at the room. Nothing had moved since he was last there. So far as he could see.

'Do you have children?' she asked.

Kang gestured at her with the gun. 'Shut up or I will gag you and the boy again.'

'Okay,' said the woman. 'I'm sorry.' She closed her mouth and forced a tight-lipped smile. Kang took one more look around the room and then went back downstairs. He stopped at the bottom of the stairs and listened for a few seconds, then went into the sitting room.

Zhang and Huang were leaning towards the television, their eyes glued to the screen. 'Come on, come on,' Zhang was saying, his hands gripped into tight fists. 'Come on.'

'What's the score?' asked Kang as he took off his ski mask but before anyone could answer he saw the numbers in the top corner of the television. 0-0. No score.

'Come on!' said Zhang, louder this time.

Kang headed for the sofa but before he could sit down there was a flurry of action on the screen and the ball rocketed into the back of the Chelsea net. 'Who scored?' asked Kang.

'United,' said Huang. 'The black fellah.'

'Babacar,' said Zhang. 'He's from Senegal.'

'Where the fuck is Senegal?' asked Huang.

'Africa,' said Zhang.

'So 1-0 to United,' said Kang, sitting down and reaching for his brandy glass. 'CK is not going to be happy.'

CHAPTER 48

Babacar was doing a moonwalk behind the goal as the home fans cheered him on. Reid was taking credit for the pass that Babacar had scored from but Gabe knew that the ball had cannoned off the shoulder of one of the Chelsea defenders before Babacar had slammed it into the back of the net. It had been one hell of a goal, one that came close to justifying the player's two hundred thousand pound a week salary. The Chelsea keeper was standing with his hands on his hips and a look of disgust on his face, shaking his head as if Babacar had done something wrong, but it had been a perfect goal. The keeper had done nothing wrong, he had placed himself in the centre of the goal and was anticipating the shot to come from Moretti, who had been calling for the ball. Truth be told, Reid had aimed his cross at the Italian but hadn't seen the Chelsea defender running across the penalty box. The ball had glanced off the defender's shoulder and shot across to Babacar who had reacted instinctively, swiveling on his back foot and putting his whole bodyweight behind a kick that sent the ball into the top left hand corner of the goal before the keeper had any time to react.

Gabe flinched as an arm fell across his shoulder. 'Fuck me!' shouted Michael Devereau in his ear. 'That was a fucking goal and a half!'

Gabe forced a smile. 'Yeah.'

'Come on, smile, captain!' shouted Devereau. 'Fifteen minutes in and we're one nil up!' He punched the air and ran over to hug Reid.

Babacar had stopped his moonwalk and was raising his arms in salute to the fans, beaming with pleasure. There was no better feeling than scoring a goal in front of a home crowd, Gabe knew. The love and admiration that poured out of the fans was like nothing else, though it could just as easily turn to vitriol and hatred when things weren't going their way. Gabe took a deep breath as he looked at the cheering fans, most of whom were now on their feet waving their scarves. He wondered how they would react if they knew that he was going to have to do whatever he could to make sure that United lost.

'Bloody hell, Gabe, smile!' shouted Maplethorpe behind him. The defender jogged over and drew back his hand for a high-five. Gabe hit his hand, open-palmed but with little or no enthusiasm. 'You okay?' asked Maplethorpe.

'Let's not get over confident,' said Gabe. 'The match has only just started.'

'Fucking hell, you got out of the wrong side of the bed today,' said Maplethorpe. 'We're going to demolish them, mate. Fucking demolish them!' He ran over to Babacar and gave him a high-five, then stood in front of the screaming fans with his arms above his head.

Gabe turned away and jogged back to the middle of the pitch. One-nil. One fucking nil.

CHAPTER 49

CK Lee poured himself a slug of brandy and drank it down in one. A big screen TV on one wall of the box was showing three pundits discussing the game. A former English international was explaining why he thought United were on target for a 3-0 victory. 'You know nothing!' Lee shouted at the TV in Cantonese. The picture switched back to the game. Chelsea were kicking off. He looked through the full-length glass windows down to the pitch. It took him a few seconds to pick out Gabe Savage, standing close to the centre spot with his hands on his hips.

His mobile phone buzzed in his pocket and he took it out. It was Yung Jaw-Lung. There was no small talk from the man. 'A United win is no good to me,' said Yung. 'I made that clear. Chelsea have to win this match.'

'It's okay, I have it in hand,' said Lee.

'You are sure? I have your word?'

'They will lose, there is no doubt.'

'You had better be right. For your sake.'

The line went dead. Lee poured another brandy and downed it in one as he looked down at the pitch. Chelsea were in possession but their midfielders didn't seem to know what to do. They were passing it back and forth and making no progress.

Lee looked for Gabe Savage again and found him in the middle of the pitch, moving aimlessly from side to side and making no attempt to intercept the ball. It had been fortuitous that Savage had been acting captain in place of LeBrun. The captain was the lynchpin of any team and Savage knew that if his team won, his family would be dead. Lee sipped his drink. It was more than a threat, Lee had every intention of killing the man's wife and son if United didn't lose. There was no point in making idle threats. If word got around that Lee didn't keep his promises, then before long no one would take him seriously. He poured himself another brandy. The big question was what would happen to the wife and son if Savage did as he was told and United lost? Lee had no qualms about killing women and children. He'd had it done before and he would no doubt do it again. He sipped his drink. If United lost, Yung Jaw-Lung would be pleased. Or at least he would not be angry, which is probably all that Lee could hope for. Yung Jaw-Lung wouldn't care one way or the other what happened to the wife and son. He was a pragmatist and would probably take the view that the fewer witnesses the better, but he would leave the final decision up to Lee.

Lee had told Teddy Kang to make sure that the woman and the boy never saw the faces of their captors. Providing Kang and his men did their job properly, the hostages shouldn't have any information that would help the police so freeing them wouldn't cause Lee any problems. And if he did have the family killed, Savage would certainly go to the police and tell them everything. Yung Jaw-Lung's involvement in football gambling was well known, at least within the Chinese community, so an investigation into game fixing would throw up his name sooner or later. And that was definitely something that would make Yung Jaw-Lung angry.

Lee stepped through the sliding glass doors to the seating area where two of his men were sitting in high-backed chairs watching the game. They raised their glasses to him in salute and he nodded an acknowledgment. He sipped his drink again as he watched the Chelsea midfielders pass the ball between them. They seemed unsure of what they should be doing and Lee shook his head in disappointment. They deserved to lose, the way they were playing. As he watched, one of the United forwards managed to intercept the ball and the crowd roared. It was one of the Italians. Moretti. Moretti was a good player but he had been a better fit at Liverpool, Lee knew. The manager, Guttoso, had brought him into the team but Lee always thought the man had been thinking with his heart and not his head.

Moretti ran with the ball, then stopped and looked around. Babacar had made his run but had two Chelsea defenders sticking to him like glue. The Argentinian was running but he was slow and had too much ground to cover. Moretti saw Gabe over on the left and he sent the ball skidding across the grass, about twenty feet ahead of him. Gabe sprinted towards the ball but was a fraction of a second late getting to it and the moment he trapped it he was shouldered to the side by one of the Chelsea midfielders. Gabe lunged at the ball but the midfielder was too quick and he twisted around and passed it to a teammate who dribbled it towards the United goal. Gabe gave chase but was too slow, Chelsea were back in possession. Lee raised his glass to Gabe down on the pitch. 'Just do what you're supposed to do, my friend, and everything will be all right,' he said.

CHAPTER 50

'I'm scared,' said Ollie. 'The man might hear me.'
Ollie was sitting on the couch, facing her. Laura
had wriggled into a sitting position with her back to
the headboard.

'He'll be watching the game on television,' she
said. 'All you have to do is move very slowly. You don't
have to jump, just shuffle your feet very slowly.'

'Can't we just wait, mum?'

'We need to do this, Ollie,' said Laura. 'Are you
sure you can't cut the tape yourself?'

His eyes brimmed with tears. 'I'm sorry.'

Laura forced a smile. 'It's okay, don't worry.'

Ollie had managed to get a pair of nail clippers
from the bathroom. It had taken him ages and he
had got back to the couch just seconds before the
man in the ski mask had come into the room. Ollie
had been clasping the clippers in his hand and the
man hadn't seen them. When the man had gone
back downstairs, Laura had asked Ollie to try to cut
the tape around his wrists with the clippers but he
just hadn't been able to do it. 'I'm useless,' he said.

'You're not useless, honey,' she said. 'You did really well to get the clippers, now all you have to do is get them to me.'

'But I'm scared I'll fall over.'

'You won't, not if you're careful,' she said. 'You've got great balance. You know you have. Now stand up. Nice and slowly.'

Ollie bit down on his lower lip and he slowly stood up.

'Good boy,' said Laura. 'Now shuffle over, very slowly. Bit by bit.'

Ollie nodded. He began to swing his feet from side to side, inching forward using his toes to dig into the carpet.

'Good boy,' said Laura. 'You can do it.'

CHAPTER 51

Ray found the box mid-way down the corridor on the second level. The name CK LEE was typed on a card and underneath it three Chinese characters, He grabbed the handle and threw open the door. There were four men in the entertainment box, all Chinese. Two of them were obviously heavies, big men in leather jackets and jeans, the other two wore suits. The heavies were standing by a buffet table covered with dishes of Chinese food and bottles of spirits and beer. The two men in suits were watching a large screen television. Ray glanced at the screen and saw that United were winning 1-0. That wasn't good news. He slammed the door shut behind him. 'Which one of you fuckers is CK Lee?' he shouted.

The two men in suits turned to look at him, their mouths open in astonishment. They were both in their sixties, one with glasses, the other shorter and almost bald. They were both holding balloon glasses.

'Which one of you is CK Lee?' he shouted, louder this time. 'I won't fucking ask again.'

Both men looked towards the outside area where there were three more men, all Chinese. One of them stepped into the room. He was in his fifties, tall for a Chinese and wearing a black suit. He opened his mouth to speak but before he could say anything, the two leather-jacketed heavies moved towards Ray. One of them was reaching inside his jacket so Ray went for him first, punching him in the face. The man's nose spurted blood as he staggered back and slammed into a table laden with plates of Chinese dumplings.

The second heavy kicked Ray, his foot slamming into his back. Ray lost his balance and he fell forward. The first heavy took the opportunity to pull out a gun from a shoulder holster, a Glock by the look of it. The man swung the gun around but before he could point it at Ray, Ray had a hand on the man's wrist. He twisted the hand down and then quickly jerked it up, feeling the bones crack. The man yelped in pain and the gun fell from his nerveless fingers. He clawed at Ray's face with his free hand, his fingers curled like talons and Ray swayed backwards to avoid the blow, then he grabbed the man's wrist with both hands and swung the arm around in a circle, bringing the man crashing to the ground. There was a popping sound as the shoulder dislocated. Ray released his grip on the man and stood up just as the second heavy moved towards him, holding a bottle of brandy above his head. Ray blocked the arm with his left forearm then stepped forward and thrust the palm of his right hand under the man's chin.

The man's head jerked back and Ray followed it up with a slash across his throat that left him gasping for breath. The man dropped the bottle and sank to his knees, clutching at his throat, his eyes bulging from their sockets. Ray punched the man on the side of the head to make sure and he slumped to the ground.

Ray turned to face the men in suits, who were huddling against the wall by the television. 'Which one of you is CK Lee?' barked Ray.

One of the men started gabbling in Chinese and Ray held up a hand to silence him. 'Do I look fucking Chinese?' he said. 'Speak fucking English.'

'They don't speak English,' said a bald Chinese guy in a black suit who had stepped into the box from the outside viewing area. He bent down and picked up the gun and pointed it at Ray's chest.

'Are you Lee?' asked Ray.

'I'm the one with the gun so I should be the one asking the questions,' said the man. 'Who are you?' The two Chinese heavies who had been sitting outside were now standing behind Lee looking menacing. Or at least they were trying to. Ray wasn't fazed by them in the least. Looking menacing and actually being menacing were two different things.

'Gabe Savage's brother, I'm here to get his wife and kid back.'

Lee grinned showing greying teeth. 'That doesn't seem to be working out well for you, does it?'

Ray nodded at the gun in Lee's hand. 'You think that'll stop me?'

'It seems to be working so far.' Lee chuckled and pointed the gun at Ray's face. He spoke to the men in suits in Chinese and one of them put up his hand and turned up the volume of the television. A commentator was excitedly describing what was happening on the pitch below. Chelsea were on the attack. The volume was almost deafening and it was clear from Lee's eyes that he was determined to shoot. Ray knew that he had less than a second to react. Lee was a good six feet away from him, too far for a kick or a punch so he had to move but as he sprang forward the door to the box opened to reveal a waiter holding a tray of Chinese food.

Lee hurriedly put the gun away then rushed towards the door. He collided with the waiter and the tray went flying as he staggered backwards. Dumpling and noodles splattered across the carpet as the tray clanged against a chair. Lee hurtled out of the door. Ray rushed after him but his foot slipped on a dumpling and his knee twisted awkwardly. He ignored the searing pain that shot through his leg and headed for the door

A hand grabbed his arm and Ray turned and thrust his elbow into the face of the Chinese heavy who had grabbed him. The nose cracked and blood spurted down the man's face. Ray chopped him across the throat with the side of his hand and the man released his grip on Ray's arm. The second heavy was stepping into the box so Ray grabbed the man with the bloody nose and threw him across the room. The two men collapsed in a heap on top of the waiter. Ray ran out into the corridor.

CHAPTER 52

Chelsea had the ball and were getting ready to make their move. One of their forwards made a break for the United goal but Michael Devereau was on him, as close as a shadow.

Johnnie Reid lunged at the ball and managed to get his foot to it and it skidded across the grass towards Fernandez. The Argentinian trapped it, turned, and headed towards the Chelsea goal. At the same time Babacar made his move, feinting left and breaking right. The defender marking him was wrong-footed and Babacar was on his own. Before he could shout for the ball, Gabe yelled at Reid. 'To me, Johnnie!'

Reid hesitated, saw that Babacar was unmarked, but then Gabe shouted again and Reid chipped the ball to him. Gabe ran with it, tapping the ball from foot to foot. He spotted a gap to his right and he went for it. Babacar had crossed across the penalty box and was now on the left of the goal, frustration etched into his face. He was being marked again and as Gabe looked over he saw the defender grabbing Babacar's shirt.

Gabe drew back his right foot and sent the ball curving through the air towards the goalmouth. Babacar moved to intercept it but the defender yanked him back and the goalkeeper beat him to it, snatching the ball from the air, taking a step and kicking it high and hard towards the middle of the pitch. Babacar appealed to the referee but the referee was already running after the ball. Babacar glared at Gabe and threw up his hands. Gabe ignored him and jogged towards the centre of the pitch.

CHAPTER 53

Ray ran down the corridor, arms pumping, his rapid footsteps echoing off the walls. Lee was at the far end, heading for the stairs. When Ray reached the end of the corridor he couldn't see if Lee had gone up or down. He listened but all he could hear was the roar of the crowd. He knew he had to make a decision. In times of danger people tended to go up, he knew that, but he also knew that all the exits were down. He headed down the stairs. He took a quick look along the corridor on the first level. There were stewards there and a couple of guys in suits heading for the toilets but no sign of Lee. Ray ran downstairs to the ground level.

Two female stewards looked at him inquisitively and Ray slowed to a walk. 'You okay, sir?' asked the elder of the two stewards, a heavyset brunette with her hair tied back.

'Looking for one of our clients,' said Ray. 'Chinese guy in a black suit. Bald, sixties maybe. He's supposed to be in our box but I think he's got lost.'

'You just missed him,' said the steward. She pointed down towards the toilets. 'He went that way just now.'

'Did he go in the toilets?'

The woman shook her head. 'I don't think so.'

'Thanks,' said Ray. He jogged in the direction she'd pointed. A roar went up from the pitch, followed by a massive collective groan and catcalls. A whistle blew.

As he turned the corner he saw Lee. He had his hand inside his jacket, concealing the gun. There were several stewards hanging around and CCTV cameras everywhere. Ray headed towards him. Lee hurried away, past a stall selling pies, then turned into another stairwell. There was a sign above it that read EMPLOYEES ONLY. By the time Ray got to the stairwell, Lee had gone through a door with another sign on it, this one saying MAINTENANCE TUNNEL. Ray grabbed the handle and pulled open the door. Beyond was a concrete-lined tunnel that ran under the pitch, allowing access to the irrigation and drainage systems. A line of fluorescent lights ran down the middle of the tunnel, flooding it with a clinical white light. There were pipes criss-crossing the roof and running down the sides. Lee was about fifty feet inside, hurrying as fast as he could. Ray let the door close behind him and started jogging down the tunnel.

CHAPTER 54

Laura smiled encouragement at Ollie. 'Come on, honey, you're almost here.' Ollie was about three feet from the side of the bed she was sitting on. There were tears of frustration in his eyes and he kept looking fearfully over at the door. 'Keep looking at me, honey. Just look at me.'

'My feet hurt,' he whispered. 'My feet hurt so much.'

'I know they do, honey,' she said. 'But try to think like Daddy. Every time he goes out on the field to play, his legs hurt. You know they do. But he pushes himself and he gets through. You can too, honey. I know you can.'

Ollie smiled. 'Okay.' He started moving again, an inch or so at a time. His toes clawed into the carpet, he shuffled forward, and then he relaxed. It had taken him more than ten minutes to move a few feet, but he was making progress and the carpet was muffling any sound.

She kept her eyes fixed on his as he slowly made his way towards her. 'Good boy,' she whispered. 'I'm so proud of you.'

It took another five minutes of inching towards the bed before he was close enough and she told him to turn around and put the clippers on the bed. It took him almost two painful minutes until his back was to her. She could see the clippers in his right hand.

'Okay, honey, just lean back and toss them onto the bed.'

'I can't, mum, I can't.'

'Yes you can, honey. You can do it.'

He drew back his hand and flicked it and the clippers arced through the air but they fell short, hit the side of the bed and fell onto the carpet. 'I'm sorry, I'm sorry, I'm sorry,' he said. Tears ran down his face. 'I'm so stupid.'

'No you're not,' said Laura. 'You're very clever and you're very brave. There's no need to cry. Look at me, honey. Come on, turn and look at me.'

He did as he was told and slowly turned around.

'Look at me, honey,' said Laura.

Ollie raised his eyes and blinked away his tears. Laura ached to be able to hug him and kiss him and wipe the tears away but that wasn't an option. Ollie had to get a grip on himself because he was their only hope.

'Listen to me, honey. It's going to be all right, I swear. We'll be home and Daddy will be there and everything will be okay.'

Ollie nodded tearfully. 'All right.'

'Here's what you need to do, honey, okay? Very carefully go down on your knees. Then sit down. Be quiet. Be very quiet. When you're sitting down you'll be able to reach the clippers. Then you stand up again.'

'I'm scared, mum.'

'I know you are, honey. But you can do this. I know you can.'

CHAPTER 55

Ray reached the halfway point of the maintenance tunnel. Lee was sixty feet away, jogging and breathing heavily. There was an electrical junction box on the wall with a sign that said – WARNING ELECTRICAL HAZARD. Leaning against it was a long-handled wooden brush. Ray grabbed it as he went past.

Lee stopped and turned to face Ray, pulling out his gun. He pointed it at Ray. He held it with one hand and it wavered as he tried to aim at Ray's chest. 'What do you want?' he asked.

'I told you what I want,' said Ray. 'Gabe's family.' He walked towards Lee, swinging the brush. 'Where are they?'

Lee pulled the trigger but the shot went wide and ricocheted off the wall near Ray's head. Ray ducked even though ducking would have done no use at all if the gun had been on target. Ray guessed that Lee wasn't used to handling guns, which was handy. But even a shit marksman would eventually get lucky in the confines of the tunnel.

When he realised he'd missed, Lee turned and started running and Ray figured that was a mistake. Lee must have realised by now that Ray wasn't armed, his best option would be to just walk towards Ray and shoot him. Not that Ray was complaining; he was more than happy to have Lee running away from him.

Lee was obviously a man who was used to getting others to fight his battles whereas Ray's background was more hands on. Ray was younger and fitter and was no stranger to physical violence. Ray was gaining on Lee but the man was still thirty feet or so ahead of him when he stopped and turned and brought up the gun. Ray kept running and threw the brush. It span through the air and Lee fired wildly, the bullets hitting the ceiling in a shower of sparks. The brush hit him on the shoulder and Lee pushed it away, cursing. It clattered to the floor.

Ray was still running and by the time Lee had steadied himself Ray was just a few feet away. Lee's eyes were wide and his hand was shaking but his finger was tightening on the trigger. Ray dropped down and slid the last few feet, his right foot catching Lee's left ankle. Lee fell and Ray rolled out of the way. As Ray pushed himself up, Lee was on his side, the gun still in his hand.

Ray used the wall to steady himself as he got to his feet. Lee was gasping for breath, stunned from his fall. Ray stamped down on the man's wrist and Lee's hand opened, releasing the gun. Ray kicked it away.

Lee lashed out with his foot and caught Ray behind the knee and he lost his balance, falling against the wall. By the time Ray had straightened up, Lee was standing in the middle of the tunnel, gasping for breath and holding the brush in front of him like a broadsword.

Ray couldn't help grinning. 'Seriously?' he said. 'You're giving me the brush off?'

Lee frowned, not understanding. He faked a blow to Ray's head but Ray stood his ground. Lee lashed out again, harder this time, and Ray swayed back. Lee drew back the brush for a third time and Ray rushed him, grabbing the pole with his left hand and thrusting his right palm up under Lee's chin and forcing his head back. Ray kept his momentum going and slammed Lee against the tunnel wall. The brush slipped from his grasp and clattered to the floor. Ray drove his knee into Lee's groin and Lee howled in pain. 'Where's Laura?' shouted Lee. He grabbed him by the lapels, swung him around and slammed him against the other wall. Lee clawed at Ray's eyes and Ray let go.

Lee put up his hands and took a fighting stance, but he was clearly hurt and exhausted.

'Are you fucking serious?' asked Ray. 'You want to fucking fight me? I'm younger, stronger, fitter and I've been doing this for years. Stop fucking about and just tell me where they are, or I swear I'll kick the living shit out of you.'

Lee lashed out with his right leg but he was slow and there was no power behind the blow. Ray caught the leg easily and held it, forcing Lee to hop back, arms flailing. Ray punched Lee in the face, keeping a tight grip on the leg with his left hand.

'Where is Laura? Where's the kid?'

Lee's nose was bleeding but he didn't answer. Ray punched him again. And again.

'Where the fuck are they, Lee?'

Lee shook his head and Ray punched him again.

Lee tried to claw at Ray's face again but Ray's next punch was so hard that Lee's head snapped back and he collapsed. Ray let go of the leg and took a step back as Lee fell to the floor. Lee's head hit the ground hard and his eyes closed. Ray kicked him in the side, hard, but there was no reaction. Ray cursed. He knelt down by the unconscious man and patted him down. He found a wallet in his right trouser pocket and he pulled it out and flicked it open. There were several credit cards, a wad of fifty pound notes, and a UK driving licence. He tossed the wallet down and squinted at the address on the licence. North London. He straightened up and slipped the driving licence into his back pocket, then picked up the gun, ejected the magazine and checked the clip. It was empty. He tossed the gun onto the body. Dead or unconscious? Ray didn't care. He started running down the tunnel, back the way he'd come.

CHAPTER 56

Mancini chipped the ball over to Gabe. Gabe trapped it and turned in one smooth movement, feinted left and went right. He took the ball twenty feet closer to the Chelsea goal, unchallenged. There were two Chelsea defenders in front of him, waiting to see which way he'd run. Gabe slowed. Off to his right, Moretti was trying to find space but failing. Off to the left, Reid was shouting for the ball. Reid had a clear run for the Chelsea goal and was the obvious choice. Babacar was standing still, a Chelsea defender to his right. Babacar had no clear shot for goal and would have to break to his left, which was his weaker side.

The defenders rushed forward and Gabe sent the ball high towards Babacar. Gabe saw the look of confusion on Babacar's face. The striker had obviously assumed that the ball would be going to Reid and he hesitated for a fraction of a second before jumping for the ball. He managed to get his head to it and nod it towards Moretti. Moretti ran for it but he was shoulder-charged and lost his balance. By the time he'd recovered, Chelsea had the ball and were heading for the United goal. There were catcalls and boos from the fans, mainly aimed at the defender who had hit Moretti.

McNamara was shouting from the sideline but his voice was lost in the crowd. Gabe looked over at Babacar. Babacar was standing with his hands on his hips, shaking his head in disgust. Gabe shrugged an apology and jogged back to the centre line.

Chapter 57

'I can't get it mum, I'm sorry,' said Ollie. He was lying on his side on the floor so Laura couldn't see him. 'I just can't reach it.'

'Keep trying, honey,' said Laura. 'Take your time.'

'But I can't move my hands. They've gone numb.'

'Try wiggling your fingers, honey. That'll get the circulation going.'

'I'm sorry, mum.'

'Honey, you've got nothing to be sorry about. Just keep trying.'

Ollie sniffed. 'Okay.'

She heard him move, then sigh, then move again. 'Mum, I've got it!' he whispered excitedly.

'Good boy. Now stand up. Quietly. Okay?'

'Okay, mum.'

Laura heard several soft grunts and she felt him bang against the bed.

'Quietly, Ollie!' repeated Laura in a harsh whisper.

'Okay, okay.'

Laura heard him grunt, then she saw the back of his head appear above the side of the bed. He pushed with his feet and slowly stood up. Laura's eyes widened when she saw the stainless steel nail clippers in his right hand. 'Well done, Ollie!' she said.

'I'm so tired and my hands hurt,' he said.

'I know,' she said. 'But we're almost there. Now sit down on the bed so that they don't fall back on the floor.'

Ollie did as he was told.

'Now flick them back as far as you can,' said Laura.

Ollie tossed the clippers onto the bed. They landed a few inches away from Laura's stomach.

'Well done, Ollie!' she whispered. She wanted nothing more than to hold her son and kiss him and make it all better, but that wasn't going to happen for a while.

'I'm so tired, mum,' he said.

'I know you are honey, but now you have to get back to the sofa.'

'My feet hurt.'

'Just take it nice and slowly,' she said.

'I want to stay here with you on the bed,' he said.

'The man might come back,' she said.

'I don't care,' said Ollie. He sniffed. 'I just want to be with you, mum.'

Tears pricked Laura's eyes. 'Okay,' she said. 'Lie down for a while.'

'Really?'

'Sure.'

Ollie swung his legs up onto the bed and lowered his head to the pillow. Laura moved closer to him and she kissed him on the cheek. 'I'm so proud of you,' she said.

'I'm really scared.'

'It's going to be all right,' she said, though she wished she was as confident as she sounded. Even if she did manage to cut the duct tape, they were still trapped in a house with armed men, armed men who were threatening to kill them if Gabe didn't do what they wanted.

CHAPTER 58

Ray hurried towards the exit. Two stewards were standing at the gate and they looked quizzically at Ray. 'Are you okay, Sir?' asked the elder of the two, a grey-haired man holding a transceiver.

'I need to get out,' said Ray.

The steward looked at his watch. 'It's not even half time yet,' he said.

There was a roar from the stand behind them, followed by groans and catcalls. 'I know, family problem,' said Ray. 'Can you let me out?'

'Just go through the turnstile,' said the steward.

'Cheers,' said Ray. He pushed through the turnstile and started running down the pavement.

'Hey mate, can I have your ticket?' shouted a young man wearing a Chelsea shirt. Ray ignored him and ran on. Behind him he heard the crowd roar, followed almost immediately by howls of despair.

CHAPTER 59

One of the Chelsea defenders kicked the ball upfield but he mistimed it and the ball cannoned off Maplethorpe's leg and bounced over the sideline. Gabe jogged over to the sideline in preparation for the throw in. Babacar joined him. 'What the fuck's going on, Gabe?' asked Babacar.

'What do you mean?'

'I've not had a decent cross from you all game,' said the striker. 'Are you trying to make me look bad?'

'They're on you like shit on a shoe,' said Gabe. 'You need to make more space.'

Babacar shook his head. 'Just give me the ball when I've got a chance of getting it,' he said. 'I'll do the rest.'

Gabe nodded but didn't reply. He looked over at the referee. The referee blew on his whistle and a Chelsea player ran with the ball, stopped and threw it hard and high. Gabe and Babacar gave chase. The ball landed at the feet of one of the Chelsea strikers who headed off towards the United goal.

Michael Devereau rushed towards the player with the ball and forced him to veer left where Mancini executed a perfect sliding tackle that sent the ball spinning back towards Gabe. The crowd roared as Gabe trapped it, turned on the spot and ran towards the Chelsea goal. Babacar was to Gabe's right, slightly ahead of him, shouting for the ball. Gabe tapped it to Babacar, a perfect pass that Babacar couldn't complain about.

Off to the right, Moretti was making a run but he was far too early so Babacar turned and tapped it back to Wood before running towards the Chelsea goal. The crowd began to roar, sensing that something was about to happen. Wood passed the ball back to Maplethorpe, Maplethorpe sent it across to Mancini and Mancini ran with it, passing two Chelsea players on the left wing before crossing it to Gabe.

Gabe was unmarked and was able to take the ball into the Chelsea half before he faced any opposition. Babacar was on the edge of the penalty area. The goalkeeper was on his line, moving from side to side, shouting at his defenders.

Babacar twisted around, feinted left and then ran towards the goal, his eyes on Gabe. Gabe heard heavy breathing behind him and he dribbled the ball to the left, turned to the right, and sent the ball high in the air towards Babacar. Babacar was lined up to head the ball into the right hand corner of the goal but Gabe had kicked the ball to the striker's other side. Babacar changed direction and managed to get his head to the ball but he was off balance and the ball went over the crossbar. Babacar landed awkwardly, slipped and fell. The United fans groaned in unison. Babacar got to his feet and rubbed the dirt from his hands.

The goalkeeper retrieved the ball and the referee blew his whistle for the goal kick and Babacar jogged out of the penalty box. Gabe looked up at the clock atop the scoreboard. It was almost half past three. United were still ahead which meant that somehow Gabe had to make sure that Chelsea scored at least twice.

Chapter 60

Ray ran full pelt through the city streets, knowing that time was running out. It had to be half time now. Forty-five minutes plus injury time to go. He slowed as he reached the garage. His BMW was parked where he'd left it, but there were two men leaning against it. Men he recognised. Mike Tyler and Barry Chisnall. Their black Range Rover was parked at the roadside. Ray cursed but forced a smile. 'Hello guys,' he said amiably. 'What's up?'

'Don't fuck around, Ray,' said Mike. His hand moved inside his jacket.

'That hand appears with a gun in it and you and I have a problem,' warned Ray.

'Don't make this any more difficult than it has to be,' said Barry. His hand was also inside his jacket.

'How the fuck did you find me?' asked Ray.

'Are you serious?' said Mike. 'The amount of mayhem you've been causing, you think no one has noticed? You've gone rogue, Ray, and Den's had enough.'

'I've spoken to Den, I've explained.'

Mike shook his head. 'No you haven't, mate. You haven't explained anything.'

Ray held out his hand. 'Give me the keys, Mike.'

Mike nodded at the Range Rover. 'Get in the car, Ray. Don't make this any more difficult than it has to be. All you have to do is talk to Den. Smooth things over.'

Ray reached into his jacket for his phone. Barry pulled out his Glock and pointed it at Ray's chest.

'For fuck's sake, Barry, can't you see he's going for his phone,' said Mike.

Ray took out his phone and sneered scornfully at Barry. 'Fine, I'll talk to him.'

'Face to face, Ray,' said Mike. 'He wants a face to face.'

'I don't have time, Mike. Now give me the fucking keys.'

'I've had enough of this shit,' said Barry, waving his gun. 'Get in the fucking car.'

'Yeah, you're going to fucking shoot me?' said Ray.

'I will if I ...' Ray moved so quickly that his hands were a blur. His left hand slapped Barry's gun to the side. His right hand slapped into Barry's wrist and twisted. Barry's fingers opened involuntarily and Ray's left hand grabbed the barrel. Ray stepped back, transferring the gun to his right hand. It had taken less than a second.

'For fuck's sake, Ray,' said Mike. He raised his hands to show that he had no intention of reaching for his own gun.

Ray kept far enough away from the two men so that neither of them could grab the weapon.

Barry stared at the gun in amazement, trying to work out what had just happened.

'Krav maga,' said Mike. 'The Israeli self defence program. Ray's a bit of an expert.'

Ray stepped forward and lashed out with the gun, catching Barry on the side of the head. Barry slumped to the floor without a sound. 'When he wakes up, tell him not to stand so close when he pulls a gun on someone.'

'Will do,' said Mike. 'Den's going to be furious, you know that?'

'He is already, right?'

Mike shrugged and slowly lowered his arms.

'Give me the keys, Mike.'

Mike slowly reached into the pocket of his trousers.

'On second thoughts, give me the keys for the Range.' Ray tucked the gun into his belt and held out his hand.

'You're stealing my fucking car?'

'It's Den's car. And I'm not stealing, I'm swapping. You're right, I've been attracting attention in the Beamer. So you take it and I'll take the Range.'

Mike sighed and handed over the keys to the SUV. 'Are you sure you know what you're doing, Ray?'

'No,' said Ray. 'I'm not. But I don't have any choice. Now keep the fuck away for me, next time I won't be so pleasant.'

Mike raised his hands in surrender and kept them in the air as Ray jogged over to the Range Rover and climbed in. As Ray drove off with his tyres squealing, Mike squatted down next to Barry. Barry moaned and moved his head from side to side, then his eyelids flickered open. 'Who was that masked man?' groaned Barry.

Mike grinned and patted him on the shoulder. 'I'm glad you've still got your sense of humour because when Den finds out what just happened he's going to tear you a new one.'

'Did he take my gun?'

'Yes, he took your gun.'

'Fuck.'

'Yeah. What were you thinking, pulling a gun on Ray Savage? That was only ever going to end one way.'

Barry groaned. 'I got caught up in the moment.'

'I think you'll need to come up with something better than that for Den,' said Mike. 'You might want to give it some thought.'

CHAPTER 61

Laura rubbed her forehead against Ollie's shoulder. 'Honey, you're going to have to go back to the sofa.'

'I want to stay here with you, mum.'

'I know, but if that man comes back and finds you on the bed he's going to be angry. You need to go back to the sofa.'

'I'm tired, mum.'

She kissed his shoulder. 'I know, honey. But you can rest on the sofa.'

'Okay,' said Ollie. He sniffed, then slowly swung his legs off the bed. He stood up, sniffed again, and began shuffling back to the sofa.

Laura rolled onto her right side and groped for the nail clippers. She rolled them into her right hand, closing her eyes and trying to picture them. One of the handles had to be swung around so that pressure could be applied to the blades. She bit down on her lower lip as she concentrated. Eventually she managed to do it and used her thumb to click the cutters closed. Her heart was racing and she took a couple of deep breaths to steady herself.

She twisted the clippers around in her hand, trying to find the duct tape by feel. She clicked the blades closed but they didn't bite down on anything. She twisted her hand more and clicked again. Still nothing. She took another deep breath and tried again. This time the clippers slipped from her sweating fingers and she cursed.

'Are you okay, mum?' asked Ollie.

'I'm fine,' she said. 'I'm trying to use the clippers.' She groped around with her bound hands and found the clippers. She took them in her right hand and swivelled them around. 'Keep going honey. You need to get on the sofa.'

'Okay, mum.'

Laura pushed the clippers against the duct tape and pressed down with the thumb. There was no resistance and she realised she'd missed the tape. She tried again and this time she felt the clippers bite against the tape. It was going to work, she realised. It would take time, but it would work.

CHAPTER 62

Ray tapped in the address from Lee's driving licence into the Range Rover's SatNav as he drove, one eye on the road and one eye on the screen. He pressed the button for the route and smiled thinly when he saw that Lee's house was just sixteen minutes away, providing he didn't hit traffic. He stamped on the accelerator. He reached a set of lights just as they turned to amber and he pressed down on the accelerator. He went through on red and he saw the junction was covered by CCTV cameras. It wasn't a problem. Den Donovan's cars were as disposable as Ray's.

A black cab pulled out in front of him and Ray swerved around it, narrowly missing a double-decker bus. The bus driver sounded his horn but Ray had already gone. The Range Rover wasn't the most responsive of vehicles but Ray kept his foot down as he powered through the traffic, overtaking where he could. There were two buses ahead of him and the road narrowed so he ignored the SatNav, turned into a side street and did a series of quick right and lefts. The SatNav kept recalibrating but Ray paid it no attention.

Five minutes later he was back on the main road and he smiled as he saw the two buses in his rear-view mirror. He reached another set of lights but they were already on red and there were several cars ahead of him. He sat drumming his hands on the steering wheel for a few seconds, then swore out loud, pulled around the two cars and drove through the red light. A white van had to break to avoid hitting him and a motorcyclist swerved out of his way. The bike and the van driver sounded their horns angrily but Ray was totally focussed on the road ahead of him.

CHAPTER 63

The referee blew his whistle and awarded a free kick to Chelsea. The tackle by Fernandez had looked okay to Gabe, but he had been on the other side of the pitch. Fernandez was protesting vociferously but the referee waved him away. Fernandez wouldn't accept the decision and he ran around to get in the ref's face, shouting and waving his arms around. Gabe ran over to placate Fernandez. Bad decisions were a fact of life, there was no point in getting upset about them, especially if they resulted in a yellow card or a sending off.

Tim Maplethorpe had joined in, shouting that the tackle had been legal, but the referee waved him away too.

The player who had gone down was massaging the back of his leg and wincing, but it looked like play-acting to Gabe.

'Are you fucking blind?' Maplethorpe screamed at the referee. 'He didn't touch him. He played the ball and he got the ball.'

The referee was red-faced and clearly upset. His hand went to his pocket, presumably to pull out a yellow card, but Gabe rushed in between him and the players and pushed Maplethorpe and Fernandez away from the official. 'Let it go, guys,' he said.

'The tackle was good,' said Fernandez. 'I never touched him.'

'Referees make mistakes,' said Gabe. 'Get over it.'

'I didn't touch him, Gabe.'

'I believe you. Just let it go.' He ushered Fernandez away. One of the Chelsea players put the ball down, the referee blew his whistle and the kick was taken, a quick chip to one of the Chelsea midfielders who ran with it to the half-way line. There he passed it to a teammate on the right wing who was promptly shouldered by Mancini. Mancini got the ball but the player shouldered him back and as the two men struggled the ball rolled over the sideline.

The referee ran over and awarded the throw in to Chelsea. It was a long throw and caught United by surprise – A Chelsea midfielder snapped it up and sprinted towards the United goal. Devereau moved to intercept and managed to take the ball off him before quickly back-heeling it to Mancini who then booted it all the way up the field. It all happened so quickly that the entire Chelsea team were wrong-footed.

Gabe realised that the ball was coming straight to him and that the nearest Chelsea player was twenty feet away. He jumped to trap the ball on his chest, let it drop to his feet and then turned and started running. There was one defender in front of him and Gabe slowed. Babacar had sprinted down the opposite wing and was unmarked. Gabe couldn't see that he had any choice other than to pass to Babacar, but if he did there was a good chance that he'd score.

He continued to move forward, then kicked the ball towards Babacar, but he sent the ball behind the striker so that he had to reverse direction to get it. Babacar saw what was happening and tried to stop his run but he was too slow and the ball bounced over the sideline, a good six feet behind him. Tens of thousand of disappointed fans groaned as one. Babacar shook his head in disbelief.

The referee blew his whistle and a Chelsea player threw it in, straight to the head of a teammate. The ball cannoned past Moretti, straight to the feet of a Chelsea striker who ran full pelt towards the United goal with Moretti in hot pursuit.

Ronnie Watts moved off his line, his arms outstretched. The striker was fast and pulled away from Moretti. Devereau and Mancini ran to intercept the player but before they reached him he took his shot. It was a blistering volley that Watts made a valiant attempt to reach but his headlong dive missed by inches and the ball powered into the back of the net.

The Chelsea fans went wild, cheering and whooping, while the United supporters sat in stunned silence.

The referee blew his whistle. He was to Gabe's left and as Gabe looked over the official took his whistle from his mouth and grinned. 'Nice one,' he said, before running over to the centre spot. Gabe stared after him, wondering what the man had meant. Had he realised that Gabe had deliberately fluffed his pass? And did his comment mean that he knew why Gabe had done it. The men who wanted United to lose the match had kidnapped his wife and child, had they also got to the referee?

CHAPTER 64

Ray glanced over at the SatNav. Lee's house was twelve minutes away. The Range Rover was caught in traffic again and Ray couldn't see any rat runs on the screen. He tapped the steering wheel impatiently. The hold-up was a van unloading office supplies. The driver had parked on double yellow lines and didn't seem in the least concerned about the tailback he was causing. When he returned from a shop and started pulling a box from the rear of his van, Ray got out and jogged over to him. He was big with a shaved head and the tattoo of a cobweb across his neck, with puffy ears that suggested he'd been a boxer at some point, and not a good one. He was wearing dark blue overalls with the name of a courier on the back.

Ray tapped him on the shoulder. The man turned, a massive beer gut straining at the material of the overalls. Ray saw that he had LOVE tattooed across the knuckles of his left hand and HATE on the right. Ray needed his game face on and he had to resist the urge to smile. He had never yet come across anyone with tattoos like that who didn't fold at the first punch. 'You need to move your van now, mate,' said Ray.

'What are you, a fucking traffic warden?' sneered the man.

Ray punched him in the face, hard enough to make his nose bleed but not hard enough to break it. The man stepped back, blood streaming down his chin. 'For fuck's sake!' he said.

'Move it,' said Ray.

The man looked at the blood on his hands in amazement. 'You hit me,' he said, as if he couldn't believe what had happened.

'And if you don't move that fucking van now I'll break your fucking legs,' said Ray, pointing at the man's bloody face. 'Now fucking move it.' Ray took a step towards the man and he stumbled back against the van.

'Okay, okay,' said the man, wiping his nose with his sleeve. He slammed the rear doors shut and hurried to the front of the van. Seconds later he was driving down the road.

Ray went back to the Range Rover. Two of the drivers in front of him gave him a thumbs-up but a middle-aged woman shook her head disapprovingly. By the time Ray got back into his car the road was clear and he was soon powering along at 50mph, well over the speed limit.

CHAPTER 65

Chelsea had the ball in the middle of the pitch, tapping the ball back and forth as they probed for an opening. One of their strikers was just outside the penalty box but Tim Maplethorpe was on him and cutting him no slack. Ronnie Watts was moving up and down the goal line, calling for Devereau to move to the side. A Chelsea midfielder made his run and hared down the left wing. The cross was perfect, low and fast and straight to his feet. He took three steps then sent it in a high curving pass towards the striker but Maplethorpe had it covered and the two men jumped at the same time and the striker fell forward. Watts scooped up the ball, ran and kicked it with all his might. The ball arced up into the air and almost made it to the half-way line. Wood trapped it, swerved by a Chelsea defender and sent it skimming across the turf to Gabe. Gabe's way was blocked by two Chelsea players so he tapped it to the left, to Armati. Armati did a cute backheel and spin to shrug off the player marking him and kicked it across to Wood. Babacar had made his run and was at the edge of the penalty box. Wood feinted left then went right and kicked the ball high towards Babacar. The crowd was roaring in anticipation of a United goal but the ball was still in the air when the whistle blew, long and hard. Half time.

CHAPTER 66

Laura felt the jaws of the clippers grip the duct tape and she pressed down with the thumb. The jaws clicked. She pulled at her wrists but the tape felt just as secure as when she'd started cutting the tape. She had no way of judging her progress, all she could do was to keep cutting as best she could. Her hands were dripping with sweat and several times the clippers had slipped from her fingers. Her hands were hurting and her right wrist was sending lancing pains up through her arm. Tears of frustration ran down her cheeks but she tried not to make any sound because she didn't want to worry Ollie.

She took a deep breath, then twisted her hand and tried to find the duct tape with the clippers. She closed her eyes as she concentrated, visualising the tape around her wrists and the jaws of the clips closing on it. She felt resistance against the clippers and pressed down with her thumb. There was a faint clicking sound but she had no way of knowing whether she'd cut the tape or not. She strained at her bonds but they held tight. She blinked away the tears and tried again.

CHAPTER 67

Gabe was the first into the changing rooms and he hurried over to his locker. He had just opened it when he felt a shove between his shoulders. He stumbled against his locker door and turned to see Babacar glaring at him. 'What the fuck are you playing at, man?' hissed Babacar.

'What do you mean?' said Gabe.

'You know what I fucking mean,' said Babacar. 'Every pass you sent me out there was off. Late or early. You trying to get me killed?'

'Don't be fucking stupid,' said Gabe, pushing him away.

Babacar pushed him back and Gabe slammed against his locker door. 'You need to get your fucking head straight because I got hit twice out there because of you,' said Babacar. 'And I got hit fucking hard.'

'Don't blame me because you're having a bad game,' said Gabe.

Babacar shoved Gabe again this time Gabe pushed back hard with both hands sending Babacar staggering backwards. Babacar bunched his right hand into a fist and launched himself at Gabe but

Michael Devereau grabbed him from behind and pulled him away. 'Cool it. Omar,' he said.

The door opened and McNamara walked in. He frowned when he saw Devereau struggling with Babacar. 'What the fuck's going on?' asked the coach.

Devereau let go of Babacar and held up his hands. 'Just horseplay,' he said.

'Omar?' asked McNamara.

Babacar shrugged but didn't say anything. He went to grab an energy drink.

Gabe turned away and opened his locker door.

McNamara went over to Babacar. 'What's going on?'

Babacar shrugged. 'Nothing, he growled as he twisted the cap off the bottle. He drank greedily and wiped his mouth with the back of his hand. 'All good, Joe.'

'You sure?'

Babacar nodded. 'I'm sure.'

McNamara walked into the middle of the changing rooms. 'Right, listen up,' he said. 'The boss'll be in any moment, but I want to get my two pennyworth in first. I know that didn't go as we'd expected, but one all is no bad thing providing we go in hard in the second half. We had a few good opportunities out there and we could easily be 3-1 right now. Let's get our heads straight and go back out there fighting. Okay?'

There were nods and a few 'yeahs' from the team. Gabe picked up his phone. There was a text message from an unknown number. His heart raced as he pressed the screen to read it.

A DRAW IS NO GOOD. YOU MUST LOSE IF YOU WANT TO SEE YOUR FAMILY AGAIN.

Tears pricked Gabe's eyes and he tossed the phone back into his locker and slammed the door shut.

The door to the changing room was pushed open and Piero Guttoso strode in. The manager had taken off his overcoat to reveal a Savile Row dark blue suit, a blue silk shirt and a dark blue tie. Gold cufflinks peeped from under his sleeves. He strode into the middle of the room and stood with his feet splayed out as he waited for quiet. His cheeks were more flushed than usual, and Gabe figured the wine had been flowing freely in the owner's box.

'Well, at least we're not losing,' said Guttoso. He flicked back his mane of grey hair. 'That's about all I can say. The owner isn't happy, obviously. Like me he thinks we should be winning this game. He doesn't understand what's going wrong and frankly I'm at a loss. We made too many mistakes out there, right Joe?' He looked over at the coach and McNamara nodded in agreement. 'Small mistakes, stupid mistakes, mistakes that we shouldn't be making. We should have had this game in the bag by now. We are by far the better team. You need to take a breath, you need to compose yourselves, then you need to go out there and kick the shit out of them. We are the better team. By far. Just go out there and prove it.'

Several of the team cheered, but Gabe sat with his back against the locker, his hands in his lap.

The manager looked over at him. 'Gabe, how are the knees?'

Gabe forced a smile. 'All good, Boss.'

Guttoso jutted his chin at him. 'A few times out there you looked as if you were struggling.'

'That's one way of saying it,' said Babacar sourly. McNamara flashed him a warning look and Babacar turned away and drank from his bottle.

'I lost focus for a bit, Boss,' said Gabe. 'It won't happen again.'

'You're the captain, Gabe. Lead from the front.'

'Yes, Boss.'

Guttoso nodded, then turned to McNamara. 'Joe, maybe go over the throw-ins on the playback. They're catching us unawares with those long throws.'

'Will do, Boss,' said McNamara.

Guttoso nodded. 'Okay, I'll leave you to it. I'll go and keep the owner sweet. But trust me, if we don't pull this game round, he'll be on the warpath.' He turned and walked out of the room. Gabe leaned back and banged his head against the locker door.

CHAPTER 68

Tommy Kang stood up and stretched. Billy Huang waved his glass at the television. 'What do you think? Do you think Chelsea will win?'

Kang shrugged. 'You can see that Savage is doing his best,' he said. 'United could have scored but he fucked up the pass and then Chelsea got the throw in and scored. If he can do that again...' He went over to the sideboard and poured himself another brandy. He sipped his drink and then turned to look at Zhang and Huang. 'We need to get this tidied up before CK gets back.'

'When will he be here?' asked Zhang.

'Game finishes at quarter to five. The traffic will be bad.' He shrugged again. 'Half five, maybe.'

Huang pointed at the ceiling. 'What about them? Do we deal with them before he gets here?'

'I don't know,' said Kang. 'I guess that depends on who wins.'

'We're really going to let them go?' asked Zhang.

'I don't know,' said Kang. 'It'll be CK's call.'

'What do you think?' asked Huang.

'They haven't seen our faces,' said Kang. 'They don't know where they are. If we do release them then there's a good chance Savage will keep quiet about it. If we finish them off...' He didn't finish the sentence.

'But if United win...' said Zhang.

'Then we'll be offing them for sure,' said Kang. 'CK doesn't fuck about. And nor does Yung Jaw-Lung.' He took another sip of brandy. 'There's another possibility, though.'

'What's that?' asked Zhang.

'If Chelsea do win, if Savage does as he's told, maybe he'll kill them all anyway. Savage and his family.'

'You think he'd do that?' asked Huang.

'The fewer witnesses the better,' said Kang with a shrug. 'Me, I'd feel safer if they were all dead. But it's not my call. I'm just a footsoldier in this.' He looked at his watch, then put down his glass. 'I'm going to check on them.'

He went upstairs, then paused in the hallway and listened. There was no sound from the bedroom. He pulled on his ski mask and pushed open the door.

CHAPTER 69

The SatNav showed that Lee's house was a few hundred yards ahead. He was in a quiet road, lined with trees, with large detached houses hiding behind high walls. There were no cars parked in the road and no pedestrians, it wasn't an area where people walked. Ray slowed the car as he drove by Lee's house. He couldn't see much of the building itself, but could see several SUVs parked in the driveway. There were two ornate wrought iron gates that were more than ten feet tall and to the left a wooden door set into the high brick wall. Ray couldn't see any CCTV cameras but he figured they must be there. He drove the full length of the wall and when he reached the neighbouring house he did a U-turn and drove back. He took a longer look at the gate and this time spotted a Chinese man in bomber jacket and jeans. The wooden door led into a single story building to the left of the gates, which he guessed was probably where security were based.

He couldn't see a back entrance which meant the gates were the only way in. He pulled over at the side of the road and checked the gun he'd taken from Lee. He put the Glock on the centre console between the two seats and unclipped his seat belt before pulling another U-turn and driving back to the gates. He pulled up at the side of the road just past the driveway and climbed out. He looked up and down the road as if he was lost, then walked towards the gates. The man in the bomber jacket stood in the middle of the driveway looking at him. He was in his thirties with a crop of old acne scars across his cheeks. 'Is this number 19?' he asked.

The man frowned. 'What?'

'Number 19. I'm looking for number 19.'

The man was wearing a black leather jacket and as he shrugged Ray caught a glimpse of a gun in a shoulder holster. 'No number,' he said.

'Every house has a number,' said Ray. 'That's how the postman knows where to deliver the mail.' He knew the house did have a number – 16 – because it had been on Lee's driving licence.

'You're not a postman,' said the second heavy. He had been standing in the building beyond the gate. He had a wrestler's build and a shaved head. He was wearing a long coat and from the way his right hand was twitching the garment was concealing something and that something almost certainly spat bullets when the trigger was pulled.

'No, that's right. But I have to collect a passenger.'

'You're a taxi?' asked Long Coat.

'Uber,' said Ray.

'What's the name of the passenger?'

'Hunt,' said Ray. 'Mister Hunt.'

Long Coat wrinkled his nose and shook his head. 'No one called Hunt here. And we don't use taxis.'

Ray sighed and peered through at the house. It was a modern steel and glass mansion, two glass-fronted wings either side of a main entrance that looked more like an upmarket car dealership than a family home. There were three black SUVs that he'd seen from the road and beyond them a silver Mercedes. 'Who owns this place, then?' he asked. 'Must be worth a fortune.'

The man in the long coat took a step closer to the gates and this time Ray saw something black hanging from a nylon sling. A gun. A big one. An Uzi, maybe. 'You should go,' said the man. 'This is private property.'

Ray couldn't see anyone else in the building behind the man in the long coat. So just two guards, both armed.

CHAPTER 70

Laura looked over at the door as it opened, her heart pounding. It was the same man who had given her water earlier. He was holding his gun and she swallowed nervously, her mouth so dry that she almost gagged. 'Is everything okay?' she asked. Was the game over? Had United won? Was he there to kill her and Ollie? She had cut through most of the duct tape but her wrists were still bound.

'It's half time,' he said, walking over to Ollie.

'What's happening?' asked Laura.

'It's a draw so far,' he said. 'One-one.'

Laura didn't know what to say.

'You better hope your husband does as he's told,' said the man. He stood over Ollie and checked the duct tape around the boy's ankles. Then he rolled Ollie over and looked at his taped wrists.

Laura's breath caught in her throat. If he checked her bonds he wouldn't fail to notice that she'd been cutting away at the tape. The man straightened up and walked towards her. 'Can I have some water?' she asked.

'I gave you water before.'

'I need more,' she said. 'My mouth is so dry.' She coughed, hoping that would prove her point. She needed to distract him, to stop him turning her over and looking at her wrists.

He sighed, then picked up the bottle of water from the bedside table. He put down the gun, unscrewed the cap and held the bottle to her mouth. She drank slowly until he took the bottle away. 'Thank you,' she said.

He put the bottle back on the bedside table and picked up his gun.

Laura squeezed the clippers in her right hand. There was no way he would fail to spot them if he rolled her over.

'I need to use the bathroom,' she said.

'That's impossible.'

'I need to pee.'

He shook his head. 'Pee on the bed,' he said.

'I can't do that.'

He shrugged. He walked to the foot of the bed and tugged at the duct tape around her ankles.

'Please, just help me to the bathroom.'

'I can't do that without untying you and I'm not going to untie you.'

'Please,' she said. 'You don't have to untie me, just carry me to the toilet.'

'The game will be over in forty-five minutes. You can wait.'

'That's what I'm telling you. I can't wait.' She paused but it was clear the man wasn't convinced.

'Is this your house?' She pressed him when he didn't answer. 'It's not, right? If I pee on the bed, the owner's not going to be happy, is he?'

'It's forty-five minutes. Not even an hour.'

'I need to pee now. Or at least put a towel under me.'

'A towel?'

'From the bathroom. Put a towel under me so that the bed won't get wet.' Getting him to put the towel under her was a risk, but with any luck he'd be so busy doing it that he'd forget about checking the duct tape.

The man muttered under his breath, and walked over to the bathroom.

CHAPTER 71

Ray got back into the car and started the engine. He looked ahead and checked the mirror to make sure there was no traffic in the vicinity, then he put the car in reverse. He pressed the button to lower the passenger side window and did the same with the driver's side. The two heavies were watching through the gate and he waved at them. 'Thanks guys!' he shouted. 'You have a great day.'

They stood impassively. Leather Jacket's right hand was patting his stomach. Long Coat's right hand was clenching and unclenching.

Ray started to reverse slowly, steering with his left hand as he reached for his gun with his right. He swung the wheel and pulled into the driveway, hoping that the heavies would assume he was just reversing so that he could drive back the way he'd come. He watched them in the rear view mirror. Long Coat was saying something to Leather Jacket. Ray straightened up the Range Rover, took a quick look left and right, then slammed on the accelerator. The engine roared and the car shot backwards, smashing through the metal gates. Long Coat dived to the left of the car and Leather Jacket broke right. Ray hit the brake as he brought his gun to bear on Long Coat. As the man got to his feet he reached into his coat and started to pull an Uzi on a nylon sling. Ray fired twice and both shots hit the man in chest and he went down.

As Ray looked to his right he saw Leather Jacket pull out a handgun. Ray hit the accelerator again and the car leapt back as the man fired. The shot went over the bonnet and the man was swinging the gun back towards Ray as Ray brought his gun across his body and pulled the trigger, firing through the open window and hitting the man in the throat, more by luck than judgment. Blood spurted down the man's chest and he staggered back, arms flailing.

Ray reversed another few metres down the driveway, then climbed out of the car. He hurried over to Leather Jacket. The man was clearly dead, his eyes wide and staring. Ray picked up the man's gun, a Smith & Wesson, and put the safety on before tucking it into his belt, then he dragged the man across to the gatehouse. He pulled the man inside. There was a sofa and a small table with two chairs and a window overlooking the gate.

Ray dumped the body on the floor and then went out to get Long Coat. Long Coat was also dead, one of the shots had gone through his heart and he had bled out in seconds. Ray pulled him into the gatehouse, then picked up the man's Uzi. He checked the magazine. It normally held 25 rounds but from what he could see through the slits in the side there were about half that. He slotted the magazine back in place and started running towards the house. He had no idea how many others there were inside, but he was sure they would have heard the shots and would be expecting him.

CHAPTER 72

Kang came out of the bathroom, holding a towel. He had heard a loud crashing noise and what sounded like gunshots. He dropped the towel on the bed and hurried over to the window. He peered through the blinds but the bedroom was at the back of the house and all he could see was the rear garden. He hurried over to the door. 'What the fuck is happening?' he shouted downstairs in Cantonese. There was no answer. 'What the fuck's going on?' he shouted. He moved cautiously along the hallway, looking down the stairs.

Huang appeared, holding his Uzi. 'There were shots, at the gate.'

'Get out there and find out what's happening?'

Huang nodded and rushed down the hall to the front door. Kang looked behind him at the bedroom door, unsure whether to go down or stay with the hostages.

CHAPTER 73

There was a flight of black marble stairs leading up to the front door but Ray ran instead to the side of the house. He knew he had made the right call when within seconds a heavyset Chinese man ran out holding a handgun. The man stood at the top of the steps, looking towards the front gate and frowning when he saw the Range Rover. Ray whistled softly and when the man turned, Ray shot him twice in the chest with the Uzi.

The man collapsed in a heap and his gun hit the floor. The man was wearing a jade ring, a match to the one that Ray had seen in the screenshots Gabe had sent him. He smiled. That was a good sign, a sign that he was on the right track. Ray moved around to the front of the house just as two other men came running out, both holding handguns. Ray fired a single shot that blew away the face of the first one, then put two shots in the chest of the second man. They were both dead before they hit the floor.

Ray's ears were ringing from the shots as he stepped into the house. He listened intently, moving his head from side to side as he moved across the tiled floor. He heard footsteps to his left and a man appeared with a Glock. He was moving fast and Ray kept his finger on the trigger, spraying the man with bullets until the magazine emptied. The man flew backwards and fell over a sofa, smearing it with blood. Ray dropped the Uzi and pulled the Smith and Wesson from his belt as he moved into the room. A big screen television was showing the United-Chelsea game, with Chelsea scoring. It was a replay, Ray realised. Half time. Ray saw the score – 1-1 – and grimaced. The room was empty but there were four brandy glasses on the coffee table. Four glasses and so far three heavies. That left one unaccounted for. He turned and went back into the hallway.

CHAPTER 74

McNamara looked at his wristwatch and blew his whistle 'Two minutes, guys,' he shouted. Gabe was sitting in front of his locker, holding an energy drink. McNamara went over to him. 'You okay, Gabe?' he asked.

Gabe shrugged. 'I know you're pissed off at me,' he said.

McNamara sat down next to him. 'I just know you can do better, that's all. You were the obvious choice for acting captain, but maybe you didn't need the pressure.'

Gabe sipped his drink. There was no way he could tell McNamara the reason for his lackluster performance.

'You just need to focus, Gabe. It could be a lot worse, we could be going out there one –nil down. A draw is like starting afresh. Go in with the right attitude and we could be 2-1 up in no time.'

Gabe stood up and tossed his bottle into a bin. He nodded at McNamara and headed out to the corridor where the Chelsea players were already filing out of their changing room.

CHAPTER 75

Ray looked up the stairway and listened. All he could hear were the commentators on the TV in the room behind him. He realised he hadn't checked how many rounds were in the Smith and Wesson's magazine. He wasn't familiar with the model and he figured it could hold anywhere between eight and twelve. He didn't want to take the risk of ejecting the magazine so all he could do was to hope for the best.

He moved across the hallway to the room opposite. He eased the door open then moved inside quickly, moving the gun around, his heart racing. It was a book-lined library and it was empty.

He moved back into the hallway. At the far end was a single door. Ray held the gun with his right hand, barrel pointing at the ceiling as he opened the door with his left. It was a large kitchen with gleaming white cupboards, stainless steel appliances and black marble worktops. A man was sitting at an island in the middle of the kitchen, his back to Ray, nodding his head back and forth to whatever he was listening to on Beat headphones connected to an iPhone that was on the work surface. Next to the iPhone was a Glock, similar to the one he had in his holster.

Ray scanned the kitchen but there was no one else there so he upended the Smith and Wesson and slammed the butt down against the back of the man's head. He slumped forward, his head smashing into the island. Ray hit the man again to make sure, then tossed the man's gun into the sink. He went back into the hall, stopped and listened again for several seconds, then went slowly up the stairs.

CHAPTER 76

The referee blew his whistle and Chelsea sprang into action. The captain kicked the ball across to the forward on his left, he kicked it back and a Chelsea midfielder sprinted with the ball towards the United goal. He didn't get far; Wood tackled him and sent the ball skidding across the grass to Gabe. Gabe tapped the ball to Moretti. The Italian turned to kick the ball towards the United goal but he turned back, feinted left and went right, catching Chelsea by surprise. Before they realised what was happening, Moretti was haring down the right wing. Babacar was running in parallel. Gabe hung back as Babacar shouted for the ball. Moretti's pass was perfect, low and fast and straight in front of Babacar.

A Chelsea defender tried to tackle Babacar but the striker shook him off. Gabe saw a gap in front of him but he didn't go for it. He ran to the right, towards where Armati was being closely marked.

Babacar had two defenders in his way so he chipped the ball to Moretti. Moretti caught it on his chest and immediately kicked it across to Fernandez who was making a run down the centre. Gabe ran with Fernandez and called for the ball. The Argentinian ignored him and flicked the ball to Moretti. Moretti headed it across to Babacar who did a flying kick that sent the ball hurtling towards the Chelsea goal. The keeper was wrong-footed and leapt across the goal-mouth, arms outstretched. He managed to touch it with his right hand and tipped it over the crossbar before crashing to the ground.

The crowd roared its disappointment. Gabe ran to take the corner kick. Jason Wood had the ball but Gabe took it from him. 'I thought I was doing the corners,' said Wood.

'Change of plan,' said Gabe. He didn't look over at McNamara, knowing that the coach wouldn't be happy. They'd been practising with Wood's corner kicks for the best part of a month and Wood was right, that was his role. But Babacar was on fire and the last thing Gabe wanted just then was for United to go 2-1 up.

Wood shrugged and jogged over to the penalty box. Babacar said something to Wood and then stared over at Gabe, clearly wondering what was going on.

The keeper was shouting instructions at his defence. Maplethorpe and Devereau jogged up to within a few yards of the penalty box but were imme-diately closely marked. Gabe took a few steps back, looked over at the goalmouth, then ran and kicked. The ball went high and curved towards Babacar but it was on his wrong side and though he managed to get his head to the ball he couldn't do anything but nod it towards Devereau. Devereau was shouldered by a Chelsea defender and another Chelsea player captured the ball and headed for the United goal.

Babacar glowered at Gabe but Gabe ignored him and jogged up the pitch. He heard McNamara calling his name and Gabe looked over at him. The coach held up his hands and bunched them into fists. 'What was that?' McNamara yelled.

Gabe looked away and carried on running.

CHAPTER 77

Ray reached the top of the stairs. There was a hallway running left and right and all the doors he could see were closed. He gritted his teeth in frustration and took a quick look at his watch. It was just after four. The match would have restarted by now. He was running out of time. He looked right, then left. He wasn't even sure that Laura and Ollie were upstairs, if they were in the house they could just as easily be in the basement. He took a deep breath as his mind raced. He could go through the rooms slowly and methodically, but that could take forever. Fast and furious would be more dangerous, but it would get the job done quicker. He turned left, grabbed the handle of the door closest to him, and threw it open. It was a bedroom and by the look of it the bed had never been slept in. The bed linen was pure white and there were framed seascapes on the walls, but it was as cold and lifeless as a furniture shop display. He pulled the door shut and tried the second door. Another bedroom. This one with Oriental furniture and wallpaper with a bamboo design. It was as soulless as the first room, and just as empty. Ray pulled the door shut. As he turned to walk down the hallway he heard footsteps on the stairs. A Chinese heavy with a handgun appeared. He had a plaster across his nose and Ray recognised him from the Chinese gambling den. The heavy brought his gun to bear on Ray but Ray was quicker and put two shots in the man's chest. The man fell back against the wall and slumped to the floor.

Chapter 78

Moretti was making a run down the left wing. He'd found himself unmarked and called for the ball from Devereau. Devereau's cross had been perfect and Moretti managed to run well into the Chelsea half before he met any opposition. He flicked the ball to Wood in the middle of the field, and Wood chipped it to Gabe. Gabe trapped the ball and looked around. Babacar was just outside the penalty box, but he was closely marked. Armati was unmarked, off to Gabe's right. He heard Fernandez shout his name and looked over his shoulder to see the Argentinian making a run. Gabe kicked the ball towards him but he put sidespin on it making the ball difficult to trap. Fernandez managed to get the ball under control but he had to slow his run and one of the Chelsea midfielders took the opportunity to get in front of him and block his way. Fernandez tried to get by but he was tripped and sprawled on the ground.

Armati and Wood appealed for a foul but the referee ignored them. The ball was scooped up by one of the Chelsea midfielders and kicked towards the United goal.

Fernandez got to his feet, shaking his head in disappointment. Wood clapped him on the back and the two men jogged towards the United penalty box. Gabe followed them.

Chelsea kept on the pressure, probing the United defence, then one of their strikers took a blistering shot that hit Mancini in the back and cannoned into the net. Ronnie Watts had no time to react and all he could do was stand on his line shaking his head in disgust. It wasn't Mancini's fault, it was pure bad luck, but the Italian sank to his knees and held his head in his hands.

The Chelsea fans were cheering wildly but they were pretty much drowned out by the jeers and cat-calls of the United supporters. Gabe stood close to the centre spot and looked up at the scoreboard. 2-1. Gabe took a deep breath. He took no pleasure in losing, but at least it meant he had a chance of seeing Laura and Ollie again.

CHAPTER 79

Ray reached the door at the far end of the corridor. He put his ear to it, heard nothing, and twisted the handle. As he pushed the door open a bullet thwacked into the wall by his head. He dived to the side, rolled over and came up with the both hands on the Smith and Wesson. A man wearing a black ski mask was standing next to Laura. Laura's hands were behind her back and her ankles were bound with duct tape. Ray kept the gun aimed at the man's head but he relaxed his finger on the trigger.

The man shoved the barrel of the gun under Laura's chin. Her eyes were wide with fear. 'Drop your gun,' said the man. Ray recognised the tattoo on the man's hand. It was Teddy Kang.

'Throw down your gun or I'll put a bullet in her head,' said Kang.

'There's no need for this, Teddy,' said Ray.

The man stiffened. 'Who the fuck are you?' he said.

'It doesn't matter who I am,' said Ray. 'But I know who you are. Teddy Kang, CK Lee's enforcer. A red pole.'

'How do you know that?'

'I just do. And you have to know that this is over now. I know who you are; no matter how this pans out you're in deep shit.'

Kang tilted his head on one side but he kept the gun pointed at Laura's head. 'Who sent you?'

'No one sent me,' said Ray. 'It's over, Teddy. Let her go and I'll let you walk out of here alive.'

'You're not telling me what to do,' said Kang, his finger tightening on the trigger.

'I need you to listen to me very carefully, Teddy,' said Ray. 'You've got a gun, and I've got a gun. I'm pointing my gun at you and you're pointing yours at her. So that's a stalemate. What do they call it? A Mexican standoff?'

'What the fuck are you talking about?' Tears were running down Laura's cheeks.

'What I'm talking about is what happens next. If you pull that trigger then she dies, but so do you. Because the second, the absolute second, that you pull that trigger I will start shooting I won't stop until every single bullet is in your head. Do you understand that?'

'I understand, but she'll be dead. And I don't think you want that.'

'You're right. I don't. So why don't we stop this now. You let her go and I let you walk away. I don't give a fuck about you, Teddy. Either way. Alive or dead, it's the same to me.'

Kang tapped the gun against Laura's temple and she winced. 'Why don't you walk away and I'll let her live?'

'She and the boy are coming with me,' said Ray. He waved the gun at Kang. 'The only question is whether you are able to walk away, or not.'

'You shoot me and I'll still pull the trigger,' said Kang.

'Maybe,' said Ray. 'Or maybe I pull the trigger and you die instantaneously. Like flicking a switch.'

Kang nodded. 'It's a gamble. Are you prepared to risk her life on a gamble?'

Ray shrugged. 'I'd prefer not to.'

'So go away,' said Kang. 'Go away and the woman lives.'

Ray shook his head. 'She's coming with me.'

Kang said nothing for several seconds. 'The men downstairs,' he said eventually. 'What have you done to them?'

'One of them's out cold. The one in the kitchen. The others...' He shrugged.

'You killed them?'

'It was them or me,' said Ray.

Kang gritted his teeth.

'Let her go, Teddy.'

'Fuck you.'

'Yeah, fuck you too. Teddy, either you pull that trigger and I shoot you. Or you try to shoot me and I shoot you. Either way, I shoot you. The only way I don't shoot you is if you walk away now.' He pointed his gun at Kang's head. 'Now stop fucking about and let her go.'

CHAPTER 80

'Shoot!' shouted Moretti at the top of his voice. 'What the hell are you waiting for?' The Italian was at the edge of the penalty box, two defenders between him and the Chelsea goal. Moretti had made a long run after getting the ball from Wood, outrunning three Chelsea players before chipping the ball across to Gabe, who had been running parallel to him.

The Chelsea goalkeeper had been wrong-footed and had slipped as he'd changed direction, sprawling across his goal line. Gabe had trapped the ball smoothly enough but had hesitated and given the keeper chance to spring to his feet. He made to pass the ball back to Wood but then swivelled and kicked the ball at the keeper. To the spectators it might have looked as if Gabe was trying to score but the keeper had no problem in pushing the ball above the crossbar.

Moretti ran over to Gabe, red-faced and angry. 'What the fuck was that?' asked Moretti. 'You had an open goal.'

Gabe smiled thinly. 'Sorry, mate. He was up like a fucking jack-in-the-box.'

Moretti shook his head scornfully. 'You had an open goal,' he repeated.

Gabe shrugged and jogged away. This time Wood retrieved the ball and placed it by the corner flag. Gabe waved at him. 'I'll take it, Jason!' he shouted.

Wood picked up the ball and held it to his chest. 'Joe says I'm to take the corners.'

'Yeah, well today I'm captain and I'm taking the kick.'

Wood shook his head. 'Gabe, Joe told me to take the corners. He wasn't happy with the way you took that last one and he said it wasn't to happen again. If you want to argue with him, that's up to you.' He nodded over at the touchline. Gabe turned to see McNamara standing on the pitch, shouting and pointing at Wood. His shouts were lost in the noise of the crowd, but it was clear the message he was trying to convey. Gabe shrugged. 'Fine,' he said. 'Whatever.'

He turned his back on Wood and jogged to the far corner of the penalty box. Moretti and Babacar were already in position, jostling for space. Armati and Fernandez had moved up and as Wood put the ball down on the ground and moved back, they broke left and right.

Wood took three quick steps and sent the ball across the grass to Fernandez who immediately turned and passed it to Maplethorpe who had made a run from the halfway line and was unmarked.

Maplethorpe charged forward with the ball seemingly glued to his feet until a defender ran to block his way. Maplethorpe feinted right but went left and as he passed the defender he chipped the ball high to Fernandez. Fernandez nodded the ball down to Armati and the Italian took one step before crossing it to Babacar. Babacar turned on the spot and hit the ball with so much force that the sound was heard at the back of the stadium. The ball shot through the air but the keeper was already jumping for it and it cannoned off his glove and over the crossbar. The United fans roared in frustration as Wood went to retrieve the ball again.

Gabe wiped the sweat from his forehead with his sleeve. He looked up at the clock on the scoreboard. It was five minutes past four. Time seemed to be crawling at a snail's pace. If he could just keep the score at 2-1, then everything would be all right. Maybe.

CHAPTER 81

Laura blinked away the tears' knowing that she had to do something if she and Ollie were going to survive. Ray was pointing his gun at Kang but she didn't believe that he would pull the trigger, not while Kang had his gun pressed against her head. She was fairly sure she had cut through most of the tape and that if she really made an effort she could break free of her bonds. But if she did that there was a good chance the man in the ski mask would pull the trigger.

She stared at Ray, trying desperately to get eye contact. He was staring at the man by her side, his eyes hard.

'Ray,' she said quietly.

He looked at her. 'Don't worry, Laura. I've got this.'

'Just put your gun down like he says, Ray.'

'If I do that, he'll shoot me. Then you. I know what I'm doing, darling. Just be cool.'

She narrowed her eyes, then stared at the floor. Back to him. Then to the floor. He frowned, wondering what she was doing. She gritted her teeth in frustration. Why didn't he understand what she was trying to tell him? She stared at the floor again. Then back at his eyes. Then the floor. Then she let the clippers fall from her fingers.

CHAPTER 82

The United defence had been caught off guard and were scrambling to get after the Chelsea striker as he made his run down the right wing. The pass had been unexpected, more by luck than judgement, Gabe thought, but the striker was taking full advantage of the confusion.

Maplethorpe was on the man's heels and tried a tackle that would almost certainly have merited a yellow card if it had connected but the striker easily avoided it and sped on towards the United goal. Ronnie Watts was just in front of his goal line, his arms out to the side as he bounced on his tiptoes. He was totally focussed on the player with the ball, ignoring all the shouting and jostling that was going on around him. The player drew back his right foot to kick and Watts crouched, but then he flicked the ball to his right where another striker was charging across the penalty box. The pass was perfect, straight to the man's head, and he hit it with a powerful snap that sent the ball powering towards the goal. Watts leapt and just managed to tip the ball over the crossbar and collective sighs wheezed around the stadium, followed by an outburst of tumultuous hand-clapping and cheers.

Watts picked himself up and acknowledged the applause from the crowd as Gabe gritted his teeth in frustration. Chelsea were still ahead but 3-1 would have been so much better than 2-1 because if United scored just one more goal then Laura and Ollie would be dead.

One of the Chelsea forwards retrieved the ball and got ready to take the corner. Gabe started jogging towards the United goal but McNamara screamed at him to stay where he was. Gabe stopped and looked over at the coach. McNamara pointed towards the centre spot. 'The defence can handle it!' shouted McNamara. 'Stay put!'

Gabe nodded and stood with his hands on his hips. The United defence clearly could handle it, that was the problem.

The corner kick was high and wide and bounced a good ten feet away from the nearest Chelsea player. Mancini pounced on it and carefully passed it to Watts who kicked it towards the Chelsea goal. Armati snapped it up and started his run. Gabe knew that he should be running flat out to keep pace with the Italian but he ran just slowly enough so that Armati drew ahead. Armati looked over his shoulder to see where Gabe was and as he did a Chelsea defender shouldered him and he span around and rolled onto the grass. The defender got the ball under control and passed it to a midfielder who sent it back to the Chelsea keeper.

Armati got to his feet and rubbed his hands on his shirt. He glared over at Gabe. 'Where the hell were you?' he shouted, but Gabe turned away without answering.

CHAPTER 83

Ray saw the metal object fall behind Laura and land on the carpet, soundlessly. His frown deepened. What was it? He still had his gun aimed at Kang's head, his finger on the trigger, but he glanced down at the floor by Laura's bare feet. Nail clippers, he realised. She'd been holding nail clippers. And she'd dropped them deliberately which meant she was trying to send him a message. He smiled at her. Clever girl. 'How do we end this, Teddy?' he asked.

'You drop your gun. Then you get the fuck out of the house.'

'I need to take her and the kid with me.'

Kang shook his head. 'They stay.'

'How do I know you won't kill them?'

'You don't have any choice, because if you stay they're going to die anyway.'

Ray nodded slowly, then lowered his gun. 'Okay,' he said. 'I'm going.'

Kang gestured with his chin. 'Throw the gun away. Do it.'

Ray sighed. 'Okay,' he said. He tossed the Smith and Wesson onto the bed.

Kang laughed harshly and pointed his gun at Ray. 'How fucking stupid are you?' spat Kang.

Laura grunted as she pulled her arms apart. The last of the duct tape parted with a ripping sound and she reached up with both hands, pushing Kang's gun away so that it pointed at the wall. He screamed at her but she gripped his wrist so tightly that her nails bit into his flesh.

Ray pulled the Glock from his shoulder holster and pointed it at Kang's head. He pulled the trigger twice. The ski mask collapsed and the back of his head splattered across the wall. Kang fell to the floor in a crumpled heap, his gun still in his hand.

Laura lost her balance and started to fall but Ray rushed forward and caught her. He lowered her back onto the bed, put his pistol back in its holster, picked up the nail clippers and used them to cut away the duct tape binding her ankles. 'Ollie,' she gasped.

'Are you okay?' asked Ray.

Laura stood up and hurried over to her son. She bent down and kissed him on the forehead. 'Oh honey,' she said. 'It's okay, it's all okay now.'

Ray went to join her at the sofa and cut the tape around the boy's legs and then rolled him onto his side and cut the tape fastening his wrists. As soon as he was free, Ollie sat up and hugged Laura. 'I was so scared,' he said, his voice faltering.

'It's all right now, honey,' said Laura, hugging him so hard that he gasped.

Ray looked at his watch. It was almost ten past four. 'We have to go,' he said.

'Who is he, mum?' asked Ollie.

'This is your Uncle Ray.'

'My uncle. I thought Uncle Jake was my uncle.'

'Uncle Jake is my brother,' said Laura. 'Uncle Ray is your daddy's brother.'

Ray solemnly stuck out his hand. 'Pleased to meet you, Ollie,' he said.

Ollie shook his hand, his uncertainty showing in his face.

'I'm going to carry you downstairs now, Ollie,' said Ray. 'I need you to do something for me.'

'What?'

'I'm going to pick you up and carry you to the car,' said Ray. 'I want you to cover your eyes with your hands.'

'Why?'

'Because there are some people downstairs who got hurt and it's best you don't see them.'

'They're not zombies?'

Ray laughed. 'No, kid, they're not coming back to life, that's for sure.' He scooped up the boy. 'Now cover your eyes.'

Ray looked over at Laura. 'Stay close to me,' he said. 'There's no one downstairs who can hurt you but it's not pretty.'

She swallowed nervously and nodded. 'Okay.'

'We're going to go downstairs and outside. We're going to get into my Range Rover and we'll go to the stadium.'

'Why don't we just call the police?'

'Because I'm in no mood to start explaining what happened here today. And Gabe needs to know that you're okay.'

He held Ollie with his left arm and took his gun out with his right hand.

'I thought you said there was no one downstairs,' said Laura.

'Better safe than sorry,' said Ray, heading for the door. 'Stay close.'

CHAPTER 84

Babacar had the ball and was charging towards the Chelsea goal. Gabe was over to his right and he called for a pass, but Babacar ignored him. A burly defender moved to block Babacar's way but the Senegalese managed to get the ball between the man's legs and past him in less than a second. The crowd roared its approval as yet again Babacar demonstrated why he was worth his £32 million transfer fee. Babacar drew back his leg to kick the ball to Moretti over on his left but it was a bluff and he started running to his right. Gabe shouted for the ball but Babacar ignored him.

The keeper was off his line and shouting for back-up. He had his arms out and was on the balls of his feet, then he took two steps closer to Babacar, trying to limit his options.

Babacar reached the edge of the penalty area and the keeper moved closer, waving his gloved hands. Gabe shouted again for the ball but Babacar paid him no attention. He went left, then right, then drew back his leg to shoot but before he could make the kick he was hit from behind by one of the Chelsea midfields, a wicked sliding tackle that took his left leg from underneath him.

The ball rolled away and was scooped up by the keeper. Babacar rolled onto his back and held his injured ankle, his face contorted in agony. The referee blew his whistle and indicated a free kick, just outside the penalty box. Moretti was immediately in the referee's face, shouting that the infraction had happened well inside the box and calling for a penalty. He was joined by Armati and the two Italians were waving their hands and shouting at the top of their voices. Gabe knew that they were right – Babacar had easily been inside the box when he had been brought down. The referee's incongruous decision backed up Gabe's suspicion that the man was also behind the plan to make sure that United lost.

More United players crowded around the referee and he blew his whistle and waved them away. Gabe jogged over. 'Guys, let it go,' he said. 'We're wasting time here.'

'The referee's fucking blind!' shouted Armati. 'We all saw what happened.' He glared over at the defender who had brought Babacar down and made a cut-throat gesture with his finger. The defender looked away.

'It's his call,' said Gabe. 'Right or wrong, he calls it as he sees it.'

'He's an idiot,' said Armati. He pointed at the referee. 'You're a fucking idiot!' he shouted. He grabbed his own crotch. 'Mangia la minchia!'

The referee's face reddened and he walked over to Armati, pulling a yellow card from his shirt pocket. 'You think I don't know Italian?' he shouted, waving the card in Armati's face. 'You're booked. And you tell me to eat your dick again and you'll be off. Are we clear?'

Armati glared at the referee and then turned and jogged away.

'Take the free kick,' the referee said to Gabe. 'And keep your team in line.'

One of the Chelsea defenders kicked the ball over to Gabe and he placed it on the ground. The Chelsea defenders formed a line in the penalty box, most of them covering their groins. The keeper was back on his goal line shouting instructions. The players shuffled forward and the referee blew his whistle and pointed for them to get back beyond ten yards.

Babacar got to his feet, tested his injured foot, then limped over to the edge of the penalty box. One of the midfielders jogged over to mark him. Moretti was over to Gabe's right, also closely marked.

The crowd was buzzing in anticipation. The defensive wall was shuffling forward again. Moretti was jostling with the defender, pushing him back and trying to tread on his feet.

Gabe took two steps back, and took a quick look over towards Babacar. Babacar was testing his injured foot. He caught Gabe's look and shook his head. He didn't want the ball. Gabe looked over at Moretti. A defender was pulling Moretti's shirt and the Italian was jabbing him in the chest with his elbow.

Gabe started his run, hit the ball with all his might, and sent the ball powering over the wall and over the cross-bar. The keeper made a token jump but it was clear to everyone that the shot was going over. The Chelsea defence jeered at Gabe but he was already running back up the field. McNamara was standing at the side of the pitch, his arms outstretched. He was screaming something at Gabe but whatever he was shouting was lost in the noise of the crowd.

CHAPTER 85

Ray reached the bottom of the stairs. 'You're doing great, Ollie,' said Ray. 'We'll soon be in the car.' He kissed him on the side of the head. 'Keep your eyes tightly closed.'

Laura looked into the sitting room and shuddered when she saw the bloody body sprawled over the sofa. 'Don't look,' said Ray.

'Too late,' she said. She looked up at the television. Chelsea were putting the United defence under pressure. She looked for Gabe but couldn't see him. Then she saw the score. Chelsea were winning 2-1.

'Come on,' said Ray. As he carried Ollie towards the front door he heard a noise in the kitchen, followed almost immediately by a scream from Laura. Ray twisted around. The heavy he'd hit in the kitchen was on his feet, running towards them with a carving knife held above his head. Ray fired instinctively and the bullet smacked into the man's chest. The man kept coming but the second bullet hit him in the middle of his face and he dropped like a stone.

Laura pressed herself against Ollie. Ray could feel her trembling. 'You're doing fine, Laura,' he said. He holstered the Glock and hurried down the hall and out of the front door.

CHAPTER 86

Chelsea were on the attack but they weren't making much progress, the ball had been passed more than a dozen times, backwards, forwards, side to side, and they hadn't been able to take it beyond the half-way line.

The United defence was waiting for them to make their move, and no one seemed to be in any hurry. Gabe took a quick look up at the clock on the score board. Ten past four. Thirty-five minutes to go, plus injury time. Gabe made a half-hearted run for the ball but it was passed back to the Chelsea defence.

The crowd began to boo. One of the defenders kicked the ball high and long and it was trapped by one of the Chelsea mid-fielders who began his run down the middle of the pitch. Gabe was the closest to him and he ran at full pelt to intercept. They ran neck-and-neck for almost twenty yards and then Gabe stuck out his foot and tripped the man over. He hit the grass hard and rolled over several times. Gabe took possession of the ball but the referee was already blowing his whistle. Gabe stopped and raised his hands. The crowd whistled and cat-called as Chelsea prepared to take the free kick. Gabe wasn't happy at having to foul the man, but at least it gave Chelsea time to regroup.

Tim Maplethorpe jogged over to Gabe. 'You ok?' he asked.

'Why?' replied Gabe.

'You seem ... I don't know ... a bit tense.'

'Fuck off, Tim.'

Maplethorpe raised his hands in surrender. 'Just asking,' he said.

'We're 2-1 down, of course I'm tense,' said Gabe. He wiped his forehead with his sleeve. 'I don't like losing.'

'Nobody does,' said Maplethorpe. 'But we can win this. We're the better team, by far.'

The referee blew his whistle and Chelsea took the kick. Gabe and Maplethorpe hared after the ball.

CHAPTER 87

Ray opened the back door of the Range Rover and helped Ollie onto the back seat. Laura climbed in next to her son and Ray slammed the door shut. He got into the front and started the engine. 'Okay?' he asked, taking a quick look over his shoulder. She nodded but didn't reply. 'Ollie, are you okay?' The boy nodded solemnly.

Ray put the car in gear and edged forward. He looked left and right. A white van and two cars drove by and then he pulled out and turned left.

'So, Ollie, let's go and see your dad, shall we?' asked Ray. He looked in his rear-view mirror. He was pale and biting down on his lower lip, obviously still in shock, which wasn't surprising considering what he'd been through. Laura put an arm protectively around her son.

A white SUV was coming towards them and Ray kept the Range Rover over to the right. He glanced down at his speedometer. Just above forty. He reached over to tap on the SatNav and input the stadium as the destination. When he looked back he gasped as he saw the SUV had moved over into his lane. A second vehicle, a black Porsche SUV was in the other lane. Ray cursed and slammed on the breaks. Laura and Ollie weren't wearing seatbelts and they were thrown forward. The tyres squealed and Ray knew they were going to hit the white SUV if he didn't do something so he wrenched the steering wheel to the right and the Range Rover bucked across the grass verge before slamming into a hedge. The airbag went off, obscuring his vision. He twisted around in his seat. Ollie was on the floor behind the front passenger seat and Laura bent down to help him. 'Are you okay?' asked Ray.

'What happened?'

'Some idiot ran us off the road.' He tried to deflate the airbag but it was like a living thing in his hands. He groped for the door handle with his right hand. Just as he found it the door was wrenched open. A Chinese heavy punched him in the face and then grabbed his arm and pulled him out of the vehicle. Ray tried to pull his arm away so that he could reach his gun but a second heavy had appeared and grabbed his left arm and twisted it. The two men had come from the white SUV. A third Chinese had stayed behind the wheel.

Ray stamped on the foot of the man who was holding his right arm and was rewarded with a scream of pain, but the man didn't release his grip. The second heavy kneed Ray in the stomach and the air exploded from his lungs. When he straightened up he saw that the Porsche SUV had pulled up behind the Range Rover. Ray could see Lee in the front passenger seat. The rear doors opened and two more Chinese heavies in leather jackets and jeans piled out. They ran to the Range Rover and pulled open the rear doors. 'Laura!' shouted Ray, but then he was kneed in the stomach again. He bent over in pain but he pulled his right arm in and the man fell against him. Ray thrust his elbow up and caught the man under the nose. The man grunted and released his grip. Ray kicked the man behind the knee and the man went down.

The second heavy was holding Ray's left wrist with both hands and his eyes widened when he saw what Ray had done to his colleague. Ray reached for his gun in its holster but the man was quicker than he expected and he kicked Ray in the chest. Ray fell back and the man sprang forward, throwing fast punches to Ray's face. Ray blocked the first couple of blows but the third hit him on the chin and knocked him back.

Ray blocked the next punch with his left hand and then pulled out his gun with the right. The heavy threw up his hands and screamed and Ray pulled the trigger. The gun clicked but there was no explosion and no recoil. The heavy grinned in triumph and then began throwing punches again. Ray dropped the gun and blocked as many of the blows as he could, keeping his hands high and his head low. He managed to get a jab to the man's chin that knocked his head back, but he kept attacking.

Ray heard Laura scream and he looked over at the Range Rover. The two heavies had pulled Laura and Ollie from the vehicle and were dragging them over to the Porsche. The driver of the white SUV climbed out. He was holding a machete and he raised it as he ran towards Ray.

Ray blocked a blow from the heavy in front of him, then kicked the man in the stomach. The man saw the kick coming and twisted sideways, avoiding most of the blow, then grabbed Ray's leg and swung him around. Ray lost his balance and fell on his back. The heavy grinned in triumph and raised his leg, preparing to stamp on Ray's face. Ray reached up, grabbed the man's foot and twisted it, throwing the man off balance, then Ray kicked up with his right leg, driving his foot into the man's groin so hard that he lifted him off he ground. The man fell backwards, arms flailing.

Ray tried to push himself up but the heavy with the machete was almost on top of him. The blade flashed down and Ray rolled to the side. The blade sparked on the pavement just inches from Ray's shoulder. The driver raised the blade again. Ray locked eyes with him and the man grinned in triumph as he swept the machete down. This time Ray rolled the other way and again the blade struck the pavement. Ray grabbed the man's wrist and lashed out with his foot, kicking the man's elbow. The man yelped but didn't let go of the weapon so Ray kicked his arm again. The man wrenched himself free from Ray's grip and staggered back, off balance, giving Ray time to leap to his feet.

Laura screamed again and Ray looked over at the Porsche. One of the heavies had pushed her into the back of the vehicle, the other had lifted Ollie off his feet and was swinging him inside. 'Laura!' Ray shouted, taking a step towards the Porsche, but he stopped as the driver swung the machete around. Ray ducked and the blade missed the top of his head by inches. Ray got in two quick punches to the man's chest and he staggered back. Ray grabbed for the man's wrist but he was too quick for him and he took a step back, raised the machete above his head and brought it down in a blur. Ray dived to the side, hit the road and rolled over his shoulders and came up into a fighting crouch. The driver raised the machete again and Ray launched himself at the man, two quick steps followed by a pile-driving side-kick to the man's stomach that sent him sprawling. The machete flew from his grasp, span through the air and landed on the grass by the Range Rover. Ray looked over at the Porsche. The two heavies were in the back now with Laura and Ollie and both doors slammed shut.

Lee climbed out of the front passenger seat of the SUV. He was grinning confidently and holding a large semi-automatic which he pointed at Ray's chest. 'Game, set and match,' said Lee.

'This isn't fucking tennis,' said Ray.

'Either way, I've won and you've lost,' said Lee.

The driver picked himself up off the ground and grabbed Ray's right arm. Ray ignored him and continued to stare at Lee. 'Let them go, or I swear to God I'll kill you with my bare hands,' said Ray.

'Good luck with that,' said Lee, his finger tightening on the trigger. The driver of the Porsche blipped the accelerator and the engine roared.

The heavy holding Ray's arm gripped him tighter. Ray continued to stare at Lee but he reached over with his left hand and grabbed the heavy's right wrist. Lee snarled and started to pull the trigger and as he did Ray yanked the heavy off balance. The heavy staggered in front of Ray and Lee's shot hit the man in the chest. He grunted and his legs sagged. Ray threw his left arm around the man's throat, holding him up as a shield.

Lee cursed in Chinese and aimed his gun again but Ray kept the heavy in front of him. The driver blipped the engine again. Lee swore, then got back into the Porsche and it drove off. Ray saw Lee glaring at him and then Laura's terrified face, her eyes wide and her mouth open. Then the car was gone, accelerating down the road towards London.

Ray released his grip on the heavy he was holding and the man slumped to the floor. A white van slowed as it drove by, then accelerated away quickly as Ray looked over at it. Ray picked up the empty Glock and he put it back in its holster as he ran over to the SUV. He pulled open the driver's door and cursed when he saw the key wasn't in the ignition. That was when he heard the sound of an approaching motor-cycle. He turned to see a motorcycle policeman on a powerful BMW bike.

Ray slammed the door shut and waited for the cop to park his bike and dismount. The cop looked at the SUV, then at the Range Rover on the grass, then walked stiff-legged over to Ray. He kept his full-face helmet on but flicked up the tinted visor. 'What's going on here?' asked the cop.

Ray shrugged. 'Road rage.'

'Which one is your vehicle, Sir?' asked the cop.

Ray gestured at the Range Rover. The cop frowned. 'How did that happen?'

'They ran me off the road.'

The cop went over to the heavy that Ray had knocked unconscious. The man was breathing heav-ily, with blood trickling from between his lips. Then he checked the heavy that Lee had shot. He knelt down, took off his right glove and felt for a pulse in the man's throat. His frown deepened as he looked at the man's chest injury. 'That's a gunshot,' he said. He looked up at Ray. 'You did this?'

Ray shrugged but didn't say anything. He looked over at the cop's motorcycle. Then down the road.

The cop straightened up and put his hand to his radio. Ray punched him just below the sternum and the breath exploded from the cop's throat. He bent over, gasping. 'Sorry, mate,' said Ray. 'Needs must.' The helmet limited Ray's options so he punched the cop in the gut again. The heavy motorcycle jacket absorbed much of the blow so he followed it up with a knee to the cop's groin. That did the trick and the cop collapsed and curled up into a foetal ball, gasping for breath.

Ray ran over to the motorcycle. The engine was still running. He climbed on, kicked it into gear and roared off down the road.

Chapter 88

Gabe was running down the middle of the pitch, Babacar to his right. Babacar's limp had gone but Gabe could tell he was a fraction slower than usual. A Chelsea defender appeared in front of Gabe and he flicked the ball across to Babacar before running around the man. The defender's shoulder caught Gabe as he went by but Gabe barely felt the blow. He called for the ball and Babacar tapped it back.

Gabe trapped the ball and looked around. Babacar was making his run but had his back to Gabe, Moretti was being closely marked and Fernandez and Reid were still in the United half.

The Chelsea defender he'd beaten a few seconds earlier came running up behind Gabe and Gabe sidestepped, did a full 360 and smiled to himself as the man hurtled past.

Babacar was looking at him now and had space, though he wasn't in a scoring position. Gabe chipped the ball across to him and ran towards the penalty box. Moretti was making a move too, bobbing left and right and forcing his defender to move with him.

Then Moretti sprinted towards Babacar, shouting for the ball. The Chelsea keeper was on his line, shouting for his defence to get their act together. The crowd was roaring, sensing a shot was coming.

Babacar sent the ball skimming across the grass to Moretti. Gabe saw an opening but held back. Moretti looked over at him, a look of confusion on his face when he realised that Gabe wasn't making a run, then Jason Wood screamed for the ball. He was running full pelt down the middle of the pitch, unmarked. Moretti chipped the ball to Wood and Wood trapped it on the move, the crowd screaming with excitement. Wood reached the penalty box, stopped for a second, then took his shot. The keeper dived but his fingertips missed the ball by inches. The ball hit the post and bounced back towards Babacar. Babacar trapped it on his chest, dropped it and volleyed it. The keeper was on his knees but managed to get one hand to it. The ball bounced down and was kicked away by a Chelsea defender.

Gabe's heart pounded as he saw the ball was coming towards him. He was unmarked, everyone's attention had been on the scramble in the penalty box. He got the ball and ran parallel to the box. Babacar was at the left of the goal, Moretti on the right, the keeper standing between them with his arms outstretched.

Gabe stopped and put his right foot on the ball, his mind racing as he considered his options. Babacar was the best bet, the lanky Senegalese was perfectly positioned for a header. Moretti, too, had a good chance of getting a header in, though he'd also be able to get a volley past the keeper if Gabe placed the ball high and to the Italian's left. Moretti was as good with his left foot as he was with his right and he had a knack for volleying under pressure. Wood had his arms raised over his head and was calling for the ball. Gabe moved forward a few feet, then trapped the ball with his foot again. The crowd was screaming for Gabe to pass the ball or shoot. Gabe took a deep breath, knowing that whatever he did had to look good, but at the same time there was no way he could risk a goal being scored. Not when it meant the death of his family.

Babacar ran across the goalmouth, his arms outstretched, signalling he wanted the ball at chest height. Gabe knew what would happen if he did what Babacar wanted – the Senegalese was in position to perform one of his turning volleys, his trademark shot.

Wood was still shouting for the ball. He was good with his head and from where he was standing he'd have a good chance of getting one in the net. On any other day Gabe would be excited at the prospect of a goal, but this wasn't any other day.

He ran a couple of yards and stopped again. He was just a few feet from the penalty box and the crowd was urging him on. He was going to have to do something, and soon, and he figured the best way out of his predicament would be to shoot and miss. He drew back his right foot which is when he was hit from behind in a brutal tackle that swept his legs from underneath him. He fell awkwardly, his left leg buckling under his full weight and he screamed in agony as he hit the ground. He was barely aware of the referee blowing his whistle and the crowd roaring its disappointment.

CHAPTER 89

It had been a few years since Ray had been on a motorbike but the BMW was easy to ride. It was responsive despite its size and after just a few seconds he realised he should have taken the cop's helmet. His eyes were watering from the battering slipstream and he narrowed them to slits as he powered down the road.

There was a set of lights ahead and they were red. There was a switch by Ray's right thumb that operated the blue lights and siren and Ray flicked it. The siren started to wail and the blue light behind him began to flash. Traffic that was crossing slowed and Ray drove through the intersection, looking left and right to check that Lee's Porsche hadn't turned. There was no sign of it so he accelerated. There were half a dozen cars ahead of him and he overtook them, the siren still wailing, pulling over only when he saw a white van heading towards him.

He took the bike up to sixty, crouching low over the petrol tank. A few seconds later he saw the Porsche ahead of him. The car was stuck behind a slow-moving coach. Ray switched off the siren and light and slowed the bike, hoping he hadn't alerted them. He checked his rear-view mirrors. There were no vehicles behind him.

CHAPTER 90

Brian Lawrence slapped an icepack on Gabe's left knee. 'How's it feel?' the medic asked. Gabe was lying on his back, surrounded by half a dozen anxious United players. Most of the Chelsea team was huddled some distance away while the referee stood between the two groups, looking at his watch.

'It's ok,' said Gabe, a lie as his knee felt as if it was on fire.

'What do you want to do?' asked Lawrence. The medic looked over his shoulder towards McNamara, who was standing at the touchline.

'I'm fine, just let me up,' said Gabe.

'This is what I was worried about,' said Lawrence. 'Your knees can't take damage like this, Gabe. You're going to end up in a wheelchair, I swear to God.'

'I just twisted it when I fell,' said Gabe. 'I'm good to go.'

The referee walked over. 'What's the story?' he asked.

'I'm just assessing the damage,' said Lawrence.

'You're going to have to make a call,' said the referee, looking up at the scoreboard.

'I'm okay,' said Gabe. 'Just let me up.'

Lawrence removed the icepack and put it in his medical bag, then offered Gabe his hand. Gabe grabbed it and Lawrence pulled him to his feet. Gabe tested the leg carefully, placing his foot flat on the ground and pressing down slowly. A bolt of pain lanced up from his knee and he winced.

'You need to come off,' said Lawrence. He waved over at McNamara.

'No!' said Gabe. 'Give me a second.'

'Gabe, I'm not going to be responsible for you hurting yourself,' said the medic. 'You've done your bit, there's half an hour to go and you'll be holding the team back trying to play like this.'

'For fuck's sake, Brian, I'm fine,' Gabe protested. He tried the leg again. This time it didn't hurt quite so much. 'I can play.'

Lawrence picked up his medical bag. 'I think you're making a big mistake.'

Gabe bounced up and down, ignoring the searing pain in his left knee and forcing a smile. 'I'm fine, look.'

Lawrence shook his head sadly. The referee blew his whistle and pointed at the spot where the free kick was to be taken. 'I'm taking it!' shouted Gabe.

'No fucking way!' said Babacar, picking up the ball.

'I'm the fucking captain and I say I'm taking the kick,' said Gabe.

Babacar shook his head and kept the ball out of Gabe's reach.

Lawrence was listening on his headset, his right hand up by his ear. 'Gabe, Joe wants you off,' he said. 'And he wants Omar to take the kick,' he added. He pointed over at the sideline. Gabe turned and saw McNamara waving his arms. Next to him was the fourth official holding up an electronic board with Gabe's number on it – 10 – and the number of the player United wanted to substitute. Behind them was Piero Guttoso, his hands in the pockets of his overcoat.

The supporters had marked the arrival of the United manager with a chant of 'WHO ATE ALL THE PASTA, WHO ATE ALL THE PASTA?' Gabe cursed under his breath. The referee blew his whistle and pointed for Gabe to leave the pitch.

'Let me talk to him,' said Gabe, reaching for Lawrence's headset.

Lawrence slapped his hand away. 'You know it doesn't work like that,' he said. 'You've been treated for an injury, you have to leave the pitch.'

'I need to talk to him.'

'Then go and talk to him. He wants you off anyway.'

The referee blew his whistle again. 'Go, or you're booked,' he said.

'Tell Joe I'm coming off, but no substitution,' said Gabe.

'Gabe, you have to leave the pitch anyway. You know that. You're treated for an injury and you have to leave. That's the rule. No argument.'

Gabe looked pleadingly at the medic. 'Please, just tell him that, will you?'

Lawrence turned away and spoke to McNamara. He listened and nodded, then waved at Gabe. 'Off,' he said.

Gabe looked over at the sideline. The fourth official had lowered the electronic sign. He jogged over towards McNamara, trying to ignore the shooting pains in his knee.

CHAPTER 91

The Porsche was trying to get by the coach, but there were cars coming the other way and each time the driver edged out to overtake he was forced back by oncoming traffic. Ray accelerated and came up behind the SUV. He could see the back of Laura's head, but not Ollie. The heavy on Laura's left twisted around in his seat and for a second locked eyes with Ray. Ray pulled out and overtook, drawing level with the driver. The driver looked to his right, saw Ray and flicked the steering wheel to try to hit the bike. Ray saw the move coming and rolled the bike to the side. A car was heading straight for him. He braked hard but realised he wouldn't have time to tuck in behind the Porsche. There was layby to his right so he swerved in front of the oncoming car, drove along the layby and then cut across the road back into the correct lane again.

As he came up behind the Porsche the window behind the driver opened and a handgun emerged. The gun barked twice but both bullets went high. He braked and tucked in behind the Porsche. The heavy with the gun turned and aimed at the bike through the rear window. Ray doubted that the man would try to fire through the window but then the glass exploded in a shower of cubes and a bullet smacked into the bike's fairing.

Ray braked as the man fired again and the change in speed threw off his aim so the bullet went wide. The heavy leaned through the broken window and used both hands to steady his arm. Ray twisted the accelerator hard and the bike leaped forward. Ray leant to the right and overtook the Porsche.

There was a red fire extinguisher clipped to the inside of the fairing. He ripped it out with his left hand and flicked off the cover that prevented the trigger being pressed accidentally. The heavy with the gun was twisting around in his seat again. Ray slowed the bike and pointed the fire extinguisher into the window. He pressed the trigger and white foam sprayed through the gap. It hit the man in the face, blinding him and getting into his mouth making him cough and splutter. Ray accelerated and drew level with the driver. The driver twisted the wheel again but Ray saw the move coming and rolled to the right. There was a truck heading right for him but the driver's reactions were good and he pulled the vehicle to the far side of the lane giving Ray just enough room to squeeze by. He took a quick look in his wing mirror and saw Lee, his jaw tight and his eyes blazing with hatred. Ray put his left arm back and sprayed foam over the windshield. The driver switched on the wipers but the foam was so thick that it smeared across the glass. Ray sprayed for several seconds, then threw the extinguisher at the windscreen as hard as he could. He heard the glass crack but he didn't look back. He put his left hand back on the handlebars and twisted the accelerator with his right. He shot forward, pulled to the right to overtake the coach, twisted the accelerator again and got to the front of the coach, forcing several oncoming cars to swerve out of his way.

He flicked the switch to operate the blue light and siren, then drove ahead of the coach and pulled into the middle of the lane. He accelerated again so that he was about ten feet ahead of the coach, giving the driver just long enough to see the flashing light before he slammed on the brakes.

Chapter 92

Gabe put his hands together in prayer. 'Joe, please, send me back out there.' McNamara was looking over Gabe's shoulder where Babacar was preparing to take the free kick. Several Chelsea players had lined up to form a wall ten yards away from the ball and the keeper was shouting over at them.

'Your leg's fucked, Gabe,' said the coach.

'It's not,' said Gabe. He put all his weight on his left leg. It hurt like hell but he forced himself to ignore the pain. 'Look. Right as rain.'

McNamara sighed. 'You're playing like a fucking carthorse out there,' he said. 'I don't know what's wrong with you but it's as if your heart isn't in it.'

'Joe, please. Come on. I'm the fucking captain.'

For the first time McNamara looked at Gabe. 'Yeah, and how's that working out for us? We're 2-1 down on a day when we should be 3-0 up. The only thing I can think of is that your knees are hurting worse than you're letting on.'

'My knees are fine.' He gestured at the medic. 'Ask Brian.'

'Without a scan, his opinion doesn't really count for much.'

'Thanks for that,' said the medic.

'No offence, Brian,' said McNamara. 'But you know what I mean. We can't see the damage. That tackle looked as rough as fuck to me, but only Gabe knows how much it hurts.'

'It doesn't hurt,' said Gabe. 'And I want to be out there. We shouldn't be a man down. Not when I'm fit to play. And I'm still wearing that captain's armband.'

Guttoso walked over, glowering. 'What the fuck is going on out there, Gabe?' he asked.

'We've had a few bad breaks, that's all,' said Gabe.

Guttoso nodded over at the owner's box. 'You're making me look bad in front of the owner, you know that? He's got all his friends up there and he's as embarrassed as hell. He's taking it out on me and I'm taking it out on Joe and all that shit is now heading your way.'

'Boss, we can win this. Just let me back on the field.'

The referee blew his whistle and Gabe heard the ball being kicked. McNamara was looking over Gabe's shoulder again and he was gritting his teeth. The crowd roared and Gabe turned to see Moretti with the ball, rushing past the wall. The keeper was off his line and clearly flustered. Moretti hit the ball hard and it hit the left post and cannoned back into play. Babacar pounced and hit it into the net with his left foot. The crowd erupted and McNamara pumped the air with his fist. 'Now that's what I'm talking about!' he shouted.

Gabe forced a smile and high-fived the coach. Tommy Brett was screaming with joy and jumping up and down excitedly. He rushed over and hugged Gabe. 'The tide has turned!' he shouted. 'The tide has fucking turned.'

The scoreboard changed, from 2-1 to 2-2. A draw. The last thing that Gabe wanted to see just then. He broke away from Brett and put his hands on McNamara's shoulders. 'Joe, let me go back out there.'

'You're in pain, Gabe. I can see it.'

'I'm fine.' He looked up at the clock on the score-board. 'Come on, there's half an hour to go. Just give me half an hour.'

'I shouldn't,' said the coach, but Gabe could hear the lack of conviction in his voice.

'I won't let you down,' said Gabe. He looked over at Guttoso. The manager was smiling for the first time that day as he looked over at the owner's box. The owner was standing and pumping his arms in the air, clearly delighted. 'Boss, please, I'm the cap-tain. Let me back on.'

McNamara looked over at Guttoso. The man-ager shrugged, leaving the decision up to the coach. McNamara sighed and waved at the pitch. 'Go,' he said.

Gabe patted him on the shoulders and ran onto the pitch. The crowd's cheers intensified when the supporters realised that Gabe was rejoining the game, but Gabe took no pleasure from the applause. He wasn't running on to the pitch to help his team, but to betray them.

Chapter 93

The heavy with the gun was flailing around, trying to wipe the foam from his face with his sleeve. 'Get down, Ollie!' shouted Laura.

Lee turned around and glared at her. 'Shut up!' he shouted.

Ollie hesitated so Laura grabbed him by the scruff of the neck and pushed him down behind the front passenger seat.

The heavy on her right was spitting foam from between his lips as he wiped his eyes with the back of his right hand. The barrel of the gun was pointing at her and she pushed it away with both hands.

'Sit down!' shouted Lee but Laura ignored him.

The heavy tried to pull the gun away from her but she twisted it back, making him yelp as his fingers involuntarily released their grip on the weapon. Laura whooped in triumph but as she did the gun slipped from her grasp and fell to the floor. The heavy used both his hands to wipe the foam from his eyes as Laura reached between his legs to try to recover the gun.

A hand grabbed at her shirt and yanked her up. It was the heavy on the other side of the car. Laura screamed and clawed at his eyes. Her nails bit into the top of his nose and she scraped them down his face, drawing blood. The man screamed.

Lee pulled a gun from inside his jacket and pointed it at Laura. 'Stop!' he shouted at the top of his voice and that was when there was a squeal of tyres skidding on the Tarmac and the Porsche slammed into the back of the coach.

CHAPTER 94

The coach hit the back of the bike sending it sprawling across the road. Ray rolled off and got to his feet. The coach had lost most of its momentum before hitting the bike and the damage was minimal. Ray ran onto the pavement and down the side of the coach. He reached the Porsche, which had hit the coach full on, exploding all the airbags. He pulled open the rear passenger door. The heavy there had hit the seat in front of him and blood was pouring down his face. Ray grabbed him by the scruff of the neck and yanked him out onto the pavement. He looked into the back. Laura was staring at him, her eyes wide. Ollie was on the floor behind the front passenger seat. The heavy on the far side was moaning and shaking his foam-covered head. There was a red patch in the middle of the foam, his head had smacked into the back of the driver's seat.

'Get out!' he shouted, then punched the heavy he was holding in the back of the neck. The man fell to the floor and Ray stamped on him, hard.

Laura picked up Ollie and pushed him through the open door. Ray grabbed him and held him as Laura scrambled out. The foam-covered heavy wiped his eyes with his sleeve and then lunged at Laura, grabbing the collar of her shirt. She screamed as he yanked her back. Ray leaned into the car and punched the man in the face and he fell back, out cold. Ray held Laura's arm and helped her out of the car, then handed Ollie to her.

The front door opened and Lee's left leg appeared but before he could get out, Ray grabbed the door and slammed it against the leg. Lee grunted in pain. Ray opened the door and smashed it shut again and this time Lee screamed. Ray threw the door open wide, grabbed Lee and pulled him out. Lee was still groggy from the crash and when he reached for his gun his hand was shaking. Ray punched him in the face and Lee fell back against the car. Lee pushed Ray away with both hands and Ray hit him again, and this time he felt the man's nose break. He punched him twice in the chest and then elbowed his chin so hard that Lee's head snapped back. Lee's eyes were half-closed, and blood was pouring down his chin. Ray grabbed the man's throat with his left hand and drew back his right, bunching it into a tight fist. Lee's arms fell to his sides. All the fight had gone out of him.

'Ray!' shouted Laura.

Ray held his fist where it was as he looked over his shoulder. Laura was hugging Ollie, his arms wrapped tightly around her neck. 'Enough, Ray,' she said. 'Please.' She hugged Ollie tighter and kissed his neck.

Ray nodded, then turned back to look at Lee. 'You don't know how lucky you are,' said Ray, shoving him against the car. He released his grip on Lee's throat and the man sank slowly down to the ground.

Ray went over to Laura. 'Are you okay?' he asked.

She blinked away tears. 'Not really,' she said.

'We have to get to the stadium,' he said.

'How?' she asked.

Ray took out his phone. 'Uber,' he said. 'But first we have to get away from here. Someone will have called the cops, for sure.' He took Ollie from her and the boy wrapped his arms around Ray's neck. Ray smiled at Laura. 'Come on,' he said. 'Stick close to me.' They hurried away from the Porsche and jogged down a side road. In the distance, a siren began to wail.

CHAPTER 95

Gabe looked up at the clock. It was half past four. Fifteen minutes to go, plus added time. And if the score stayed at 2-2, Laura and Ollie would be dead. Chelsea had to score again. They had to.

Fernandez had the ball, close to the centre spot, Wood to his left and Maplethorpe to his right. Babacar was trying to break free of the man marking him but the defender was sticking to him like a shadow and the Senegalese was tiring. Moretti was also heavily marked, jostling for position on the edge of the penalty box.

Fernandez started running with the ball and Gabe went with him, to his left and slightly behind. Fernandez kept going as long as he could then passed it to Gabe. The crowd was screaming in anticipation as Gabe took possession and sidestepped a Chelsea defender. Fernandez was free again but Gabe only faked a pass to him and then continued his run, fast enough to look good but not so fast that he couldn't be intercepted.

A Chelsea player appeared at his left and Gabe took the ball the other way but then allowed himself to be shouldered. He shouldered back and used his hand to push at the man's head. It was a clear foul and the referee blew his whistle immediately.

Gabe moved away as Chelsea got ready for the free kick. 'Come on guys!' he shouted. 'Let's get fucking serious!'

Chelsea took the kick and the ball went soaring into the United half where it was snapped up by one of the Chelsea forwards. Gabe stared after him, willing him to score, but the man's run lasted less than twenty feet before Mancini tackled him and sent the ball spinning over the sideline. The referee blew his whistle and awarded the throw-in to Chelsea. Gabe gritted his teeth. If Chelsea didn't get a grip on the game he was going to have to put the ball in his own net, and that would open up a whole can of worms that would almost certainly spell the end of his career.

CHAPTER 96

The Uber driver's name was Mohammed and it was clear he knew that something was wrong by the way he kept glancing at Laura and Ollie in his rear-view mirror. Ray was sitting in the front passenger seat of the Toyota Prius, his arms folded. According to the SatNav, they were just four minutes away from the stadium. Mohammed saw Ray frowning. 'You know the game is almost over,' he said.

'Yeah,' said Ray, stretching out his legs as far as they would go. 'I know.'

'Do you want to listen?'

'Sure, why not?'

Mohammed reached over with his left hand to turn the radio on, then pressed the tuning buttons until he got a station that was broadcasting the match. An excited commentator was describing a Chelsea attack on the United goal, reeling off the names of the players as they touched the ball.

'Come on, what's the score?' muttered Ray.

The commentator described the United keeper falling on the ball, then kicking it upfield to Gabe.

'Daddy!' shouted Ollie from the back.

'Hush, honey,' said Laura, putting his arm around her son.

Gabe ran with the ball, passed it to Luca Moretti who kicked it back to Gabe. Gabe sent the ball over to Fernandez but Fernandez lost the ball to a sliding tackle. Chelsea then spent a minute or so passing the ball between them. Eventually the commentator gave the score. Two-all.

'They're drawing,' said Ray.

'Does the score matter any more?" asked Laura.

'It does to me,' said Ray. 'I don't want those bastards getting their way, not after what they did to you and Ollie.'

CHAPTER 97

Chelsea had been awarded a throw in and this time the United midfielders were prepared for the long throw. Fernandez intercepted the ball and passed it immediately to Wood who ran down the centre of the pitch and into the Chelsea half. Gabe ran with him, a few yards behind, but he was closely marked and the Argentinian looked left and right, desperately looking for someone to pass to before he hit the Chelsea defence.

Armati headed for the left wing and then broke right, shouting for the ball. Fernandez sent it to him and ran right. Babacar was also in the mix, having broken free from the player who had been marking him. Babacar reached the edge of the penalty box and turned with his arms outstretched. Armati had stopped and when he saw Babacar he lobbed the ball to him. Gabe's heart was in his mouth as Babacar trapped the ball on his chest, let it bounce once and then turned and volleyed in one smooth movement. The ball hit the right goalpost and ricocheted back towards Babacar but, as he drew back his leg to kick it again, a Chelsea defender thrust his arm across Babacar's neck and pushed him backwards. Babacar's arms flailed as his legs buckled under him and the ball rolled towards the keeper who scooped it up and booted it up the field. It looked like a clear foul to Gabe but the referee didn't acknowledge it and he kept his head down and ran after the ball. The crowd clearly wasn't happy and nor was Babacar, who got to his feet, rubbed his chin and cursed. The defender who'd hit him had moved over to the far side of the penalty box and was studiously ignoring the United striker. 'You okay, Omar?' asked Gabe.

'You saw what happened?' said Babacar. 'He practically punched me.'

'Heat of the moment,' said Gabe. 'Shit happens.'

'Yeah, well if he tries that again shit is going to be happening to him,' he said. He spat onto the pitch, then wiped his mouth with the back of his hand. 'We should be winning this fucking game.'

'There's still time,' said Gabe. He looked up at the scoreboard. Twenty minutes to four. Five minutes to go, plus added time.

'Let's do it,' said Babacar, and he sprinted towards the United half where Chelsea seemed to have lost momentum and were back to passing the ball aimlessly to and fro, as if they were warming up and not in the final minutes of a match with the score 2-2.

CHAPTER 98

Mohammed brought the car to a halt on double-yellow lines close to the stadium. 'You give me five stars, okay?' he asked Ray, who was already reaching for the door handle.

'Sure, mate.'

Mohammed smiled broadly and nodded enthusiastically. 'Good. I will give you five stars also.'

Ray got out and helped Laura and Ollie out of the back. Ray picked up Ollie and headed towards the Players Entrance as Mohammed drove away. Laura followed him. 'We're too late,' she panted.

Ray looked at his watch. 'No, there's added time,' said Ray. 'For stoppages, injuries and substitutions. It's not over yet.' There were two stewards at the Players Entrance and they weren't the ones that he had seen before. They were both men in their twenties, one black and one Asian. 'We need to get in,' Ray said to them, putting Ollie down. Ollie held out his hand and Laura took it and smiled down at him.

'That match is pretty much over, mate,' said the Asian steward. 'They're in to injury time.'

Ray put up his hands. 'I get that, but I have to get in there, now.' He gestured at Laura. 'This is Gabe Savage's wife.'

The Asian shrugged. 'We get that a lot, mate. Sorry. Even if you had a ticket we couldn't let you in now. The stadium'll be emptying any minute.'

'Is Gerry around? Gerry McGee?'

The two stewards looked at each other, frowning in confusion.

'Just get Gerry for me,' said Ray. 'Now.'

CHAPTER 99

The referee pointed for Chelsea to take the throw-in and the crowd booed its disapproval. Jason Wood and a Chelsea midfielder had jostled for the ball close to the sideline and it was pretty clear that the Chelsea player had been the last to touch the ball but the referee was adamant. Gabe was sure now that someone had gotten to the referee, one way or another.

The throw in was good but Fernandez's anticipation was better and he intercepted the ball, turned on the spot and started running for the Chelsea goal. A Chelsea midfielder ran towards Fernandez and the Argentinian chipped the ball to Babacar who immediately sent it across the field to Moretti who was completely unmarked. The crowd roared, sensing a goal, and Gabe's heart raced. He ran down the middle of the pitch, shouting for the ball but Moretti's attention was totally focussed on the Chelsea goal.

He beat one defender, then another, then sent a blistering shot towards the goal that the keeper only just managed to get to. The keeper's left hand pushed the ball to the side of the post and the crowd groaned. Gabe stopped running and stood with his hands on his hips as he stared up at the scoreboard. There were only minutes to go and all the attacks seemed to be coming from United. He gritted his teeth. He would do whatever it took to make sure that Chelsea scored again. No matter what it meant for his career and his reputation. All he cared about was Laura and Ollie and getting them back safely.

CHAPTER 100

G erry McGee was confused to see Ray outside
the stadium again, but he greeted Laura and
Ollie enthusiastically. 'The match is almost over,
Mrs Savage,' he said.

'I know, Gerry, but can you let us in. We promised
Gabe we'd be here.'

'Of course,' said McGee, ushering them through
the turnstile.

Ray looked at his watch. It was twenty minutes
to four. The game would soon be over. 'What's the
score, Gerry?'

'Two-all,' said the steward. 'I dunno what's wrong
with United, they should have had this game in
the bag.'

Ray reached for Ollie's hand and the boy took it.
'Can you take us as close to the pitch as we can get?'
asked Laura. 'I want Gabe to know we made it.'

'Sure, but there isn't much time,' said the steward. He took them away from the turnstile and
towards the main stand. Ray tensed as he saw two
Chinese men walking towards them. They both wore

overcoats over suits, but they had the look of hard men who would have no trouble getting down and dirty. 'Gerry, I need you to wait here with Laura and Ollie,' said Ray, but before the steward could reply one of the men slid his hand out of his coat pocket, just enough to show he was holding a gun.

The second man had his hand inside his coat and he drew it back to show what he was carrying. His gun had a bulbous silencer screwed into the barrel. 'You're to come with us,' he hissed. 'Any trouble and we're to shoot the boy first.'

Ray nodded. 'There won't be any trouble.' McGee had begun to tremble and Ray patted him on the shoulder. 'Don't worry, Gerry, these guys just want a word with me.' He smiled at the steward's obvious discomfort. 'Just take deep breaths, everything will be okay.'

Laura picked up Ollie and looked anxiously over at Ray. 'Ray?' she said.

'It's okay, darling. Don't worry. I've got this.'

'Like fuck you have,' said the heavy with the silencer. He nodded towards the executive boxes. 'This way,' he said. 'And if you try anything, I'll shoot the boy.'

'I heard you the first time,' said Ray.

Chapter 101

Chelsea had the ball but again they seemed at a loss as to what they should do with it. They got it to the halfway line and then lost momentum, passing it back and forth as the seconds ticked by. Gabe looked up at the scoreboard clock. It was 4.42. Three minutes to go, plus injury time, maybe eight minutes in total. It was more than enough time for another goal to be scored, the problem was that all the attacking was being done by United.

Wood and Fernandez launched a joint attack on the player with the ball, Wood with a sliding tackle and Fernandez with a brutal shoulder charge. The ball rolled away and Fernandez chased after it but Maplethorpe got to it first. He ran up the middle of the field and saw Gabe off to his left. Gabe nodded and Maplethorpe kicked it over to him, a near perfect pass that meant Gabe was running at almost full speed when the ball reached his feet. He dribbled it out to the sideline, then brought it in towards the Chelsea penalty box.

Babacar was in position for a shot and was scream-ing at Gabe for the ball. Gabe heard the thud of boots to his right. He drew back his leg to shoot but braced himself for the tackle that he knew was com-ing. The defender slammed into Gabe's side, send-ing him sprawling. The crowd jeered but Gabe knew the tackle was good. As he rolled over he saw the defender retrieve the ball and start running towards the United half. Gabe ignored the stabbing pain that shot through his left leg as he stood up. The defender reached the half-way line and seemed to run out of steam, looking around anxiously for someone to pass to. Gabe cursed under his breath. 'For fuck's sake,' he muttered. 'If you carry on like this I'm going to have to put the ball in the back of the net myself.'

CHAPTER 102

The heavy with the unsilenced gun walked ahead of Ray, his coat flapping behind him. McGee was on Ray's left, ashen-faced, and Laura and Ollie were to his right. The heavy with the silencer was one step behind them and Ray had no doubt that if he did try anything Ollie would be the first target.

'What do we do, Ray?' whispered Laura.

'Just do as they say for the moment,' said Ray. The heavy behind him pushed the barrel of the gun into Ray's back and hissed for him to keep quiet. Having the gun that close was a mistake, Ray knew. He knew from experience that he could turn and push the gun away faster than the man could pull the trigger. But the fact there were two men with two guns meant the odds were in their favour.

Ray wasn't surprised in the least when they arrived at CK Lee's box. The heavy in front opened the door and nodded for them to go in. Ray went in first. There was a small Chinese man standing at the windows looking out over the pitch. He could have been anywhere between sixty and ninety with parchment-thin wrinkled skin and coarse dry hair that looked like dead grass. He was wearing a grey suit that looked as if it had come from Savile Row, and gleaming black shoes. He turned to look at Ray, his hands behind his back. 'You're the brother?' he said, his voice a flat monotone.

Ray winked. 'Ray Savage, at your service,' he said.

'You think this is funny?'

'I try to keep my spirits up.

Laura and Ollie came in behind him. Ray waved at a sofa at the side of the room. 'Why don't you and Ollie grab a seat?' he said to Laura.

McGee came into the box, followed by the heavy with the silenced gun who shut the door behind him and stood with his back to it.

Ray folded his arms. 'So I'm guessing you're Yung Jaw-Lung. What are you, a hundred and twenty?'

Yung chuckled dryly. 'It sometimes feels like that,' he said.

'And I'm guessing Lee called you, did he?' Ray pulled a face. 'I knew I should have finished him.' He looked over at Laura. 'See what happens when you leave loose ends, darling? They end up biting you in the arse.'

Yung looked out through the full length windows towards the scoreboard. 2-2 with less than a minute to go. Plus injury time. Another five minutes, perhaps. 'This is not going well,' he said.

'How much do you have riding on this game?' asked Ray.

Yung shrugged. 'Twenty million dollars.'

'Hong Kong dollars?'

'US.'

Ray nodded. 'That's a lot money.'

'There are a lot of gamblers in Asia.' He turned back to look at Ray with his watery eyes. 'Your brother didn't come through for us, so now his family will have to pay the price.'

'Don't give me that, you were never going to let them go,' said Ray.

'That's not true,' said Yung. 'If your brother had lost the match like he was supposed to, we would have let his wife and son go. But now, after everything you've done ...' He shrugged.

'Don't blame me for this,' said Ray.

'Your brother made a mistake, asking you for help,' said Yung. 'Now you will pay the price. And so will he.'

Ray stared at Yung, his eyes narrowing. 'Then I'll pay,' he said. 'Do what the fuck you want with me, but let Laura and Ollie go. They're civilians.'

'Sometimes civilians get hurt,' said Yung.

'If you want to take your anger out on someone, I'm here for you,' said Ray, holding his hands to the side. 'Hurting Gabe and his family doesn't help you. It won't bring back the money you lost. Or bring back the men who died.'

'No, but their deaths will serve as a lesson to others. A warning.' He waved at the heavy with the silenced gun and said something in Cantonese. The heavy grunted a reply and walked up to Ray, keeping the gun pointed at Ray's face. It was a Glock. The gun was just two feet from Ray's face. The heavy grinned and Ray grinned back. Two feet was close enough. More than enough. Ray's smile widened. The heavy frowned, confused.

'Laura?' said Ray, still staring at the heavy.

'Yes?' Her voice was trembling.

'Cover Ollie's eyes.'

Chapter 103

Gabe dribbled the ball across the line into the penalty box. There were two defenders in front of him but he had a clear shot to the top right hand corner. He instinctively switched into shooting mode but the reality of his situation kicked in and he tapped the ball to his left. The keeper was shouting furiously and one of the midfielders ran into the box.

Babacar was by the left post, screaming for the ball. Gabe turned around and took the ball out of the box, then ran parallel to the line. One of the defenders lunged at the ball but Gabe tapped it to the side and shielded it with his body. They bumped shoulders but Gabe stayed on track, keeping the ball at his feet. He pulled a 180, running back the other way as the defender floundered. He had an opening again, the right hand of the goal was completely clear, but he hesitated and almost immediately the keeper was in position and ready for the shot.

The crowd was screaming now, desperate for a goal. Fernandez came running up on Gabe's right and he passed the ball to him. The Argentinian took the ball two steps and then sent it spinning across the box to Babacar. Gabe's mouth opened in surprise and horror as Babacar went for it with his head. The ball went high and hit the cross-bar, then bounced to the right where Fernandez hit it with all his might, a blistering shot that turned the ball into a blur. The keeper reacted instinctively, throwing up his hands and deflecting the ball over the bar as the crowd went wild.

Jason Wood went to retrieve the ball for the corner kick. Gabe looked over at the sideline. McNamara was standing between Tommy Brett and Martin Jessop. There was no sign of Guttoso, presumably the manager had gone back to the owner's box. Gabe knew he couldn't insist on taking the kick so he moved to stand on the edge of the penalty box.

Babacar and Moretti were getting busy on the goal line and the keeper was screaming at the top of his voice. One of the defenders pulled Moretti's shirt and the Italian Jabbed him in the ribs, swearing profusely in his own language. Maplethorpe ran into the box, closely followed by Johnnie Reid.

The crowd was at full volume, sensing blood. Gabe glanced up at the clock. There was one minute to go, then they would be in injury time. His heart was pounding but he felt light-headed, as if he was losing his grip on reality. It would be all over within minutes and the way things were going it looked as if there was no way that Chelsea could win. And if they didn't... He gritted his teeth in frustration.

Wood took a few steps back and composed himself. The keeper was still screaming at his defence. Fernandez stepped back and deliberately trod on the foot of the defender behind him. Wood began his short run, then kicked it high and towards Gabe. Gabe was relatively open, the nearest defender was six feet away, and he trapped the ball easily on his chest and dropped it to his feet. He took it across the line into the penalty box, then turned to the right. His best chance of getting the ball in play for Chelsea was to kick the ball at the keeper and let him clear it. With most of his teammates on the attack, there was a chance – a slim one – that a sudden Chelsea attack might catch United by surprise. Babacar and Moretti were both screaming for the ball but Gabe ignored them. He turned again, looking for a gap so that he could hit the ball to the keeper, but Maplethorpe was in his way. A defender shouldered Gabe but he turned and avoided most of the blow, the ball still at his feet. He realised he had a clear view of the keeper and he drew back his right leg to take the kick when the defender lashed out and caught Gabe just behind the knee. A bolt of pain paralysed his right leg and he went down, screaming in agony.

Chapter 104

'Are you ready?' asked Ray as he stared into the eyes of the man holding the gun. Yung said something in Chinese and the man grunted but kept his eyes fixed on Ray's face. His finger began to tighten on the trigger.

Ray's hands blurred as he moved. His left hand slapped the silencer to the man's right. Ray's right hand slapped into the man's wrist and Ray's left hand grabbed the barrel. He twisted the gun out of the man's hand and stepped back, transferring the weapon to his right hand. It was a move he'd practised a thousand times but he was always amazed at how effective it was. The heavy was frowning, trying to come to terms with what had happened. Ray winked at the man and then shot him twice, above and below the heart. He slumped to the ground, red flowers blossoming on his shirt.

The second heavy was caught by surprise and his gun was down at his side as he leant against the door. He started to raise it but Ray's finger was already tightening on the trigger as he turned to face him.

He put two shots into the man's chest. He would have preferred a head shot but they tended to create a lot of mess in enclosed spaces.

Gerry McGee was standing with his mouth wide open, flecks of blood across his fluorescent jacket. 'Gerry, are you okay?' asked Ray, keeping the gun trained on Yung.

McGee nodded but couldn't speak.

'Good man,' said Ray. 'Take Ollie and Laura outside for a minute,' he said. He dragged the body away from the door, smearing glistening blood across the carpet.

McGee nodded again but didn't move.

'Gerry, take them out. I won't be long.'

McGee shook himself as if he was waking from a dream. Laura had her hands over Ollie eyes and she kept them covered as McGee ushered them into the corridor.

Yung stared at Ray with watery eyes, his face a blank mask. 'We're not so different, you ...' Ray pulled the trigger and shot him in the throat. Red froth bubbled from the wound as Yung sank to his knees.

'Mate, I don't give a fuck what your last words are,' said Ray. He put a second bullet into the man's heart. Yung fell face forward and hit the floor with a dull thud. Ray wiped the butt of the Glock with a serviette and tossed it onto Yung's body.

The steward was waiting in the corridor outside with Laura and Ollie. 'Right, all sorted,' he said brightly. 'We need to let Gabe know you're here.'

CHAPTER 105

Gabe struggled to his feet. The defender who had brought him down had moved to stand by the keeper and was pretending to ignore Gabe. The referee pointed at a spot outside the penalty box and signalled a free kick. Moretti was in his face immediately. 'Are you fucking blind?' screamed the Italian. 'Cazzo che ti fotte!'

The referee's jaw tightened and he pulled a yellow card and waved it in front of Moretti's face.

Gabe limped over and got in between the two men. 'Leave it, Luca,' he said.

'Why the fuck are you defending him?' shouted Moretti. 'You were well over the line.' He pointed at the referee. 'This fucker has it in for us.'

'Luca, mate, he'll send you off if you carry on like this.'

'I don't give a fuck.' He struggled to reach the referee and Gabe pushed him back. 'Luca, as captain I order you to walk away.'

'Captain?' shouted the Italian. 'A fucking armband doesn't make you captain. If you want to be captain, act like a fucking captain!'

Gabe pushed him again. 'Get the fuck back, Luca!' he shouted.

Luca shoved Gabe in the chest, then Babacar grabbed him and dragged him away. The referee used his spray can to mark where he wanted the kick to be taken, a good three feet outside the box and several yards from where Gabe had actually been tackled. Then he used the can to mark a line ten yards from the spot and waved for the Chelsea players to get behind it. Gabe looked around for the ball. The whole North Stand was jeering now, lambasting the referee for his decision.

Maplethorpe was in the referee's face, shouting at him and waving his arms around.

'Tim, leave it!' said Gabe.

'He's been making crap decisions all game!' shouted Maplethorpe. 'He's got it in for us.'

One of the Chelsea defenders rolled the ball towards Gabe. He trapped it and placed it where the referee wanted. The Chelsea defence formed a wall inside the penalty box.

Jason Wood came up behind Gabe and grabbed his shoulder. 'Don't do it, Gabe,' said the midfielder. 'It's the wrong call and he knows it. You were well over the line. Well fucking over.'

'He's the referee,' said Gabe. 'It's his call.'

Wood shook his head. 'He's not the only referee.' He pointed over to the sideline where the assistant referee was waving his arm and pointing to the penalty spot. As Wood and Gabe watched the assistant referee ran onto the pitch. He was in his thirties, ginger-haired and freckled. 'He saw it,' said Wood. 'So did she.' He pointed over at the opposite sideline where the other assistant referee – a blonde woman with her hair tied back in a ponytail – had also run onto the pitch. They both reached the referee at the same time and began arguing that he should be calling for a penalty.

The Chelsea players gathered around the referees, shouting and gesticulating. Moretti tried to force his way through but was pushed away and fists started flying before the Italian was dragged away by his teammates. The spectators were all on their feet and a chant began in the North Stand that quickly spread around the entire stadium 'YOU DON'T KNOW WHAT YOU'RE DOING! YOU DON'T KNOW WHAT YOU'RE DOING!'

Gabe shoved his way through the Chelsea scrum, holding the ball to his chest.

The referee was red-faced and perspiring, his whole body shaking. The female referee was standing in front of him, talking to him calmly, as if she was soothing an injured horse. 'I'm serious, Davie,' she said. 'You have to call this as a penalty or they're going to be asking questions. It was well inside. Not just inches, not just feet. It was yards, Dave. Fucking yards. You call this as a free kick and your refereeing career will be over.'

Scott glowered at the two assistants but seemed lost for words.

'It's going to be on the TV, Davie,' said the other assistant. 'They're going to be asking what the hell came over you.' He shrugged. 'Your call. We've told you what we saw. And we know what the spectators saw.' He waved at the chanting crowd. 'Just listen to them. I tell you, you call this as a free kick and they won't let you off the pitch alive.'

The referee swore, stamped his foot, then pointed at the penalty spot and blew his whistle. The crowd roared its approval and half a dozen Chelsea players surrounded the referee, disputing his change of heart.

Gabe hugged the ball and looked over at the clock. There couldn't be more than a few minutes to go at most. Tears of frustration pricked his eyes and he blinked them away.

The referee shouted at the Chelsea players to get out of the penalty box, but it was only when his hand moved towards the yellow card in his pocket that they obeyed. The referee walked over to Gabe, his face ashen. 'You know what you've got to do,' he muttered. 'Don't fuck it up.'

Gabe's eyes narrowed, wondering whether the referee had been paid off or if like Gabe he was acting under duress. Not that it mattered. All that mattered was there was hardly any time left and even with a draw his family were dead. His mouth had gone dry and he had trouble swallowing.

He heard his name being called. At first he thought it was Joe McNamara and so he ignored it, knowing that the coach would almost certainly want to veto him taking the penalty.

He walked over and placed the ball on the penalty spot. The crowd went quiet as Gabe took three slow paces back.

'Gabe!'

Gabe frowned. It was coming from the stand to his right, not the touchline. He looked over. There was a steward at the bottom of the stand, waving to attract his attention. It took a couple of seconds for Gabe to recognise him. It was Gerry McGee. McGee stopped waving and pointed up into the stands. It took another couple of seconds for Gabe to realise what McGee was pointing at – the family box. Gabe turned to look, shading his eyes with his hand. He saw Laura, standing close to the window. Ollie was in front of her and she had both hands on his shoulders as if he was scared she would lose him. Relief washed over him like a cold shower and a smile broke across his face. Ollie waved and Gabe waved back. The referee blew his whistle and Gabe took a deep breath, exhaled, and started his run.

His mind raced at lightning speed. The keeper usually went to his right, Gabe's left, and he'd know that Gabe would have realised that which meant that he'd expect Gabe to go to the keeper's left. That was where Gabe focussed his body on – right, right, right – but as he planted his left foot he switched and powered the ball to the bottom left of the goal. The keeper was already diving the wrong way and there was no way he could stop – the ball rocketed into the net and the crowd went wild.

Gabe stood with his hands on his hips but he was only allowed a second or two of relief before his team engulfed him. He was grabbed and hugged and his hair was ruffled. Tens of thousand of people were chanting 'Savage, Savage, Savage!'

Babacar appeared in front of Gabe, his eyes wide with excitement. 'You fucking star!' he screamed at the top of his voice, then grabbed him and kissed him on both cheeks.

Maplethorpe pushed Babacar to the side and took his place, hugging Gabe and sticking his tongue in his ear. Gabe laughed and pushed him away. Gabe caught a glimpse of the referee walking away, his shoulders hunched as he stared at the ground. Then more players crowded around Gabe and he was thumped on his back so hard that his teeth rattled.

Eventually the back-slapping stopped and they jogged back to take their places for the kick off. The Chelsea players were already in position but it was clear from the look on their faces that they knew it was all over. The clock on the scoreboard showed 4.50pm.

The referee blew his whistle and the Chelsea captain kicked the ball to his left. All the Chelsea team raced forward but almost immediately the referee blew his whistle long and hard, signalling the end of the match. The stadium exploded in a collective roar of triumph.

CHAPTER 106

Ray took Laura and Ollie out of the family box and down into the main stand. The crowd were on their feet cheering as the team did a lap of honour around the stadium. As they walked down the steps to the pitch, Laura saw Gabe in the middle of the United team. It looked as if he was trying to break away but his teammates wouldn't let him. He kept looking in her direction but she couldn't tell if he could see her or not.

Ollie slipped out of her grasp and ran down the final stairs. Two stewards blocked his way but Gerry McGee spoke to them then pointed up at the stairs to her and waved. She smiled and nodded and McGee let an excited Ollie dash onto the pitch.

The United team rounded the far end of the pitch and were heading their way. Laura smiled as Ollie ran over to Gabe and jumped up at him. Gabe caught him and whirled around as he hugged the boy.

'Are you okay?' Ray asked Laura.

'I am now,' she said. 'Thank you. Thank you for everything.'

Ray shrugged. 'You're family,' he said. 'You and Ollie.'

She looked across at him. 'Ollie isn't yours, Ray,' she said quietly.

'You don't know that for sure,' he said. 'The timing's right. Unless you did a DNA test.'

She shook her head. 'There's no need to test anyone's DNA,' she said.

'Laura...' Ray began, but she silenced him with a warning look.

'Don't go there, Ray,' she said quickly. 'It was a one-night stand. I was drunk and you...'

'Don't say I took advantage of you because that's not what happened,' said Ray.

She shook her head. 'I was stupid,' she said

'Thanks,' said Ray. 'Thanks for that.'

'You know what I mean. I was young and I was stupid and I wasn't used to champagne. Gabe and I had only just started going out, you were...' She laughed. 'Well, you're you. That's never going to change.'

'I know it was only once,' he said. 'But the timing fits. Nine months later...' He nodded over at Ollie and Gabe.

'Let it go, Ray,' said Laura. 'Ollie is Gabe's son, the DNA has nothing to do with that.'

Ray nodded. 'Okay.'

'I'm serious. You're his uncle. If Gabe lets you back in our life after this, that's who you are. Uncle Ray.'

'You think he'll start talking to me now?'

Laura laughed. She reached over and took his hand and squeezed it gently. 'I can't see he has any choice, can you?'

Ray shrugged. 'He was angry as hell. He wouldn't have anything to do with me for almost ten years.'

'You slept with his wife.'

'You weren't his wife back then. You'd been going out for what, a week? It's not as if you were wearing a ring, is it?'

'I'm his wife now, Ray,' said Laura. She leaned over and kissed him softly on the cheek. 'Thank you.' She let go of his hand and walked down the steps to the pitch. She nodded at McGee. 'Thanks, Gerry,' she said.

The steward grinned and flashed her a fake salute. 'Always a pleasure, Mrs Savage.' He gestured up the stairs. 'I never knew Gabe had a brother.'

'Ray keeps to himself, pretty much,' said Laura. She walked onto the pitch and held out her arms. Gabe was forcing his way through the crowds towards her with Ollie on his shoulders. Supporters were congratulating him and slapping him on the back. Stewards were trying in vain to keep the support- ers back but they kept on coming. Eventually Gabe reached her and he hugged her tightly. They kissed for several seconds, surrounded by screaming and cheering fans. 'I love you so much,' Gabe said when he finally broke away. Over her shoulder he saw the referee, glaring in his direction. The man was clearly furious and Gabe figured he'd been bribed rather than threatened to rig the match. He was angry at the money he'd lost, and Gabe grinned over at him and flashed him a thumbs-up. The referee mouthed an obscenity and then jogged towards the tunnel.

'What are you looking at?' asked Laura, her eyes narrowing.

He smiled at her. 'The woman I love,' he said.

Laura laughed. 'Sweet talker,' she said.

'I'm never going to let either of you out my sight again.' He kissed her again, then looked up at the stand. 'Where's Ray?'

Laura twisted around to look up at where Ray had been standing. He'd gone. She shrugged. 'He'll be back,' she said.

Gabe had one arm holding Ollie's legs and he put the other around her and squeezed. 'He came through for me. I wasn't sure he'd be able to do it, but he did.'

She nodded. 'He's family.'

Gabe squeezed her again. 'Yes,' he said. 'Yes, he is.'

THE END

ABOUT THE AUTHOR

Stephen Leather is one of the UK's most successful thriller writers, an eBook and Sunday Times bestseller and author of the critically acclaimed Dan "Spider' Shepherd series and the Jack Nightingale supernatural detective novels. Before becoming a novelist he was a journalist for more than ten years on newspapers such as *The Times,* the *Daily Mirror,* the *Glasgow Herald,* the *Daily Mail* and the *South China Morning Post* in Hong Kong. He is one of the country's most successful eBook authors and his eBooks have topped the Amazon Kindle charts in the UK and the US. The *Bookseller* magazine named him as one of the 100 most influential people in the UK publishing world. Amazon has identified him as one of their Top 10 independent self-publishers. His book *The Basement* is one of Amazon's most successful self-published titles of all time. Born in Manchester, he began writing full-time in 1992. His bestsellers have been translated into fifteen languages. He has also written for television shows such as London's Burning, The Knock and the BBC's Murder in Mind series and two of his books, *The Stretch* and *The Bombmaker*, were filmed for TV. You can visit his website at www.stephen-leather.com.

Printed in Germany
by Amazon Distribution
GmbH, Leipzig